Missing Home

Michele Rankin

Michele Rankin

This book is a work of fiction. Names, characters, places, and incidents are products of the author's imagination
or are used fictitiously. Any resemblance to actual persons, living or dead, events, or locales, is entirely coincidental.

Michele K. Rankin

Printed in the United States of America

First Printing: November, 2021

ISBN: 9798769031779

This book is dedicated to my husband, Mike.

A special thanks to my writing cohort. Linda, I have learned so much from you! You've been there from the beginning of this story and helped me bring it to life!

To my readers, Kris and Cindy: You are the best (especially with commas!), and this book is better because of you!

Kris-thank you for the beautiful cover! I appreciate all your hard work.

Ray Williams and Jack Holliday, thank you for sharing your expertise.

Prologue

"Shaw!" Aaron Fletcher called to Jed as he got to his desk at the Illinois State Police Division of Criminal Investigation. "Phone for you. It's Lieutenant Horton from Chicago P.D. – I'll transfer."

"Thanks." In his office, Jed slipped out of his dark blue sport-coat, hanging it on the back of the chair as he searched his brain for any current case CPD could be calling him about. Nothing came to mind. He pushed the flashing button and picked up the phone.

"Detective Shaw."

"Detective Jed Shaw?" A woman's voice. "This is Lieutenant Allison Horton, Chicago District 12. Do you know Chelsea Winters? Our records show that you're her brother."

"Winters?" he said. "I have a sister named Chelsea." Opening up the Illinois criminal background check page he typed in the new name and stared at his sister's picture. "Um, yeah. That's her. We've been...uh...out of touch." He ran a hand over his close-cropped hair.

"I understand you and your siblings grew up in the foster system," she said.

"Yes."

"It's easy to lose track of each other when siblings are separated. That's why the policy now is to keep families together if possible."

"I'm well aware of the attempts to correct the foster care system," Jed interrupted. He scrolled through the listed offenses; drug possession, solicitation, public intoxication, all of that coming after the 14-month sentence she'd gotten for stealing their car sixteen years ago.

"What did she do now?" Then another thought hit him. "Is she...?"

"She's alive as far as we know. But she seems to have gone missing," Detective Horton spoke quickly. "A neighbor called us when her daughters came over because they were hungry. They hadn't eaten since the day before."

"Daughters?" Jed had no idea he had nieces. He hadn't seen or talked to Chelsea in almost fifteen years, and Noah never mentioned her having kids. Of course, he didn't talk to his younger brother that often, either.

"Two," the detective said. He heard fingers clicking on a keyboard. "Josephine, age 8 and Zora, five. The condition of the apartment was..." she took a breath. "It was pretty bad."

"I can imagine," Jed closed his eyes, images flashing in his memory.

"The reason I'm calling is that we're looking for any family that may have had contact with her."

"I haven't," he said. "You might try our half-brother, Noah. She was in contact with him the last time he and I talked. But that's been awhile," he admitted. He'd sent a card when Noah graduated from college, and his younger brother called to thank him. That was at least ten years ago. They'd only had sporadic email contact since then.

"Noah Denton, yes. I haven't been able to get a hold of him."

"I can try his work number," Jed said. "Where are the girls?"

"Right now they are both at Lurie Children's being examined. They suspect some malnutrition," she sighed. "The younger one has a cut on her leg with a nasty infection."

Jed's jaw tightened and he rubbed his forehead, pressing a thumb against his temple.

"We attempted to reach the children's father, a..." her voice faded and came back. "...Dante Winters, but so far, no luck. Without family the girls will go into foster care."

"I... we... my wife and I will take them," Jed said without thinking.

"Good. I was hoping you would. Hannah Wilkes from Child Protective Services is going to join us on this call, is that alright?"

"Yes, that's fine."

A bright, chirpy voice came on the line. "Hello, Mr. Shaw. I'm Hannah Wilkes and I've been assigned as Josie and Zora's caseworker. I just need to ask you a few questions, and then I can get the papers in to get you temporary custody. There will be a home-study and a hearing at a later date. It's usually within two weeks, but the courts are backed up, so it might be longer."

Jed answered her questions and gave her his email address for the forms he would need to fill out.

"The girls are getting medical treatment right now. It would be helpful if you or your wife could come to the hospital. Can you do that?"

"Yes. I'm not far from there. Do you think they'll be coming home with me tonight?"

"Probably not until tomorrow." She rattled off some information and Jed scrawled it down and slipped it into his pocket. On his way out, he stuck his head into Tom Delgado's office.

"I need to leave," he said. "Family emergency."

His boss looked up, his eyebrows knitted together in concern. "Is Natalie okay? Theo?"

"Yeah, it's my sister."

"I didn't know you had a sister," Tom said.

"It's been a long time, and it's a long story. I'll tell you over a beer sometime."

"Okay, no worries. Take the time you need. You've got the days."

In the parking garage, Jed pulled out his cellphone and called his wife, then headed into the midafternoon Chicago traffic toward the hospital to meet his nieces.

Part 1: Before

Chapter 1

Jed had a distinct memory of trying to rinse out his baby brother's dirty disposable diaper in the kitchen sink of the tiny apartment they lived in. He must've been eight or nine. He realized pretty quickly it wouldn't work, so he dressed Noah in two pairs of jogging pants and stuffed paper towels under his bottom.

"I'm hungry!" His five-year-old sister, Chelsea, tugged at the heavy refrigerator door. Jed knew the fridge was empty, just like the cupboards. Their mother hadn't been home for two days.

"We'll get something at the store," Jed told her, helping her into her too-small coat. He reached into the money jar on the counter where their mother threw her tips from the bar. It was almost empty as well, but he tucked the few bills and a handful of change into his pocket. Holding Noah in one arm and taking Chelsea's hand with the other, he trudged the five blocks to the convenience store through the Chicago snow.

In the store, Chelsea grabbed a box of Pop Tarts off the shelf. "I like 'St-awbewy."

"Okay." Jed took a half gallon of milk from the refrigerated section and chose two jars of baby food, bananas and carrots. He counted the money from his pocket. No way was there enough for diapers. "Can you hold Noah for a minute?"

His sister nodded seriously and held out her arms for her baby brother.

"Be really quiet," he told her.

His eyes darted up and down the aisle. Seeing no one around, he put the jars of baby food in his pockets, then picked the smallest pack of diapers and unzipped his jacket, stuffing them inside. Taking Noah back, he held him tight against his chest to keep the package from falling out. "You carry the milk and Pop Tarts, okay?"

Chelsea nodded again, happy to be helping. At the checkout, he paid, carefully counting out the change. They were halfway out the door, Jed about to heave a sigh of relief, when he felt a hand on his collar.

That was the first time they ended up in foster care. Lucky enough to be placed together, they thrived in a normal home. Chelsea grew chubby and pretty, her wavy blond hair free of lice for the first time. Baby Noah began to crawl and babble at eleven months old. As for Jed, he grew two inches and his grades went from low C's to A's and B's in just two months at his new school.

Their mom didn't show up for the first few supervised visits. Then she did. Theresa Shaw was full of remorse and promises. She was going to rehab. She would get a better job. She would show them how much she loved them. She directed all this at Jed, of course. Chelsea and Noah were too young to be anything but overjoyed at her presence. After seven months, the court returned them to her care.

The next two years were full of wonderful memories. Theresa followed through with her promises. Sober and happy, she had a new boyfriend who treated the kids like his own. Mitch took Jed to his first baseball game–Cubs vs. Reds–and started him collecting baseball cards. He worked with him on his swing and bought him a real leather catcher's mitt. He paid for dance lessons for Chelsea and Noah's preschool. Then everything went to hell.

Theresa hooked up with some of her old crowd and started drinking again. The fights with Mitch escalated and more than once, neighbors called the police to the apartment. Soon the drinking turned into more. Since Mitch paid the rent, he told her that the kids could stay, but she had to sober up or leave. She left. Things were fine for a few more weeks, until she showed up, temporarily sober, of course, with a 'friend' to collect 'her' kids and her stuff. There was nothing Mitch could do except hug them and slip Jed his phone number.

Theresa was staying with her new friend in a run-down duplex. The family of four had one room and two beds to themselves, which really wasn't a problem since Theresa was never there at night. After someone stole their stuff and what little cash they had while they slept, Jed took to sleeping on the floor in front of the door so he would know when his mother, or anyone else, tried to get into the room.

They moved two more times, each place worse than the one before. He learned how to scare rats and ignore cockroaches. School became impossible. He often slept through his alarm and missed the bus or fell asleep in class on the days he made it there. There was nowhere to wash their clothes, and it became a matter of choosing the least dirty items to wear or stealing money from his mom's pockets or purse to buy something clean at Goodwill. More than one teacher tried to talk to him, but he kept quiet, afraid that if they went back into foster care, protective services would separate them.

Four-year old Noah was a sweet, shy child who cried because he missed his preschool friends, but at nine, Chelsea was a terror, throwing things and having screaming fits whenever she didn't get her way. Calls from the school to Theresa resulted in slaps and threats, which only made things worse. Jed had bruises and scratch marks all over from trying to calm his sister down, but he was the one she came to crying after another fight with their mother.

Theresa was rarely sober, continuing her downward spiral. Then, one morning the summer Jed turned thirteen, Noah came to him in the filthy kitchen of their current place as Jed was trying to scrounge up some breakfast for them.

"Mama won't wake up."

When Jed went to check, he found Chelsea standing by the pull-out couch and his mother cold to the touch. Theresa Shaw was dead.

Jed tried to reach Mitch, but the number had been disconnected.

This time, when they went back into the system, Jed's fears were realized. His and Chelsea's father was long gone, but the parents of Noah's biological father came forward to claim him, filing custody papers with the court and taking him back with them to Indianapolis. His sister's emotional and behavior issues made placing her difficult, and after several unsuccessful attempts to keep them together, Chelsea went to a group home for troubled girls.

Jed landed in suburban Chicago with Tom and Susan White. As bland as their names, the Whites had two other foster children, Eric, nine, and Carla, eleven. There were few hugs and strict rules – no television on weeknights, assigned chores, and homework done and checked over before supper. Jed didn't need hugs, and he liked rules. The known parameters gave him a feeling of security he'd lacked. While he didn't exactly love Tom and Susan, he appreciated them. His grades continued to improve, and he made the high school baseball team. Tom, Susan, or sometimes both of them came to every game.

He tried to keep in touch with Noah through phone calls and letters, but eventually that tapered off to nothing. Chelsea, in constant trouble, moved around from one group home to another. By the time Jed got her contact information, it would be wrong. His siblings faded into the background.

It was the baseball team that gave Jed a genuine sense of belonging. His coach took a liking to the serious young man, giving him advice and pointing the star catcher out to recruiters. The other players respected him because he was a great catcher and understood the rules of the game better than any of them. It surprised no one when he earned a full scholarship to Northwestern.

At college, members of the baseball team roomed together in quads in one of the athletic dorms. Jed's roommates were red-headed Ryan from Ohio, the team's other catcher; Jordan, who played shortstop; and Antonio, a quick-witted, left-handed pitcher from El Paso, Texas, who instantly became Jed's best friend.

Jed was finding his way. By the time he was a junior,

his teenage dreams of a major or even minor-league baseball career had faded, but he had an academic major, criminal justice, and a new dream—law school. So he trained, played baseball, and studied. Now an upper-classman, he lived in an off campus duplex with Antonio, who had a more typical college philosophy.

"All work and no play...," Antonio said. "...is boring. Let's throw a party."

Jed wasn't much of a drinker. He'd seen his mother drunk and cleaned up after her enough times to have a natural aversion. He listened when Mr. Gibson, his high school psychology teacher, talked about heredity in addictive behavior, so Jed was careful. He enjoyed a beer, maybe two, after a run or while watching a ball game, but avoided parties where over-indulging was expected. Too bad this one was at their apartment. It was too loud, too crowded, and everyone was too drunk. There would be a mess to clean up in the morning and since he was the one who wouldn't have a screaming hangover, he knew he'd be doing most of the work. He was about to go into his bedroom and shut the door, or crawl out the window and escape.

Then he saw her.

She was gazing out the screen door into the tiny backyard, a beer bottle dangling from her hand. Unlike some of the other girls, who dressed in tight shiny fabrics and high heels, she was wearing a lacy white camisole with a short denim skirt and Doc Martens. Her chin length blonde hair framed her face like a halo and she looked as bored and out-of-place as he felt.

Jed had no trouble getting dates. He was well built and handsome, with dark brown hair and crystal-blue eyes, and there were always girls hanging around the practice field and athletic buildings flirting with the players. One-night stands were rare, but so was any relationship that lasted more than a few months, mostly because of his fading interest or the girl's unwillingness to put up with his strict training and studying schedule.

All of that assured that he wasn't usually nervous about approaching girls, but now his heart pounded and his mouth went dry. He grabbed a beer from the cooler and twisted off the cap to have something to do with his hands. He took a quick sip.

"Hey," he said, approaching her. "You alright?"

"Oh!" She looked up at him and drew in a breath. "You startled me. Yeah, I'm fine. This is more my friend's scene than mine." She gave a shrug and her eyes grazed his and then slid away. "I think I'm just going to walk back to the dorm."

"You shouldn't go alone. This isn't my thing, either.

I'll walk with you."

"And leave all this?" She made a gesture at the chaos in his living room and he laughed.

Her name was Natalie, and she liked to talk, which was fine with him since it meant he didn't have to. He learned a lot about her as they walked across campus. She was nineteen, a freshman, with no major yet. She was from a small town west of Chicago, where her father was a veterinarian and, according to her, an animal hoarder.

"He can't help himself." She talked with her hands as they walked. "He can't stand to see an animal neglected or without a home. We've had dogs, cats, miniature goats, a pony... even a parrot," she made a face. "The most annoying creature ever. His name was Stan, and he must've seen *Scarface,* because whenever he got excited he'd yell 'Say hello to my little friend!'"

Her brother, Ian, was thirteen. "Going on forty. He's an old soul."

Currently, Natalie worked as a hostess at Lido's, an off-campus bistro. "What I most want is to get a job in the kitchen," she told him. "I love to cook."

When they reached her dorm, she turned to him. "Do you want to come up and talk? If that was your apartment we just left, I don't think you're going to be getting to sleep any time soon."

He followed her up the stairs, which she took two at a time, to the fourth floor.

She slid a CD into the stereo and Jed flopped down on the futon, expecting to hear Jewel or Sarah McLachlan, surprised when the strains of Led Zeppelin's *Kashmir* filled the small room. Natalie laughed at his expression and tossed a pillow onto the floor, using it to lean against the bed.

"I'm a musical throw-back. At least that's what my parents say. I've been raiding my dad's record collection since I was ten or eleven."

"He has good taste."

She smiled, and it lit up her face. Jed felt the glow take him in as well.

She scooted closer, stretching her legs out in front of her and crossing them at the ankles. Her short skirt slid up, showing smooth tan thighs. "Hot dogs or hamburgers?" she said.

"Uh..."

"Which one do you like best?"

"Hamburgers, I guess."

"Spring, summer or fall...no one likes winter around here."

"Spring."

"Beer or wine?"

"Beer."

"Running or weights?"

"Huh. I like them both."

"Field Museum or Art Institute?"

He smirked. "Do I have to go at all?"

The questions went on, back and forth, and she scooted closer and closer. Finally, he leaned in. "I'd really like to kiss you right now."

"I know." She hopped up and scanned the CDs for several seconds before selecting one and exchanging it. Led Zeppelin was replaced by Jimi Hendrix. Not exactly make-out music.

"So, you know all about my family," she said. Reaching into the small fridge and grabbing two beers, she handed one to him and returned to the floor in front of the futon, twisting off the cap on hers. "And I know you like hamburgers, beer, spring–probably because of baseball. You love working out, and you don't like museums." She ticked each one off on her fingers, then looked him in the eye, expectantly.

Jed always dreaded this part of meeting someone new, but something in her warm brown eyes made him want to tell her everything, and by the time they finished the beer, he had – most of it, anyway. She took it all in, listening, but not becoming weepy, like some girls he'd been with, or angry at 'the system', or even overly sympathetic. She just accepted it for what it was. He wanted to do more than kiss her now. He'd joined her on the floor and leaned in again, but she saw it coming and moved away.

"Patience, young man." She laughed.

Jed briefly considered that she might be a tease, but he'd met a few and this didn't seem like that.

"What about you, then?" he asked. "Morning person or night owl?"

"Well, it's after midnight and here we are-night owl, I guess. Although, I love a morning run."

"You're a runner?"

"Cross-country in high school. I'm not fast enough for college."

"We should run together sometime."

"We should."

"Uh... hamburgers or hot dogs?"

"Pizza."

"With what on it?"

"Mushrooms, peppers, onions, all of it. Sausage, pepperoni... everything."

He searched his brain for something else to ask. "Cake or pie?"

"Pie," she said, closing her eyes. "I love pie. Lido's has wonderful banana cream pie and sometimes there are leftovers and we get to take it home."

"That's my favorite, too."

"Well, we'll have to share it sometime after a run." She smiled at him and rose to her feet. "I'm going to the bathroom. Be right back."

Jed stood up and looked at her CD collection. It was impressive. Everything from classical and Broadway to Dave Brubeck to sixties rock, Billy Joel, U2, and Third Eye Blind. Jewel and Sarah McLachlan were in there, too.

The bathroom door opened and Natalie walked over to him. "You can kiss me now."

Chapter 2

Natalie woke with the unfamiliar weight of Jed's arm around her waist. Closing her eyes, she tugged the quilt up and tried to go back to sleep, but her mind started racing. After a few minutes she took a deep breath and turned her head to look at him. His eyes were closed, his breathing soft and steady. A warmth spread through her as she thought about the night before. Slipping carefully out from beneath his arm, she used the bathroom, brushed her teeth, and pulled on jeans and a t-shirt. When she came back into the room Jed was sitting up rubbing his eyes, the quilt pooled at his waist. His love of weights and running showed in his chest and arms.

"Good morning," she said.

"Morning." His voice was rough from sleep. "What time is it?"

She pointed to the clock on the built-in dresser. "A little after ten. Are you hungry?" She shifted from one foot to the other. "I know a great place for a cheap breakfast."

"I should get back to the apartment. There'll be a mess to clean up and Antonio will be too hungover."

"Come to breakfast with me and after we can to back to the apartment. I'll help you clean up," she said. She didn't want this to end. Was she imagining him? Would he

hand. Her dark hair was flecked with gray and pulled back from her face in a loose ponytail. Lines fanned out from her green eyes. "Natalie!" she said, coming over and giving her a one-armed hug. "We haven't seen you in a while."

"This is Jed," Natalie said. "Jed, this is Chuck's wife Rosie."

"Nice to meet you," Jed said, holding out his hand.

The woman took his hand, met his gaze, and looked from him back to Natalie. "He's handsome," she said, winking.

Natalie blushed, and Jed pretended not to hear. "We'll take the booth over there." She gestured at an empty one near the back. "Come see us if you get a minute."

They slid into opposite sides of the booth, and Jed gazed across the table at her. She wore no make-up, but her cheeks were flushed pink and her greenish-brown eyes sparkled. It felt like he'd known her for years, rather than hours.

Rosie came over with her carafe and two cups. "Cream for you, I remember," she said. She looked pointedly at Jed.

"Sugar, please."

She set the sugar packets on the table and filled both their cups. "Your food should be up in a sec," she said.

"How'd you find this place?" Jed asked when Rosie moved away.

She shrugged. "When I was looking for a job, I knew I wanted to work in a restaurant. I went to every place I could find. They didn't need anyone here, but Chuck knows Dean, the guy who runs Lido's, and found out they were looking for a hostess. He put in a good word for me."

"What she ain't tellin' you," Chuck said, coming from behind the counter with two plates. "Is that not long after that, when my Rosie was sick in the hospital, this girl showed up every morning at 5 and helped me until she had to leave for classes. Wouldn't take no pay, neither."

Natalie bent her head. "It wasn't a big deal," she said.

"It was to me." Chuck set their food in front of them. "On the house. Her money is no good here, and neither is yours."

After he walked away, Jed leaned in. "So that's what you meant by 'cheap breakfast'?" He laughed.

Natalie shrugged. "Can't get much cheaper than free. But I always leave a huge tip," she added quickly.

Jed's jaw dropped at the amount of bacon on her plate. "Are you going to eat all of that?"

"I love bacon," she said, taking a bite. She chewed and swallowed. "If I was on death row, and they asked me what I wanted for my last meal, I would have a BLT with homemade mayo, fresh tomatoes, and a whole pound of bacon. And a beer," she added.

"They don't let you have alcohol."

"Well, that sucks," she took another bite. "I guess I can't kill anyone." She grinned at him.

Jed laughed. "Just don't get caught."

****

They started seeing each other steadily. Natalie joined him on his morning runs and later, after classes, Jed brought his books and laptop to the restaurant, taking over the least desirable table by the swinging doors into the kitchen. Over bowls of minestrone, pieces of pie, and endless cups of coffee, he studied and waited to take her home. He loved the glimpses he caught of her working her new spot in the kitchen, even though all she was usually doing was chopping vegetables.

One evening on her break, she slid into the booth across from him with a slice of pie. She took a bite, then scooped up another, holding it across the table for him. His mouth was full of crumbling crust and tart cherries when she said;

"I love you."

He swallowed and stared at her.

She broke the silence. "I needed to say it. I don't need to hear it," she said. "Not if you're not ready or not sure or..."

"But I am sure," he said, the words tumbling out. "I love you, too. You're all I think about." He grabbed her hand. "I want us to have a life together." He watched her face, worried that he'd said too much, taken it too far.

But she flashed that smile, the one that took him in and made him feel a part of something amazing, spread across her face. "Me, too," she said.

****

Big fat flakes fell all around them as Jed lobbed a snowball, missing Natalie by a foot. She laughed as she ran, bending to scoop up a handful of snow.

"Good thing you aren't a pitcher, Shaw!" she called over her shoulder.

Ducking behind a sign for the science building, she threw a tightly packed snowball at him, hitting him smack in the chest. While he was bent over making another, she reversed course, sneaking up behind him, using the parked cars as cover. She scooped up a handful of snow and grabbed the back of his jacket, creating enough space to slide the snow down his neck. She turned and sprinted away.

Feet pounded behind her and he was there, wrestling her

to the ground. "You," he panted. "Are evil." But his grin didn't match his words.

She giggled and looked up at him as he lowered his mouth to hers.

"Come on," he said. He pushed up and held out a hand to help her up. "Let's get back to the apartment so you can make pancakes."

She took his hand, and he pulled her to her feet. "Pancakes, huh? Do you think you deserve pancakes?"

"I'll make it up to you later," he said, giving her a wink.

"Ooooh... massage?"

"I'll massage anything you want."

She smacked his butt in response as they turned back toward the apartment.

The smell of pancakes and bacon roused Antonio and he staggered out to the kitchen in gym shorts and a sweatshirt, peering out the window into the falling snow. His gaze settled on the damp coats hanging on the hooks on the wall and the shoes sitting in puddles on the floor.

He stared at his roommate. "You been outside in this?"

"We took our Sunday morning run," Natalie said as she flipped the pancakes. She set a stack on a plate and handed it to him. "Syrup and bacon is on the table."

He shook his head. "You all are nuts."

"Your blood is too thin, southern boy," Jed laughed. He took a second plate from Nat and sat down, drenching the pancakes with syrup.

"Whatever," Antonio said, forking pancakes into his mouth. "Ummmm," He murmured. "I like livin' with a chef, that's' for sure."

Natalie took a little bow and sat down next to Jed when there was a knock at the door.

"I got it." Jed hopped up, crossed the room in two long strides and opened it.

Natalie watched, fork halfway to her mouth, as a slim, pretty girl with long blonde hair threw herself into Jed's arms.

"What are you doing here?" he said. The girl pulled away and looked at him. She wore no coat, only a hooded sweatshirt, despite the cold winter day. Her feet were stuffed into tennis shoes, bare ankles showing below the hem of her jeans.

Nat looked at Antonio, who shrugged. She placed her uneaten forkful of pancakes back on the plate and waited. After what seemed like hours, Jed backed away from the door, letting the girl inside.

"This is Chelsea," he said, his gaze on Natalie. "My sister."

A breath she didn't realize she'd been holding came whooshing out as she rose from her chair. "Hi, Chelsea," she said, her voice too bright.

"This is my girlfriend, Natalie, and my roommate, Antonio," Jed said. "We're having breakfast. Are you hungry?"

"I'm not hungry." Chelsea shook her head. "Can I talk to you... alone?"

Jed's eyes found Natalie's again, and she saw confusion and worry there. "Sure, I guess. Come on." He led his sister, who didn't acknowledge anyone else, back to the bedroom.

"Huh," Antonio said. "That's kinda weird." He went back to shoveling pancakes into his mouth.

Not knowing how much about his childhood Jed had shared with his roommate and friend, Natalie didn't reply. She'd lost her appetite. She took her plate to the sink and started cleaning up the breakfast mess. Within a few minutes, angry voices came from the bedroom.

"You told me you'd always be there for me! But now that I really need you, you're just like everyone else!"

"I told you! I don't have that kind of money! I don't even have a job. I go to college for God's sake."

There was a crash.

"What are you doing?" Jed yelled. "Stop it. Put that down!"

Something shattered.

"Dammit! Come on, Chelsea! Calm down."

Anthony pushed up from the table. "That doesn't sound good. Should I go back there?"

Natalie bit her lip. The two of them strained to hear what Jed said next.

"Sit down."

"Ow! You're hurting me!"

"No, I'm not. Sit still and listen to me. If you need clothes and stuff, I'll take you shopping. I'll try to get you whatever you need. But I'm not just giving you money."

"You don't trust me!"

"I don't know you!"

"Whose fault is that?"

"That's not fair. I tried. If you had..."

"What? If I'd been a good little girl, some family would have kept us both?"

"Chelsea..."

"Fuck you! I should have known better than to come here. You don't care about me. No one does!"

The bedroom door opened and Chelsea came storming past them, her face twisted in fury.

"Chels, come on!" Jed cried, following her out the door.

"I'm going after him," Antonio said. Natalie trailed behind them, twisting the dish towel in her hands.

They met Jed coming back up the stairs. "She's gone," he said. "There was some guy waiting for her in a beat up Civic."

"What's her deal, bro?" Antonio held the door open as they moved back into the apartment.

Jed sat down, resting his forehead on one hand. He pushed the plate of cooling pancakes aside. Natalie sat beside him and touched his arm. "I'm sorry."

"Yeah, me, too." He sighed. "I should call protective services," he said. "I'm pretty sure she's run away from another foster home. They'll want to know she was here."

"What'd she break in there?" Anthony asked.

"She threw my baseball trophy and broke the lamp," he said. "There's a dent in the wall we're gonna have to fix before the landlord sees it."

"I'll get it. Don't worry, man." Anthony clapped a hand on Jed's shoulder. "She wanted money?"

"Yeah. Five hundred bucks."

His roommate gave a low whistle.

Natalie set a cup of coffee in front of Jed. "I put sugar in," she said, giving him a smile.

"Thanks." He took a sip. "She's always had temper tantrums. When she was a baby, she could scream nonstop for what seemed like hours. She got into trouble at school, at home, at the foster homes we lived in. She was always fighting with other kids. That's why we got separated when

34

Mom died. She's right. No one wanted to deal with her."

"How old is she?"

"Sixteen, maybe closer to seventeen. She'll age out of the system soon." He leaned back in his chair and closed his eyes. When he opened them, they were brimming with tears. "What will happen to her then?"

****

Later that night, Jed and Natalie were curled next to each other on the battered futon in his bedroom as snow continued to fall outside the window. Natalie highlighted a paragraph in the book on her lap, flipped it over, and looked at him. Jed was staring at his own textbook, but hadn't turned a page in a long time.

"You're awfully quiet," she said. When Jed didn't respond, she pushed her elbow against his ribs.

"I'm sorry you had to see that."

"You mean your sister? It's not your fault."

"She's a lot. I mean, you've got to be wondering about..."

"I'm not wondering about anything," she said. "I love you."

"And I love you," he said. "But I'd understand if..."

"If what?"

"If it was too much."

"It's not too much." She kissed him. "We're in this together. Deal?"

"Deal." His lips found hers and stole another kiss. "I'm the luckiest guy in the world to have you," he murmured.

"You're about to get luckier," she said, deepening the kiss and sliding her hand down his stomach.

****

"I think I want to go to culinary school." Natalie said one morning not long after Chelsea's visit. They were sitting in the kitchen sharing a spinach, cheddar, and bacon omelet she made.

"I told you I've always loved to cook. I have wonderful memories of my grandmother-my Nonna-teaching me-and I love working at Lido's. I'm learning so much! It's a lot more fun than classes. If we have to do it forever, work should be fun; don't you think?"

His mouth full, Jed nodded in response.

So they made plans. Jed had already applied to law schools in the Chicago area, and after some intense conversation with her parents, Natalie began the process of transferring to Kendall College, a local school with an excellent culinary program. After graduation, they would get a small apartment and start their life together.

Then, a month before Jed's graduation, everything changed.

Natalie stared into the mirror, tapping her fingers on the edge of the sink, waiting for the timer to go off. When it did, she closed her eyes and held her breath, picking up the plastic stick and saying a quick prayer before looking at it. The plus sign glowed bright blue. Sighing, she tossed it in the trash with the other two and lowered herself onto the closed toilet seat. Pregnant. She was pregnant.

She thought back over the last couple of months, not understanding how this could happen when she took her birth control faithfully. But she hadn't had her period, and two days ago, the first sip of her morning coffee sent her running to the bathroom to vomit. She hadn't said a word to Jed. Now, three pregnancy tests later, she was certain. Wiping away a tear, she got up and walked into the bedroom.

"Hey," she whispered, shaking him gently. "Wake up."

When he looked up at her, she couldn't make the words come out. Instead, she burst into tears, burying her face in his shoulder.

Chapter 3

Jed wasn't as upset as Natalie thought he might be. After a trip to the campus clinic for confirmation of what they already knew, they spent a long few days thinking and talking. Together, they made the decision to get married and have the baby. Jed graduated, and the wedding was a small ceremony in her parents' spacious backyard with now fifteen-year-old Ian, Antonio, and Natalie's best friend, Katy, the only guests. Russ and Connie welcomed their new son-in-law and were thrilled to become grandparents, despite the circumstances. Neither of Jed's siblings came. Chelsea was in the wind and Noah was on a high school trip to France. Jed's foster parents, Tom and Susan White, didn't come either, but sent the newlyweds a beautiful hand-sewn quilt and invited them for a visit.

Law school became a dream deferred. Instead, a friend of his new father-in-law suggested Jed's major in criminal justice and minor in finance made him an excellent candidate for the Illinois State Police. After several interviews and an intense background check, he was hired as an investigator and began a daily commute to Chicago from Westlake, where they lived in a tiny apartment above Russ Dunham's vet clinic. The same apartment Russ and Connie lived in when Natalie was born.

Natalie worked for a local caterer throughout the pregnancy. When her water broke in the middle of preparations for a wedding reception, it took Jed over four hours in rush hour traffic to get to the hospital. He needn't have worried. It was another eight hours before Theo made his very noisy entry into the world. Placed on his mother's chest, the baby continued to howl. Distracted by the sight of his son, Jed didn't notice the doctor's distress until one nurse grabbed the baby and another directed him out of the room as Natalie was quickly wheeled away.

****

"What can they possibly be doing?" Connie wrung her hands and paced in her daughter's room.

"I'm sure it seems longer than it's been," her husband said. "Do you want me to go check?"

"Would you?"

Jed listened to his in-laws from the rocker where he sat holding his son. He kept his eyes locked on the tightly swaddled baby in his arms, not trusting himself to look up. He couldn't allow himself to consider any possibility other than Natalie being wheeled back in perfectly fine. She had to be.

Jed's father-in-law was not alone when he came back. The doctor followed Russ, his face serious, as he walked up to Jed.

"Your wife is in recovery," he said. "She had what's called a uterine atony. Her uterus didn't contract after the baby was born. Unfortunately, the minimally invasive techniques I attempted didn't work."

"But you said she's in recovery," Connie said. His throat dry, all Jed could do was stare up at the doctor.

"She is," the doctor said. "But – and I'm very sorry about this, especially since she's so young – I had to remove the uterus. She's receiving a transfusion right now to replace the blood that she lost. As soon as that's finished, we should be able to bring her back to the room so she can be with you and her baby." He put the chart on a hook on the wall and turned back to all of them. "I really am very sorry. But you have a healthy boy there, and Natalie should make a full recovery."

"Thank you," Jed managed to croak. He bent his head down to his son's. "Your mama is going to be okay," he whispered. That was all that mattered.

****

Natalie sat rocking Theo long after he'd fallen asleep. Today he took his first steps, toddling from the couch across six feet of living room carpet into his mother's waiting arms. He repeated the performance for Jed when he got home from work, crowing with delight as he crashed into his father's legs. Jed scooped him up, his eyes shining as he swung his son over his head and the baby giggled.

Now, Theo's head heavy on her shoulder, Natalie inhaled the sweet baby scent of him. In a month, he would be a year old. Tears rolled down her cheeks, but she didn't brush them away. She just rocked, patting the baby's back and humming softly.

"Hey," Jed's voice came low from where he leaned against the doorframe. "Is he asleep?"

Natalie nodded.

"What a day, huh?" He grinned and moved toward them. "I can just see him running the bases in a few years."

That did it. Natalie choked back a sob and more tears fell.

"What? What did I say?" Jed came to her, crouching, a hand on her shoulder.

"Nothing," she managed. "I just…" she swallowed another sob.

Jed lifted Theo from her arms and stood, laying him on his back in the crib.

Natalie sniffed, and he handed her a tissue. "He's the only baby we'll ever have," she cried. "And he won't be a baby much longer." She snuffled again.

Jed took her hands and pulled her to her feet and into his arms. "It'll be okay." He kissed the top of her head.

She leaned into him and closed her eyes. Waking up from surgery after Theo was born had been surreal. She couldn't remember anything after they lay the baby on her chest and didn't really absorb the fact that she couldn't have another child until weeks later. By then, she was so busy with new motherhood that she pushed it to the back of her mind. Lately, though, as Theo reached milestone after milestone, she was feeling blue.

"I wish I'd known when I was pregnant that it would be the only time. I would have paid more attention."

Jed chuckled, his chest vibrating against her cheek. "I think you were pretty observant," he said. "You had something new to tell me every day once he started moving around."

"I did?" She tilted her head and looked up at him.

"Yes, you just don't remember."

"I wish I could freeze time. Just for a little while."

"I know." He tipped her chin up and kissed her. "We just need to remember to enjoy each stage. He's only one. He's going to be your baby for a while yet."

Natalie moved to the crib and Jed joined her, putting his arm around her as they gazed down at their son.

Chapter 4

Jed stared at the two spreadsheets side-by-side on his screen. The answer was here somewhere. He just needed to find it. He rubbed his forehead and zoomed in on one column of figures.

Gary, one of the department investigators, poked his head in. "Hey, Jed, some of us are hitting Bennett's in a few for some beers. Wanna join us?"

He shook his head. "I've almost got this figured out. I'm gonna finish up and head home."

"Suit yourself," he said with a dismissive wave.

Jed knew some of the guys thought he was a stand-offish workhorse, but he took his job seriously. Since joining the Illinois State Police Division of Criminal Investigation—DCI—almost five years ago, Jed had impressed the bosses with his skills in financial analysis. His department concentrated on criminal wrong-doing by elected officials, or any government appointees at the state or local level. The first case Jed worked on resulted in the resignations of a state senator and the assistant district attorney of Lake County and the former's conviction on corruption charges. It got a ton of good press for the department.

That case and the next two he helped investigate put Jed on the fast track to Detective. His promotion came at the perfect time. With Theo growing, the apartment was becoming small. The raise that came with his new responsibilities allowed them to buy a house, one with a big backyard for all that 4-year-old energy. They'd just moved the previous weekend, and he was anxious to get home.

"There it is!" Jed said. "Gotcha!" He highlighted the transaction that would likely prove embezzlement on the part of a county clerk in the southern part of the state. Opening an email, he attached the files and sent it to his boss. Then he loosened his tie, grabbed his jacket, and headed for the door.

****

"Mom-my!" Four-year-old Theo cried. "There's a lady at the door."

Natalie came into the living room barefoot, weaving her way carefully through the boxes still stacked up from the move. She glanced down at the cut-off jean shorts and faded Northwestern t-shirt she wore, hoping it wasn't one of their new neighbors coming to introduce themselves. "Well," she thought. "Come unannounced and what you see is what you get."

She patted Theo's sun-streaked curls and peered through the screen at the woman standing on the porch. She looked vaguely familiar. "Hi," Natalie said. "Can I help you?"

The woman licked her lips, shifting her weight from one foot to the other. She was shorter than Natalie, with dark blonde hair that hung to her shoulders, framing a narrow face. She wore a dirty gray zip-front hoodie and jeans in the eighty-degree heat. A faded blue backpack, stuffed full to bulging, hung over one shoulder.

"I'm... uh... does Jed Shaw live here? This is the address they gave me at the other place."

Why was this woman looking for Jed? Natalie looked more closely at her. Was this Jed's sister? After a moment, she said, "Chelsea?"

The woman took a step back. "How do you know my name?"

Opening the screen door, Natalie stepped out onto the porch, scooping Theo up onto her hip as he followed her. He stared at the other woman and his thumb went into his mouth the way it always did when he met someone new.

"You're Jed's sister, aren't you? I'm Natalie," she said. "We met once at Jed's apartment at Northwestern. We're married now. This is our son, Theo."

Again, Chelsea licked her lips, which were dry and chapped despite the warm summer day. Her eyes flicked to Natalie's, then away. "Yeah," she said. "Right. So does he live here? I went to this other place, but they said he moved."

"Oh!" Natalie said. "You were at the apartment?"

She nodded. "That's the address I got."

"We just moved last weekend," Natalie said. "It's a mess, but you're welcome to come in and wait for Jed. He's at work. He usually gets home around six or so." She smiled. "Can I fix you a sandwich or something to drink?"

Chelsea tucked a strand of hair behind one ear. "I am kinda hungry, I guess."

Natalie held the screen door open. "Come on in," she said. "Watch your step. We're still unpacking."

"I got a swing set," Theo said, not taking his thumb all the way out of his mouth.

In the kitchen, Natalie set him down and handed him a popsicle from the freezer. "Go eat it outside on the swing," she said, shooing him out the door into the fenced-in backyard. She pulled bread, leftover chicken, mayo, and a few other things out of the fridge and started making a sandwich.

"How did you get here?" she asked.

"Huh? Oh. A friend dropped me off at that other place. Then I walked here."

"Go ahead and sit down." Chelsea sat at the small table, stowing her backpack between her feet.

"Aren't you warm?" Natalie asked. "You can take your jacket off if you want."

"That's okay." Chelsea tugged at the sleeves, pulling them down half over her hands. It made Natalie sweat just looking at her.

"Jed is going to be so happy to see you," Natalie said. "He's been looking for you for years."

"Really?" For the first time, the woman's blue eyes showed a spark of something.

"Yes," Natalie said. "Every time he thought he knew where you were, you were already gone." She finished making the sandwich and plated it with some potato chips and a pickle. She poured each of them a glass of lemonade and set the plate in front of her sister-in-law.

"Thanks," Chelsea said. She picked up the sandwich and took a bite, then another, before she swallowed the first. She wiped her mouth with the back of her hand and took a long drink of lemonade, followed by another bite of sandwich. Across the table, Natalie sipped her own lemonade and tried not to stare. This woman was practically feral. The sandwich and chips were gone in about three minutes.

"When was the last time you ate?"

Chelsea looked up at Natalie's words but didn't say anything.

"Are you still hungry? There's plenty of chicken. I can make you another sandwich."

She stared down at the table for a moment, then nodded. After a second sandwich and a glass of milk, Chelsea stood up, hoisting the backpack onto her shoulder. "Can I use your bathroom?"

"Sure," Natalie said. She glanced out the window, watching Theo on the swing as she showed the way to the bathroom. She heard the lock click as she walked away.

In the kitchen, she picked up the phone and dialed Jed's cell number.

Half-an-hour later, Theo came running in from outside. "Daddy's home!" He ran to the back door, bouncing on his toes. "Daddy!" he yelled when Jed opened the door. Jed picked him up, throwing him over his shoulder.

"Where is she?" he asked Nat as Theo giggled and screamed.

"She's asleep in the living room," Natalie said. "On the floor."

"Asleep?" He put Theo down. "On the floor?" His eyebrows squished together in confusion.

"Yep. Theo dripped popsicle all over his shirt, so I took him upstairs to wash up and change. When I came back down, she was curled up by the boxes, sound asleep." She took the empty lunch box Jed handed her. "You should have seen her eat! She had two chicken sandwiches and half a bag of chips. I don't think she'd eaten for a while.

Theo tugged on Jed's hand. "Can you push me on the swing, Daddy?"

Natalie took charge. "Mommy will push you. Daddy's going to talk to..." she paused and looked at him. He shrugged.

"...Chelsea," she finished. "Come on, let's go." She took the boy by the hand and they walked out the back door.

Jed took a deep breath before heading into the living room. His sister was here. How many times had he tried to find her? Too many when they were first separated. The counselor the Whites sent him to at Coach Drake's recommendation suggested it wasn't healthy. Then Chelsea showed up at the apartment when he was in college wanting money. Jed called the authorities. What else was he supposed to do? She couldn't stay with him. After that, she disappeared again, running away from the group home. He'd tried once or twice since then, but except for a couple of computer searches, he'd basically given up since Theo was born. His life was full and his job was busy and right now, both of those seemed like lousy excuses for abandoning his baby sister.

In the living room, he stood and watched her for a few moments. She lay on the floor, one arm under her head for a pillow, the other thrown over a battered blue backpack. Her nails were bitten to the quick, just like when she was little. Back then, they got so sore they would bleed. Jed was always bribing or scolding her to keep her fingers out of her mouth. He rubbed the bridge of his nose and sighed, kneeling beside her.

"Chelsea," he shook her shoulder gently. "Hey," he said, when she opened her eyes.

She looked up at him and swallowed, her eyes filling. "I didn't have anywhere else to go."

"I'm glad you found me," he said.

Tears rolled down her cheeks, and she lifted her arm to brush them away. As she did, the sleeve of her hoodie slid up and Jed spied bruises on her arm.

He lowered himself all the way to the floor, sitting beside her. "What happened to you?"

She quickly yanked the sleeve down. "Nothing."

"Chelsea," he said, soft. "It's me. Take the jacket off. Let me see."

She shook her head.

"Someone hurt you. That's not on you."

She cried harder and slowly unzipped the hoodie. As it slipped off her shoulders, Jed gritted his teeth and felt his face flush. There were distinct fingermark bruises on her neck, upper arms, and wrists. Several round angry red circles marred the inside of one wrist, cigarette burns from the looks of them. He wasn't an expert, but what looked like track marks dotted the other arm.

"Who the hell did this to you?"

She shook her head. "It doesn't matter."

"It sure as hell does matter," he said. "I'm going to..."

"You're going to what, Jed? Beat him up?" She laughed harshly. "He'd kill you." She lowered her head and swiped at her eyes again with the sleeve of the jacket in her lap.

"Who is he?" Something told him not to let her know yet that he was in law enforcement. "I know some cops, Chelsea, I can take care of this."

"No," she shook her head. "No cops. I just had to get away, and now I am. I want to forget about

52

it. Please?" She scooted to a sitting position and brushed the hair from her face. Blue eyes, so like his own, stared back at him.

"Please promise me you won't try to find him."

"Okay," he said, after a beat.

"Can I stay here until I..." she paused and looked away. "I mean, I'll understand if you don't want me to, but like I said. I don't have anywhere else to go."

He took her hand and turned her arm over. "Are you using drugs? Are there drugs in that backpack?"

She dipped her head again and didn't answer.

Jed heard the back door open and reached for the backpack. "I'm going to take this to the garage. I won't have it in the house where Theo could get into it."

Chelsea clutched it. "There's nothing in here but clothes and stuff," she said. "I swear."

"Fine. Let's go upstairs and empty it."

She stood. "I should just leave."

"I don't want you to leave," Jed said. "But I can't have drugs in the house."

"Please don't go," Natalie said. She walked up to them. "At least stay tonight. You can sleep in Theo's room. He'll sleep with us. It's the only other bed and you aren't going to spend the night on the floor."

"Tomorrow I'll make some calls," Jed said. "We'll find you somewhere to get clean. When you get out, we'll be there for you, I promise. You can stay as long as you need to."

Natalie took her husband's hand and nodded.

Chelsea looked from one to the other, unsure.

"I'm making spaghetti for dinner," Natalie said. "There's plenty. Please stay."

Chapter 5

While Natalie finished preparing dinner, Jed showed his sister upstairs to Theo's room. He motioned for her to put the backpack on the bed.

"Empty it," he said.

"Jed…" She crossed her arms and narrowed her eyes at him. In that pose, she looked exactly like their mother.

"I mean it. Everything out. I won't have drugs in this house with my son."

Reluctantly, she unzipped the pack and started pulling out clothes, most of them filthy. There was a tattered, stained towel, a pair of flip-flops, a sketchbook, and a couple of paperbacks with no covers.

"That's it," she said.

"I don't think so." Jed picked up the backpack and unzipped the two side pockets. In one, he found a wad of bills, mostly ones, but a couple of twenties, too. In the other was a dirty cosmetic bag. He opened it and looked inside, then up at his sister. "I'll take this."

She bit her lip, then nodded.

"There's a towel and stuff in the bathroom in case you'd like to take a shower before we eat," Jed hoped she took him up on the offer, because frankly, she reeked of cigarette smoke and body odor.

She took a black t-shirt and a pair of jeans that looked almost clean from the pile of clothing on the floor. "I'll wash up and change," she said.

"I can throw the rest of your clothes in the washer, if you want."

Chelsea nodded. "Thanks."

By the time Chelsea joined them downstairs, Natalie had set the kitchen table with four places and was serving the food.

"I wasn't sure where to put the wet towel, so I hung it over the tub," Chelsea said.

"That's fine. Feel better?"

The woman nodded.

"I always do too, after a shower," Natalie said, as Chelsea took a seat at the table. Jed joined her, helping Theo into his booster as Natalie pulled the garlic bread from the oven and sliced it.

Chelsea looked everywhere but his eyes, and Jed took a moment to study his sister more closely. Cleaned up, she looked younger than her twenty-three years. Her damp hair clung to her face and her collarbones stuck out under the thin fabric of the t-shirt. Her nose was pierced and there was a tattoo of a skull and crossbones on her upper arm, with purple daisies where the eyes should be.

Bruises, some new, others faded yellow, covered both arms. A thin red scar ran from her ear about three inches down her neck, and another bisected an eyebrow. Her hands shook when she picked up the fork, but she ate her salad, two helpings of spaghetti, three slices of garlic bread, and drank another glass of milk. Theo kept staring at her, and Natalie kept redirecting his attention to the food on his plate.

After supper, Natalie took Theo upstairs for his bath while Jed began cleaning up the kitchen. Without him asking, Chelsea started clearing the table, scraping dishes into the trash and handing them to him to rinse and put into the dishwasher. There was no conversation, but they worked in a surprisingly easy rhythm, and soon the kitchen was spotless.

Chelsea ate a cookie and watched as Jed switched her clothes from the washer to the dryer and tossed the towels into the washer for later.

"Thanks for letting me stay," she said.

"You always have a place here. We're family." He sat down across from her and took a cookie from the jar. He reached out and ran a hand lightly down her arm, ending at the bruises on her wrist. She didn't pull away. "You sure you don't want to tell me what happened?"

"It doesn't matter."

"Chels, if someone hurt you…"

"I'm really tired," she said. "If it's okay, I think I'd like to go to bed now."

"Okay." He nodded, trying to hide his disappointment. "We can talk in the morning." He led the way back upstairs to Theo's room.

Natalie appeared in the doorway, a pajama-clad Theo on one hip, his hair in ringlets from his bath. "Here's a nightgown," she said. "I thought you might not have one."

"Daddy." Theo reached out for Jed. Jed took him and the boy settled his head on his father's shoulder. "Will you read me a story?" His thumb went into his mouth.

"Sure, Bud," he said. He turned to Chelsea. "Goodnight. Sleep well."

"G'night," she said.

"Hey," Jed leaned in and kissed his sister's cheek. "I mean it. I'm glad you're here." His free arm came up around her shoulder. "We'll figure this out."

For a second, she relaxed and leaned into him, then just as quickly, the moment passed and she pulled away. Jed turned and left, and she shut the door behind him.

****

The Winnie-the-Pooh clock on the wall in Theo's room read two-thirty when Chelsea opened her eyes. She blinked, staring at the ceiling for a few minutes. Her mind began spinning, the way it always did. What was she doing here? Jed had his own life. He didn't need her butting in. If she stayed, he would make her go to rehab. She'd tried that once before. She knew would be miserable and hard and then what? Live here with her brother and his perfect little family? How long would his wife put up with that? A tear trailed down her cheek. She shouldn't have come here. It only made things worse, seeing the life she would never have.

Silently, she slipped out of bed. After using the bathroom, she dressed in the t-shirt and jeans she'd worn the night before. Taking her backpack, she crept quietly down the stairs. The nightlight on the kitchen stove gave enough light for her to find the laundry room and fish her clothes out of the dryer. She stuffed them back into the backpack, and opened the refrigerator.

Chelsea didn't remember ever seeing a fridge this full of food. She took several packages of lunch meat and cheese, a half loaf of bread, an apple, and two chocolate bars she found in the crisper. Several cans of pop and a bottle of wine went into the backpack as well. She glanced around the kitchen and saw Natalie's purse hanging off the chair. She hesitated for a minute, listening for any sound from upstairs, then she rifled through until she found the woman's wallet. Not much cash, less than fifty, but squinting at Natalie's driver's license, she figured it could pass for her if no one looked too closely. She put that and a MasterCard into the side pocket of the backpack.

Her eyes did another sweep of the room. Her brother's wallet and car keys lay on the counter. She took his cash, almost $200, but left his bank cards. Hesitating, she stared at the car keys. It had been a long time since she'd driven. Would she remember how? It couldn't be that hard, she decided, and the car would get her farther than she'd ever get on foot or by bus, not that she had any idea where she was going.

Now for her stash. Where did Jed put it? He'd mentioned the garage, but once it was out of the backpack, it was small enough he could've hidden it anywhere. She'd heard him coming back upstairs, and it hadn't taken him that long. It had to be in the house somewhere.

Not in the kitchen, she didn't think. There was no sign of any place to hide it in the dining room, either. Her heart started to pound as she thought of losing it. It wasn't that much, she'd have to find more soon, but she *needed* that bag. In the living room, she forced herself to take several deep breaths and think. He'd want it up high enough that the kid couldn't get it. She wove through the stacks of boxes toward the front door, pausing at the fireplace. On the mantle was a small wooden chest carved with flowers and the words *For Natalie and Jed, June 12, 1999, Love Ian.* It was just the right size. She lifted the lid and smiled.

Chapter 6

Natalie kissed Theo's forehead and slipped out of bed, leaving him sleeping curled next to Jed. Yawning, she walked past the closed door to her son's room and down into the kitchen. She opened the cupboard and started to make coffee. When she turned to fill the carafe at the sink, she saw the contents of her purse scattered on the counter.

"What the..." Grabbing up her wallet, she looked through it, then headed upstairs, throwing open the door to Theo's room. The bed was empty, her borrowed nightgown in a puddle on the floor. Chelsea's things were gone.

"Jed," she called. "Wake up!"

"What?" He said as she came into the bedroom. "What's wrong?"

"She's gone. Your sister is gone and so is my driver's license and all my cash." She rifled through the wallet again. "And my MasterCard!"

"Shit!" Jed said. He headed downstairs in nothing but his boxers.

"Daddy said a bad word," Theo mumbled.

Natalie lifted him and he slumped against her, already asleep again by the time they got downstairs. She held him close, letting his soft breath on her neck calm her.

Jed walked out of the kitchen, his face a mixture of anger and confusion. "She took all my cash, too," He said, then. "Sonofabitch!"

"What?"

"My keys." He opened the door into the garage and turned on the light. "She stole our fucking car!"

Natalie put a hand over Theo's ear and scowled at him. "I hope you didn't just add *that* to our son's vocabulary."

Jed was already dialing the police. "They're sending an officer to take our statements," he said. He smacked his hand on the counter. "How could I be so stupid?"

"Honey," Natalie said. "You couldn't know she was going do this."

"She just shows up here out of the blue? With drugs in her backpack? I should have suspected she was up to something. She's always been just like our mother. I *should* have known. All she ever wants from me is money."

Natalie bit her lip and walked over, putting her free arm around him. His other arm came up, and he took a breath and kissed Theo's forehead. They stood like that for a moment until Theo stirred. Natalie put him down and he crawled up into one of the kitchen chairs.

"Cinnamon toast?" She asked. He nodded, and she went to the refrigerator for the bread. "She took food, too," she said, sighing. "The bread's gone and I think there was a package of ham in here and some salami."

"Sorry, Honey," she said to Theo. "No cinnamon toast. How about cereal?"

His face puckered, and he began to cry. "I want cim-a-non toast!"

"There isn't any bread so there's no toast." Jed whirled around. "Stop crying," he snapped.

Theo's eyes widened and Natalie moved in, scooping him up and whispering in his ear before he could start really wailing.

"You don't have to take it out on him," she said to her husband. She reached into the cookie jar and broke one of her own rules, handing Theo a sugar cookie. "Here, eat this and have a glass of milk. We'll go to the store in a bit and get some bread. You can have cinnamon toast for lunch."

"Really? Theo stared at the cookie, not sure how his fortunes had turned so quickly.

"Yes," Natalie said. She plopped him back down in the chair with the cookie in his fist and poured him a glass of milk.

"Is there any coffee?" Jed asked. "Or did she take that, too?"

"I was making it when I discovered my purse. I'll finish. You'd better get some clothes on before the police get here."

She lay a hand on his arm as he moved past her. "You wanted to help her. It's okay to see the good in people, Jed."

He didn't answer, but kissed her quickly and headed upstairs.

****

"They found the car just outside the city," Jed said the next day. He slumped, elbows on the counter, and tipped up the bottle of Heineken, taking a long sip. "It's been stripped down. Tires are gone," he sighed. "It's pretty much totaled."

"I liked that car," Natalie said.

"Yeah," Jed nodded. "Me, too." It was the first new car they'd owned, and it was just a year old.

"Insurance will cover it, won't it?"

"There are some hoops to jump through, but it should."

"Dad said we could borrow the Toyota if we need to. And they have a car seat for when Mom takes Theo, so we wouldn't have to get another one right away."

"They got Chelsea's prints off the steering wheel. There's a warrant out for her."

Natalie turned the chicken and put the pan back in the oven. "So what's next?"

"Hopefully, they find her. I mean, she stole our car. She charged over five hundred dollars on your credit card."

"I told you I called the bank and the card company. We don't have to cover it."

"She's still responsible. She deserves what's coming to her."

"And what's that?"

Jed shrugged. "She's got some priors for theft; mostly petty stuff. This time it's grand theft auto. She could get as much as five years. But it will be less if she pleads out."

Natalie grabbed a beer from the fridge for herself, twisting off the cap and taking a drink. "I don't know." She sat down next to Jed. "She seemed genuinely scared."

"Yeah, and maybe it was all an act."

"Those bruises weren't an act."

"She was running from someone." He sighed. "Part of me hopes she gets far away from whoever he is. But then I'm afraid that getting caught is the only way she'll ever get clean." He rubbed a hand over his face. "I don't want her to end up like our mom."

"I know." She put an arm around her husband and leaned into him. "I love you."

He kissed her temple. "I love you, too."

****

They arrested Chelsea two days after they discovered the car. The detective on the case called Jed at work and explained the charges. Chelsea was being held in the county lock-up and would be assigned a public defender. The lawyer would likely contact him, as would the assistant district attorney in charge of prosecuting the case.

Ted Allen, the assistant prosecutor, made contact first, arranging a meeting at his office when Jed got off work.

"So," he said as his assistant finished reading aloud the statements Natalie and Jed gave to the police the night Chelsea left with their car. "Is there anything you want to add or correct? Sometimes people remember things or find other things missing...'

"No," Natalie said. "That's it."

Jed raised his eyebrows and nodded in agreement.

"Alright. It's a pretty clear case as far as I can see. The attorney of record is Nancy Beaufort. She's good. I've worked with her before. She'll probably go for a plea deal. I'll let you know."

At work the next day, Jed paced in front of his office windows. Rain pounded on the glass and dripped down onto the sills. A swath of lightning cut the sky. The weather fit his mood perfectly. Even though it was his third cup and he knew more caffeine wouldn't do anything to settle his nerves, he picked up his mug and walked down the hall to the coffee machine.

Once he was back at his computer, Jed tried working through the spreadsheet he was analyzing, but he couldn't focus. His head was too full of his sister.

"Dammit," he muttered. He dug through the pile of notes on his desk until he found the one he was looking for. When the police called to say that Chelsea had been arrested, the officer gave him a number for the public defender assigned to her case. Jed looked at the scrawl on the sticky-note and picked up the phone.

Chapter 7

"What did the lawyer say?" Natalie asked, setting a bowl of ice cream and a spoon in front of Theo. She turned to the counter and came back with two more bowls, handing one to Jed.

He glanced at Theo. The child was totally absorbed in eating his dessert.

"If we agree to it," Jed said quietly. "Beaufort thinks she can get it down to a year - maybe less if Chelsea behaves herself. Then there would probably be probation." He sighed. "I told her we would think about it."

"And," Natalie licked the ice cream off her spoon. "What do you think?"

"I guess that would be okay. It's enough time for her to get clean, anyway. What do you think?"

"I feel sorry for her, honey," she said. "I can't help it. She seemed so scared. Maybe she was afraid to tell us what she was running from."

Jed shrugged. "Maybe. She sure didn't want to tell me anything about where she got those bruises."

"Can I have some more?" Theo held up his empty bowl.

"No, sport," Jed laughed. "One bowl of ice cream is enough. But, I'll play a game with you when I'm done talking to Mom."

"Shark Tale?" Theo asked, hopefully. The PS2 game his grandparents gave him for his birthday was his current obsession.

"Sure."

Theo ran off to the living room, and Jed turned back to Nat.

"So, I'll call tomorrow and let the lawyer know we're okay with the plea deal?"

"Yes." She paused, rising from the chair and picking up the bowls. "Maybe you should go see your sister."

"I thought about that. I guess I could ask Nancy Beaufort to set something up." He stood, too, lowering his head and running a hand over his close-cropped hair. "What am I going to say?"

She set the bowls in the sink and turned to him, putting a hand on his shoulder. She tipped his chin up and met his eyes. "You tell her she's your sister and you love her. That you'll - that *we'll* - be there for her when she gets out."

Jed smiled at his wife. "You always know what to say." He kissed her.

Natalie turned back to the sink. "I'm going to put these in the dishwasher and go take a bath. Katy dropped off the new John Grisham and I'm going to read in the tub. You," she said, "are in charge of bedtime tonight. When you guys finsh playing, can you have him take a quick shower? And don't keep him up too late. He has swimming lessons at the Y in the morning."

"Got it, boss," he saluted and gave her a smart aleck grin.

She swatted him with the dish towel as he left the kitchen.

****

"What do you mean she doesn't want to see me?"

The heavy-set officer behind the counter looked back at his computer and up at Jed. "The guard's message just says *Inmate declined visit.* No reason given."

"Can you ask again? I'm her brother. I'd really like to talk to her."

The man sighed and picked up the phone. "Gibson here, can you check on Shaw; #47927 again? About the visitor? He's still here. Pretty insistent." He held the phone between his shoulder and ear and shuffled some papers on the desk in front of him.

"Okay," he said after a minute. "I'll let him know."

Turning back to Jed, he shook his head. "She doesn't want to see you. Sorry."

Jed blew out a breath. "She knows it's me, right?" He tapped his fingers on the counter.

"You deaf? I told them who you were. She's refusing the visit. That's her right. You want to see her, then I suggest you go to the arraignment hearing. Her lawyer can tell you when that is." He stared at Jed. "We're done here."

Jed swore under his breath as he was walking away. He pulled out his cell and scrolled through recent calls to find the lawyer's number. After four or five rings, he got voicemail and left a message asking her to call back with the date and time of Chelsea's arraignment.

****

Chelsea hugged her knees to her chest on the narrow bunk. Her cellmate, Rose, a skinny woman with detailed tattoo sleeves on both arms, glanced at her for the third time, then scoffed.

"If I had someone who cared enough to visit me, I'd sure as hell go. Get out of this cell for twenty minutes anyway."

"I don't want to see him and I don't have to," Chelsea snapped.

"Whatever." Rose went back to biting her nails and reading a battered paperback.

"I stole his car," Chelsea said after a minute. "And money, and his wife's credit card."

"Huh," Rose said.

"What's worse is, he probably wants to forgive me."

"How's that worse?"

Chelsea chewed her lip. "I don't deserve it."

****

Jed went to the arraignment and listened as his sister pled guilty. The judge sentenced her to fourteen months in prison. They led Chelsea out of the courtroom in handcuffs. She never even looked at him.

Chapter 8

Natalie sat at the kitchen table with Theo while he did his math homework. She opened the battered recipe book that belonged to her grandmother, smiling as she recalled all the times they had looked through it together. Turning the pages carefully, she read through the recipes, stopping once in a while to jot a note on the legal pad in front of her.

Theo looked up. "Whatcha doin', Mom?"

"I'm thinking about using some of Nonna's recipes for a party we're catering."

Two years ago, when Theo started kindergarten, Natalie took several culinary classes at the local vo-tech college. In one, she befriended a classmate who worked at a caterer that was looking for help. Natalie applied and soon had a part-time job. Since most of the events were evenings and weekends, Jed was usually home to be with Theo. So far, the arrangement worked well. Natalie got to do what she loved and bring in a little extra money, without disturbing their family life.

The previous week, a bride-to-be approached the caterer with an unusual request. Rejecting the typical chicken, beef, or fish, she wondered if they could do an

Italian menu as a nod to her fiancé's heritage, since both sets of his grandparents were Italian.

Jennifer, who ran the operation, explained that Italian food wasn't their specialty, but Natalie, who was listening, spoke up.

"I think we can do it."

Her boss looked at her.

"My mother is Italian. My grandmother taught me to cook and I have her recipes—I'd be happy to go through them and see if there's anything we might make on a large scale that you might like."

"Really?" the bride said, beaming. "That would be fantastic! Authentic Italian recipes-I'm so excited!" She clapped her hands.

After the young woman left, Jennifer crossed her arms over her chest and looked at Natalie. "You'd better not have been blowing smoke."

"Of course not!" Natalie assured her. "I'll look through the recipes tonight and come up with some ideas."

Jennifer still looked skeptical, but she waved a hand and sent Natalie on her way. "Work up the pricing for each plate, too. And get it to me by the weekend so we can send her some choices and an estimate."

"I don't get this problem," Theo said, breaking into her thoughts. He slid the paper over to his mom.

Natalie stared at the arrangement of boxes and arrows. "What is this?" she said. "What are you supposed to do?"

"I dunno. Subtract, I guess."

She studied it again. "This makes no sense. I didn't learn subtraction like this."

The door opened and Jed came in, tossing his keys and wallet onto the counter. Natalie looked up. She hadn't realized how late it was.

"Hey," he said, giving her a kiss. "What's all this?" He gestured at the mess on the table.

"Not dinner, I'm afraid," she said. "I lost track of time."

Theo piped up. "Can we go to El Taco?"

"El Taco sounds El Okay-o to me," Jed said.

Theo rolled his eyes. "Dad joke alert."

"Let me finish up while you change," Natalie said. "Oh, and see if you can figure out this math homework. I'm stumped."

Jed changed into jeans and a grey Henley and sat down next to Theo. "This is ridiculous," he said after a minute. "I get what they want you to do." He plugged the numbers into the boxes and showed his son. "What I don't understand is why. It's so much easier this way." He jotted down the problem and solved it with the traditional subtraction algorithm, the way he learned it.   "See?" he said.

"Yeah," Theo nodded. "But I'd better do it the way Mr. Willetts wants us to."

Jed ruffled his son's hair. "Yep, but now you know two ways." He stood and looked over Natalie's shoulder. "Ready for El Taco?"

She closed the recipe book and glanced at her notes. She'd found several possibilities she could make on a large scale. After supper she would go over the ingredients and figure out the cost. Hopefully, it would be within the couple's budget. "Ready," she said. "And I really want a margarita."

****

The kitchen of the reception hall was stifling. Natalie heard the party going full blast in the large ballroom, spilling out onto the patio overlooking the immaculate lawn that sloped down to the river. The sun was setting and the light slanting in through the windows only added to the heat in the kitchen.

She wiped the sweat from her forehead with a sleeve and took a long drink from the bottle of water on the counter. Dinner had been a great success. The Italian wedding buffet included eggplant parmesan, beef ragu over penne, seafood Alfredo, and chicken manicotti, along with an assortment of appetizers. Almost every pan came back to the kitchen, picked clean.

Now they were preparing trays of lemon tiramisu, roasted almond and espresso cannoli, and a dark chocolate 'Torte della Nonna'; a delicious pastry tart with a dark chocolate custard filling topped with roasted pine nuts. There would be wedding cake, of course, but the bride and groom wanted to give the entire reception an Italian flair.

She was sliding a tray of tiramisu out of the fridge when a tall, slender woman with striking silver hair pulled up into a low chignon came through the doors.

"Excuse me," the woman said in a low, melodic voice that brought to mind an old movie actress whose name Natalie couldn't recall. "I'm looking for the chef."

"Just a sec," Natalie said. She placed the tray on the counter beside the others so that the servers could grab it and turned back to the visitor.

"I prepared the food tonight," she said. "Is there a problem?"

"Not at all. The opposite, actually." She held out her hand. "Stella Danielli."

"Natalie Shaw," she said, shaking her hand.

"Your food was delicious."

"Thank you."

"I own a restaurant here in Westlake called Sorriso," she said. "I'm looking for a chef and I think you just might be a great fit."

"Sorriso?" Natalie said. "I'm not sure I've heard of it."

"Well, until about a year ago, it was called Napoli."

"Oh! The café on the corner of Oak and Culver," Natalie said. "I thought it closed."

"I closed it temporarily." She leaned against the counter. "My parents started the restaurant over thirty years ago. My father passed away and when I looked around the place, I decided it needed to be updated, so I closed down, remodeled, put in a patio, and we opened three months ago under the new name. *Sorriso* means smile in Italian."

"It all sounds lovely, and I appreciate the offer, but I'm not sure about working full time. My son is just seven and..."

"Then this may be perfect for you," she interrupted. "What I'm most interested in is beginning a lunch service. The restaurant is close enough to the courthouse and other offices that I think we might draw people in by offering something other than the usual soup and salads, but my current chef is already working forty-plus hours a week just with dinner."

"Wow, um…" Natalie reconsidered. "Lunch hours would be when Theo was in school."

"That's what I was thinking." She reached into the bag on her wrist and pulled out a card and pen. Scribbling something on the back, she handed it to Natalie. "Call me at this number on Monday. The restaurant is closed and I can show you around, give you a feel for the place. We can talk and decide if you think it would work for you."

Natalie took the card, slipping it into the pocket of her black pants. "I will," she said. "Thank you."

"I look forward to talking more." They shook hands again and the older woman exited the kitchen.

****

At home that night, she told Jed about the encounter. "And then," Natalie took a sip from her bottle of beer, "the woman gave me her card and asked me to call her. She wants me to come down to her restaurant and see if we're a 'good fit'." Natalie couldn't hide her excitement.

He tipped back his own bottle. "That's great," he said. "But won't working in a restaurant mean a lot more hours than what you're doing now? What about Theo?"

"She wants to start serving lunch," Natalie said. "That would be perfect. I could go in after I drop him off and I'd most likely be done by the time he's out of school."

"If I'm not, I'm sure Ian would be happy to pick him up." Her brother had quit college and was living back at home. He'd set up a workshop in her parent's barn where he built and refinished cabinets and other furniture. He was also dating her best friend, Katy, who was six years older and taught art at the high school.

"Sounds too good to be true," Jed said. "But I definitely think you should go talk to her. See what the job entails, then we can make a decision."

"I wouldn't be as available for room mom stuff at school," she said. "And I already told Mr. Willetts I would head things up." She sighed.

"Isn't head room mom mostly making phone calls?"

She rolled her eyes at her husband. "You have no idea."

Jed was quiet for a moment. He finished his beer and leaned across the table, taking her hand in his and brushing a kiss across her knuckles. "This is your dream," he reminded her. "I think Theo will survive if you miss a few class parties."

"I'm more worried about Mr. Willetts," she laughed. "But I've got a good feeling about this, Jed. This could be my dream job!"

Chapter 9

Natalie collapsed into one of the chairs under the striped awning on *Sorriso's* patio, slipping off her shoes and putting her feet up on a second chair. It was just the first of August, and the kitchen was already stifling tonight. She finished the bottle of water she was drinking and ran a hand through her damp hair. A slight breeze ruffled the ferns hanging from hooks at the edge of the roof and she closed her eyes and turned her face up to it. A few minutes later, her boss, Stella Danielli, came outside carrying a tray with a bottle of wine and two glasses. It was their routine since Natalie became head chef three years before, to spend some time after closing on Thursdays to catch up and plan the menu for the next week.

"I'm not surprised you're exhausted. You outdid yourself tonight," Stella said. "The *Pasta al Limone* was..." she searched for a word. "...exquisite. Something was different. What was in it?"

"It's simple, really, lemon, garlic, butter, and a little bottarga."

"Bottarga?"

"Salted, cured fish roe," Natalie said. "They call it poor-man's caviar, imported from Italy. I grated a bit on top of the pasta. It adds a richness; don't you think?"

83

Stella uncorked the bottle and poured wine into each of the glasses. "Well, whatever it adds, I ate every last bite of mine. It was a huge hit in the dining room, too. What if we put it on the regular menu?"

Natalie sipped her wine. "I don't see why not. Bottarga is expensive, but I don't use much in each dish, it's just grated on top like parmesan, and it keeps forever. The block I have should easily last us through the fall."

Stella made a note on the pad in front of her. "How *is* the fall menu coming?"

"Great," Natalie said. She was excited about several new recipes. "Jed and Theo have enjoyed sampling my creations the last few weeks."

"I see Theo worked his last shift."

"Yes, we packed the car, and he's heading out in the morning," she said. She tried to keep her face neutral but failed. She was going to miss having her son home, not to mention working with him. Theo's summer job had been busing tables and filling in as a server during busy hours and it was nice to look out and see him, handsome in his crisp white shirt and black pants, filling water glasses or carrying trays of food to the tables. He seemed to have gained a new appreciation for what she did, too. Now he was heading back for his sophomore year at Northwestern.

Stella sympathized. "I know you loved having him here with you. He did an excellent job. He can certainly come back next summer if he wants to."

"He might, unless he stays in the city. Have you hired anyone to replace him?"

"Yes, I did." She nodded and flipped a page back in her notebook. "His name is Dylan Severns. Don't know too much about him, but he had good references from a couple of places, one in Willamette and one in Evanston. She shrugged. "He was neat and polite. What he doesn't know, he can learn." She took a drink from her glass of wine, then held it with both hands. "Tell me more about the fall menu."

"Alright," Natalie pulled a thin notebook out of her apron pocket. "I'm going to do the osso buco again, but over polenta, rather than in the ravioli like last year. For the ravioli I'm imagining a chicken sausage with chili and parmigiano, in a vodka cream sauce."

"Those both sound delicious. Which one did your men like better?"

"They both liked the osso buco," she laughed. "But that's always their favorite, no matter what I do with it. I've also come up with a new appetizer... Arancino." She paused when Stella held up a finger, showing that she was thinking and didn't want Natalie to explain.

After a moment, she said. "Fried risotto balls?"

"Yes!" Natalie said. "Theo *loved* these. I couldn't make enough," she laughed. "I stuffed them with ragu, parmesan, and eggplant." She held up her hand, thumb and index finger, almost touching to show the approximate size.

"Sounds yummy. We'd offer a plate of three? With tomato sauce?"

"That sounds about right–maybe tomato and alfredo. Or a larger plate of six or eight to share?"

Stella's pen flew across the paper. "Let's do both. We'll add that to the usual fall line-up of the antipasto platter, lamb meatballs, and crostini with Caponata."

"Great." Natalie glanced back at her notes. "I was also thinking of adding a roasted sea bass–if our supplier thinks he can get what we need. It would be simple, with lemon and fresh herbs."

"I like that idea."

"I'll do the chicken cacciatore again. It's always popular." Natalie swirled the wine in her glass. "We'll keep the bolognaise sauce and shrimp alfredo on the menu." She took another drink of wine. "This is good," she said. "What is it?"

"It's called Argyle, a Pinot Noir from Oregon. I had it in the city a couple of weeks ago and liked it, so I ordered some."

"It's very light, but not at all fruity. It will hold up well with the heartier fall menu."

"That was my thought." Stella smiled and put down her pen. "I think we're set. Get me the details and write up some descriptions and I'll send everything to the printer on Friday."

"I thought we could start the new menu the first of October," Natalie said. "That's a Saturday, always a good night to launch, and hopefully the weather will be cooler by then." She fanned herself with the notepad.

"I'm going to get some bigger fans installed in the kitchen. I don't like the ones we have. They don't move enough air."

Natalie gave her a thumbs up and yawned. "If we're done, I'm going to head home."

"Get out of here," Stella said, waving a hand. "Go home to that handsome husband of yours."

"Theo, too," she said. "It's his last night at home. We probably won't see him until Thanksgiving unless we go to the city. He and Jed were going to have popcorn and watch a movie." She wrinkled her nose. "Cars will crash. Things will blow up. People will die."

Stella laughed. "At least it will keep you awake for a while."

"We can hope," Natalie said, pushing up from the chair. "See you tomorrow."

****

Jed handed a bowl of popcorn to Theo and took his place on the couch. He glanced at his watch. It was Thursday, which meant Nat would be a little later, since she always met with Stella after closing. That was fine. She wouldn't like this movie, anyway.

"You're sure you don't need Mom and I to bring anything on Sunday?"

"I'm pretty sure I got it all packed," Theo said. "If I forgot anything, you can always mail it to me."

Jed shot his son a look. "Like your mother would pass on an opportunity to come and see you."

"True," Theo said. He clicked the remote and queued up the movie.

Jed looked on as his son tipped up the bottle and took a sip of beer. He was only twenty, but Jed and Natalie harbored no illusions that he abstained while he was at school. The at-home rule was that he could have a drink with them, but if he drank anywhere else, he needed to call for a ride home. It worked well over the summer, and they'd only picked him up once, from an all-day barbeque and pool party with some high-school friends. He'd gotten in the car sunburned and happy, buzzed, but not trashed, and promptly fell asleep on the short drive home.

Jed was pretty sure they'd raised a good kid. Theo got excellent grades. He was even-tempered, dependable, and had a lot of friends. He didn't seem interested in fraternity life, which was a relief to Natalie, who'd had a few run-ins with idiot frat-boys during her short time at NW. There was no steady girlfriend, although the name Olivia came up quite a bit in conversation, always preceded by '*my friend*'. They'd yet to meet his friend Olivia, but Natalie was curious enough to stalk her Facebook page. Jed chided her, of course, but not before looking over his wife's shoulder to see what this girl looked like.

"Mom's home," Theo said as headlights hit the driveway. The garage door went up, and Finn and Charley bounded into the kitchen to greet her.

"Any popcorn left for me?" Natalie called from the kitchen.

"I'll share," Jed yelled back. On the screen, Liam Neeson aimed a gun at some idiot who had pissed him off.

Nat came through the family room, ruffling Theo's hair and giving Jed a peck on the lips. "Don't eat all the popcorn. I'm going to take a quick shower and I'll be right back down."

Theo held up his empty bowl. "Better just make some more, Dad."

Natalie leaned against him, eyes on the screen, fingers in the popcorn bowl. "That makes ten," she said. "And that's just since I came downstairs."

Theo rolled his eyes and laughed. It was a family joke that Natalie kept a body count whenever they watched one of these movies. "There were about six or seven before that, Mom," he told her.

"Thanks, sweetie. I knew I could count on you." She poked Jed. "That makes seventeen. He's killed seventeen people and we're supposed to be *rooting* for him."

"But they were bad people," Theo said.

"Very bad," Jed agreed.

Natalie yawned.

"Why don't you go to bed," Jed said. "This is almost over."

"I'd rather stay here with the two of you." She snuggled closer, and he put an arm around her. She was asleep before the next gunshot.

90

Chapter 10

"Jed," Tom Delgado said. "Can I see you in my office?"

After tossing his jacket over the chair and grabbing a file of printouts on the current case, Jed made his way down the hall to his boss' office.

"Morning," Tom said. "Did you have a good weekend?"

"Yeah, we did." He smiled. "Natalie and I are empty-nesters with Theo back in school. How about you?"

"It was good. Kayla was home, so we did some shopping for her new apartment." He laughed. "I knew college was expensive, but no one warned me it didn't stop when they graduated. Consider this your 'head's up'."

"Thanks," Jed chuckled, then opened the file folder and slid a paper across the desk to him.

"I can't find anything linking the mayor to what the auditor was doing. I don't think she knew anything about it. She looks clean to me."

"Okay, good. But that's not why I asked you in here." He sat back in his chair. "Mark Yeager is retiring as of January 1."

Jed nodded. Major Mark Yeager was head of the Special Investigations Unit and their direct boss. "I read the email. He's a good guy. Sorry to see him go."

"I'm being promoted to take his place."

"That's great!" Jed said, meaning it. Tom was dedicated to DCI and supportive of the detectives and agents he worked with. "We'll be sorry to lose you here, but you're perfect for the job."

"Thanks. And you aren't losing me. Since Tyler is a sophomore, Jenni and I really don't want to uproot him. I asked if I could work from here, rather than Champaign, at least until he graduates. Colonel Rogers agreed. So I'll be around." He cleared his throat. "I'm recommending you as my replacement."

Jed blinked slowly. "Me? But Kurt and Doug both have more years."

"They do," Tom agreed. "But neither of them is the investigator you are. This job is as much about knowing where to dig and..." He tapped a finger on the paper Jed had given him. "... when to stop digging as it is administration. You'll lead by example."

"Wow, well, I'm honored, really. Thank you."

"It's not 100% yet. Like everything, it will have to go up the ladder, but I think my recommendation will carry some weight. You can expect a call from Yeager, and probably Colonel Rogers, too. They'll want a face-to-face interview, I'm sure."

"Who else is being considered?"

"They mentioned Sarah Fletcher, from Central Command. That's the only other name I've heard, but I'm sure a few more will throw their names in."

Jed considered this. "And if Kurt or Doug is one of those?"

"You'll still have my support. You're my guy, Jed."

"I appreciate that." He picked up the file on Tom's desk. "I'll write this up and get it to you this afternoon. We should let the city council know as soon as possible that there's no involvement on the part of the mayor. After that, I'll set up an interview with the legislative aide who called the other day. What did you think of her story?"

"About the Lieutenant Governor?" Tom slipped off his glasses and rubbed the bridge of his nose. "I'm not sure. It's not a lot, really. And 'me too' is such an issue right now. We'll need to handle this discreetly. I want to be in on that interview."

"I thought maybe you would. I'll look at your schedule before I set it up."

"Thanks."

"Sure thing, and congratulations, again."

Tom smiled. "When you get *my* job, we'll have to get our wives and go out to celebrate."

"Sounds good."

****

It was a busy Saturday night at Sorriso. Natalie pulled a tray of bruschetta out of the oven and slid it down the counter to Kendall, who added the last touches, basil and a drizzle of balsamic vinegar. She loaded it onto plates and put it out for the servers.

Lily came into the kitchen and Natalie took the slip from her outstretched hand, reading it quickly. "Two lasagnas, a salmon Caesar, and one osso buco ravioli," she called out to the kitchen.

"Got it," Kendall responded. She plated the lasagna and passed both to Danie,l who poured a dipper of alfredo over the top of each one and added a sprig of Italian parsley. Janine pulled the prepped Caesar from the walk-in and waited by the grill for the salmon.

Natalie plated the osso buco herself, dropping the fresh pockets of ravioli into the boiling water and plucking them out in exactly four minutes. She topped it with the braising gravy, a pinch of parmesan, and parsley.

Janine fanned the salmon out over the salad and passed it to Lester. The newest addition to the kitchen stopped chopping carrots and topped the salad with crunchy fried onions and house-made croutons. He loaded it on the tray with the other meals, and Lily carried it out to the dining room as they prepped the next order.

Natalie put on the heavy oven mitts and checked the focaccia – sundried tomato and garlic tonight. She pulled one of the two pans out of the oven, set it on the counter, and slid a third one in.

"Table four wants more bread," Janine called.

"Got it," Lester said. He sliced a square from the hot pan, grabbed a prepared ramekin of seasoned olive oil and set it all in the ceramic serving dish, handing it to Janine.

The kitchen was running smoothly enough that Natalie grabbed a bottle of water and slipped into Stella's office for a quick break. She picked up a discarded menu and fanned herself for a few minutes while she sipped on the water.

She took out her phone. There was a text from Jed and two from her mother. She clicked on her husband's first. *Working late. Bring home dinner and we can eat together.*

She smiled as she typed back. *Osso Buco sound good?* They rarely ate that late – she wouldn't be home until ten – but tomorrow was Sunday and they could sleep in.

Before she could read her mother's texts, there was a rap on the door. "Table 7 wants the fettuccine with chicken instead of shrimp. Can we do that?"

"Yes," Natalie said. "Use the leftover breasts I pounded thin for lunch. They'll cook fast. I'll be right there to put it together."

She pocketed her phone and adjusted her jacket as she headed back into the kitchen.

Two hours later, there were just three tables finishing up and a couple eating appetizers at the bar. It was Kendall's night to close. Natalie boxed up two salads, the servings of osso buco, and a square of focaccia.

"I'll see you all on Tuesday at ten for the weekly meeting," she said. "I'm making frittatas. Daniel, can you start the washer with the towels and napkins? I'll come in tomorrow and put everything in the dryer."

"Sure, chef," Daniel said.

"I can come in tomorrow if you'd rather not," Lily said.

"Really?" Natalie gave her a smile. "That would be great! Thank you."

"Sure. I can refill the oil candles for the tables while the stuff dries. That's one less thing to do Tuesday morning."

On her way out, Natalie paused, laying a hand on Kendall's shoulder. "You're doing a fabulous job," she told her sous chef. "How would you like to plan this week's lunch special?"

Kendall turned, her eyes bright. "I'd love to! Thanks, chef!"

Natalie smiled. "You earned it. I can't wait to hear what you come up with."

****

Jed's car wasn't in the garage when she arrived home, so Natalie slipped the osso buco into the oven, set it on warm, and headed for the shower.

She stood under the spray, her eyes closed, as the hot water eased the tension in her neck and shoulders.

"Want me to wash your back?"

She startled at her husband's voice. "You scared me," she chided.

"Not the reaction I was hoping for," Jed said. His shirt already discarded, he stepped out of his pants and boxers and into the shower, wrapping his arms around her and pulling her into a kiss.

She met his tongue with her own and slid her hands down his back, giving his butt a playful smack. "That's for being such a bad boy," she teased.

"I'm sorry," he murmured, his lips skimming her ear and making her shiver despite the hot water coursing over them. "I can be good." He kissed his way down her body.

"Oh, I know you can," she said as she leaned back against the wall, her breath coming in short, quick gasps as he reached his destination.

They ate the osso buco and drank a bottle of Chianti in their pajamas, watching Chance the Rapper host Saturday Night Live.

"Theo would love this," Natalie said as the rapper segued into another number. "I wonder if he's watching."

"Yeah, he would. Afraid I'm not a fan," Jed grimaced.

She leaned her head on his shoulder. "I miss him."

"Me, too. But it's kind of nice to have the house to ourselves, isn't it?" He kissed her temple. "At least you didn't have to be quiet in the shower earlier."

"True," she laughed. "There are perks to being empty-nesters."

They enjoyed a few more of those perks the next day. After sleeping in and their usual 3-mile weekend run, Jed suggested brunch at a café Natalie had been wanting to try in a nearby town.

"This is perfect," she said as the waiter led them to a table outdoors. The patio was shaded by an awning and a large oak tree and faced a park across the street. It was shady and quiet. Natalie took a sip of her coffee and smiled at her husband.

"What are you thinking?" she asked.

"I'm thinking that it's been too long since we took a vacation. Any chance you could get some time off this fall?"

"Hmmm. Maybe. Do you have a destination in mind?" She put down her menu and set her elbows on the table, resting her chin in her hands as she looked at him.

"Well, as a matter of fact." He grinned and slipped his phone out of his pocket. Scrolling through, he found what he was looking for and slid it across the table to her.

She studied it, then looked up, her eyes wide. "Italy?"

"You've always wanted to go." He gazed at her over the brim of his cup as he took a sip. "And we never really had a honeymoon. Why not go big?"

"But... can we afford it? I mean, with tuition and..."

Jed set his cup down. "I had a meeting with Tom Delgado yesterday. He's getting promoted and he wants me to replace him."

She reached over and squeezed his hand. "That's wonderful! Why didn't you tell me last night?"

"I got a little distracted." He brought her hand to his lips and kissed it. "Anyway, it's not a sure thing yet. There will be other applicants for the job, but I have Tom's recommendation."

"When will you know for sure?"

"Tom's new job won't start until after the first of the year. So, I may not know until then, or closer to Christmas." He shrugged. "It depends on how the process works. Tom's been the captain of the intelligence division since I started, so I'm not sure how they'll do it."

"Maybe we should wait then... plan this vacation for next year instead."

The waiter arrived with their food, and Jed poured the warm syrup over his pancakes before he answered. "I don't want to wait. I want to take you away somewhere."

"It doesn't have to be Italy right now," Natalie said. She took a bite of her breakfast, a savory crepe with a fried egg, bacon, and cheese. "We could go somewhere tropical." She raised an eyebrow.

"I thought you'd be thrilled with Italy," Jed said. His shoulders dropped.

"Oh, Honey," Natalie said, realizing his disappointment. "I am! It's sweet of you to think of it. I just think we would need more time to plan that kind of trip. It's once-in-a-lifetime. We want to do it right. Stella has been there several times so she could help us."

Jed was quiet for a bit as he ate his pancakes. "I get it, I guess," he said. "I just wanted to surprise you."

"I know," Natalie said. "and I love you for that, among other things."

"Someplace tropical, huh?" His blue eyes settled on hers.

She winked at him. "Where we don't need many clothes."

Part II

Chapter 11

Stunned by her husband's call, Natalie clicked off and put the phone in her pocket. She was glad Stella wasn't in the restaurant tonight. She would want details, and Natalie had no idea how to explain the situation yet. Two little girls were coming to live with them. How was this going to work?

She turned to Kendall. "I'm going to need to leave," she told her sous chef. "Can you and Daniel finish things tonight?"

"Absolutely," the young woman said. "What's up? Everything okay?"

"Just a family thing," Natalie said. She looked around the busy kitchen, quickly taking stock.

"Everything is ready to go," she said. "There are two full pans of eggplant lasagna in the oven. It should be done in about fifteen minutes or so, and then you can just keep it on warm." Her latest variation on lasagna was their popular Wednesday night special. "The salads are prepped and in the fridge and there's plenty of Bolognese sauce for the pasta."

"I've got it. No problem," Kendall said. "You go do what you need to do."

"Thanks." Natalie gave her a grateful smile. She knew her assistant could handle it.

Natalie tossed her apron in the laundry basket and slipped her jean jacket over the black t-shirt she wore with khaki pants. She fished her keys out of her purse and tapped out a text to Jed as she walked through the darkening parking lot to the car.

She typed: *How old are they? How long will they stay?*

A bubble appeared, letting her know Jed was answering. She hoped he was using voice control and not texting while he drove.

8 and 5. I don't know how long.

Using Siri, she responded. *Should I get clothes? Toys? Do they have anything at all?*

Assume not. Pajamas, for sure. Some clothes. What do girls play with now?

I'll call Anna Calhoun down the street. Hannah is in third grade, so she'll have a good idea. Headed to Target now.

K. Love you.

She sent back a heart. As she drove to the shopping area, Natalie worried about her husband. Jed hardly ever talked about his childhood. He'd told her a condensed version of his life story the first night they met, then details leaked out here and there, but it wasn't something he discussed easily.

The last time they saw Chelsea was when she showed up out of nowhere, starving and covered in bruises, just after they bought the house. They fed her, gave her a place to sleep, and she left in the middle of the night, stealing their money and their car. When she was caught, she pled down the charges, but still ended up with over a year in prison. They had heard nothing from her since, and Jed wondered more than once if she was even alive.

Before that visit, Natalie had met Jed's sister exactly once; the time she came to Jed's apartment in college and threw a fit when he wouldn't give her money.

Still, those impressions aside, there was something so wretched and vulnerable about the woman that Natalie couldn't help feeling sorry for her. Now she was missing. What would this do to Jed? She forced herself to take a deep breath and concentrate on the task at hand. She needed to make these girls feel at home.

Once she got to Target, Natalie called her neighbor Anna, who had three daughters. She talked Natalie through the unfamiliar little girl's section, helping her choose two pairs of pajamas, one with a flowered pattern for the older girl, and another with puppies chasing balls for the five-year-old. She added several packages of underwear, t-shirts, jeans, and leggings, and a simple dress for each girl. Anna suggested waiting on shoes since sizes were too hard to predict.

Pushing the cart through the store, Natalie threw in two bright yellow comforters with daisies on them, 2 fuzzy pillows, and several stuffed animals, including a rabbit that was so soft she held it to her cheek for a moment, remembering her son's baby days. She added boxes of crayons and markers, two thick pads of drawing paper, and stickers–didn't every kid like stickers? She tapped a note into her phone to get the box of Theo's old books down from the storage space above the garage when she got home.

At the last minute, she detoured to the grocery section, grabbing things she recalled Theo liking as a child; frozen waffles, chocolate milk, chicken nuggets, and boxes of orange macaroni and cheese that made her cringe. Her phone dinged as the clerk was bagging the last of the purchases.

At the hospital. Meeting the caseworker here. I'm thinking I won't be home tonight. I might call Antonio and see if I can crash.

She texted back. *Call me when you know for sure.*

****

"This way," Hannah Wilkes said. She was young and fresh-faced, barely five-feet tall. Jed felt like he was walking with a child, but she moved confidently down the window-lined hospital corridor, her low heels clacking on the tile.

"Still no luck locating the mother–your sister. I'm sorry. It seems from the little we've been able to get from the neighbors, it isn't unusual for them to be alone. The lady across the hall says she checks on them if she hasn't seen Chelsea that day. She also told us there's a friend that sometimes stays there or takes them back to her place if it's late, but all we've got is a first name–Skylar." She looked at him as if he's supposed to know who that was.

"I haven't spoken to my sister in a really long time," he said. "I didn't even know she had kids."

They reached the elevator bay, and she pushed the button. "The girls are up on five."

Jed shoved his hands into his pockets and watched the lights move from one number to another until they arrived on the 5th floor. He wished Nat were here. What could he possibly say to these girls? He was a complete stranger to them. He'd like to throttle his sister. The doors opened and Hannah Wilkes exited, turning quickly to the right down a busier hallway. She stopped at a nurses' station and flashed her identification.

"CPD brought in two minors; Josie and Zora Winters? This is their uncle."

"Room 513," the nurse said, briefly looking up from her computer. "I'll let Dr. Montoya know you're here. She's the one taking care of them."

"Thank you." She motioned for Jed to follow her. They turned a corner past the nurses' station and found themselves in front of 513. "You ready?"

Jed paused, then nodded.

The caseworker slowly pushed open the door. Two pairs of brown eyes stared at him. The bigger girl, evidently Josie, sat on the edge of the bed, long skinny legs hanging over the edge. Her tawny brown skin was flecked with scratches and bite marks. Fleas or bedbugs, Jed thought, mentally cursing his sister again. The other child seemed swallowed up by the pillow and blankets, her hair a dark, tangled mess around her face. A shade darker than her sister, her mouth puckered when she saw him, ready to cry.

"Josie, Zora, this is..."

"Are you another doctor?" Josie interrupted the caseworker, patting her sister as tears rolled down the younger girl's cheeks.

"No," Jed said. He glanced at Hannah Wilkes and took the chair from its place in the corner, moving it so he could sit right across from her, at eye level. "I'm Jed and your mother is *my* sister – just like Zora is *your* sister. That makes me your uncle. We're family."

"Mama never told us we had an uncle. She said we don't have nobody but each other." Her mouth settled into a thin line and she stared at him.

Jed frowned, his forehead wrinkling. "Well, we haven't seen each other for a long time."

"Why?" Before Jed could answer, the other child tugged on the sheet and Josie turned her head.

"He's not a doctor," she said to her sister. Then she looked back at Jed. "She doesn't like shots."

"Neither do I." Jed swallowed, seeing something familiar in his niece's eyes. "So since we *are* family, my wife and I want you girls to come stay with us for a little while. Until..."

"Until your mother comes back," Ms. Wilkes finished.

Josie sighed and folded her arms across her chest. "Whatever."

"Has this happened before?" Jed asked.

"We stay with Skylar sometimes," she said, not meeting his eyes.

108

Ms. Wilkes spoke up again. "Does your mom leave you alone a lot?"

"I already told you." Her eyes narrowed. "She works."

Jed wished the woman would leave. "Where does she work?"

One shoulder lifted and fell. "Different places. She waits tables sometimes."

"Who takes care of you?" Ms. Wilkes again.

"You and that policeman asked me all these questions already," Josie said, rolling her eyes.

"I bet you've been taking care of your sister, haven't you?" Jed said.

Josie raised her chin, but didn't say a word.

"You're nice." Zora said, her voice scarcely above a whisper. "That other man who talked to us wasn't very nice."

The door opened and a heavy-set woman in a white coat entered. Thick dark hair was pulled into a braid that hung down her back. "I'm Dr. Montoya," she said. "Are you a relative?"

"Yes," Jed said. "I'm their uncle."

"Good. There are some papers for you to sign. I need to do a debridement of Zora's..." She glanced at her chart. "... left calf. And she should stay overnight with IV antibiotics. There's an infection."

"A debridement?" Jed glanced toward the bed, where Josie was comforting her sister, who was crying again.

"Yes," the doctor said. "We'll numb the area and remove the damaged tissue. Hopefully we won't have to go very deep, but it looks like it's been infected for a while. She's lucky it didn't get into the bloodstream."

Jed felt a tug on his jacket and turned to look down at Josie.

"I have to stay with her," she said. "She's scared."

"That's simply not...," the doctor began.

"I *have* to!" Josie said, louder, staring up at the doctor and balling her hands into fists.

Jed crouched down to her level and met her eyes. "I'll see what I can do," he said.

She looked away, pressing her lips together, then nodded.

"Will you sit with Zora while the doctor and I talk in the hall? I'll be right back." He shot a look at the caseworker and the two women stepped into the hall. Jed followed, shutting the door behind them.

Chapter 12

"Thanks," Jed said to the orderly, who handed him a pillow and blanket. "I appreciate it." The young man grunted an acknowledgement and left.

Josie eyed him from the bed where she lay tucked in beside Zora. The younger child was asleep, long eyelashes grazing her tear-stained cheeks. The debridement had gone well, from the doctor's point of view. After talking with Jed, Dr. Montoya allowed Josie and him to stay in the corner closest to the head of the bed where Zora could make eye-contact with her sister during the procedure.

"You really gonna stay here all night?" Josie asked now.

"I really am," Jed said. He already called Natalie to let her know what he was doing. He kicked off his shoes and took off his dress shirt, hanging it on the hook on the back of the door. Now in his t-shirt and khakis, he pulled the lounge chair closer to the bed and sat, cranking up the footrest, adjusting the pillow, and attempting to get comfortable. It was going to be a long night.

Reaching over, he flipped the switch on the wall by the door. Even with the lights off, the room was by no means dark. Light spilled in from the hallway, and a nightlight from the bathroom cast long shadows on the floor and across the end of the bed. Josie still stared at him.

"Why're you staying?"

"Because I don't want you to feel like you have to stay awake. You should go to sleep. I'll be right here."

Josie glanced at her sister, then back to him. "She wakes up sometimes."

"I'll be right here," he repeated.

"I'm not that tired."

"Okay," Jed said. He thought of a trick that used to work with Theo. "I'll play some music on my phone. We can just lie here and listen. Does that sound good?"

Josie shrugged. "Okay, I guess."

He pulled out his phone and scrolled through the playlists. Finding the one he wanted, he tapped it and the Eagles began singing *Best of My Love*. By the third track on *Soft Rock Love Songs,* Josie's eyes drifted closed, but Jed stayed awake, studying his nieces for a long time.

Zora woke up twice. Once, when the nurse came to check on her and again an hour or so later. "I gotta go," she whispered to Jed.

He stuck his head out in the hallway, but seeing no one, came back into the room. He carefully lifted Zora from the bed with one arm and wheeled the IV pole with the other, maneuvering into the tiny bathroom. He was grateful for the hospital gown that made it easy for her to take care of things herself.

"I'll be right outside, okay? I'll help you back to bed when you're done."

He leaned against the wall outside the bathroom and yawned. He must have closed his eyes, because a yelp from the bed startled him.

"Where's Zora?" Josie cried.

"Shh...," Jed said. "She's in the bathroom."

Josie hopped down and skittered across the floor past Jed, opening the door and slipping inside. He heard her whispering to her sister.

After a moment, Josie came out, pushing the IV pole.

"Let me get her, okay?" Jed said. Josie hesitated, so he added, "You don't want to pull out the needle and hurt her."

Both girls back in bed, Jed stretched out on the recliner again and closed his eyes, finally slipping into a restless sleep.

****

Late the next afternoon, Natalie paced back and forth in the kitchen. When she heard the garage door open, she took a deep breath and tucked a loose strand of hair behind her ear. The butterflies in her stomach started doing backflips. Somehow in her mind, welcoming these girls perfectly had gotten all tied in with her love for Jed and what he'd gone through as a kid. She wanted everything to be just right.

The kitchen door swung in, and she met his eyes first. He carried one girl, the lower half of her leg wrapped in a pink bandage. The other stood in front of him, head bowed. Jed gently set the smaller child down and she immediately reached for her sister's hand.

"This is Zora." He lay a hand on the little one's head. "And this is Josie," he said.

Natalie bent to be eye-to-eye with them. "I'm your Aunt Natalie," she said. "I'm so glad you're here. I have a room all ready for you. Do you want to see it?"

The smaller one looked at her sister, and after a moment, they both nodded.

The four of them walked through the family room and up the stairs, Natalie in the lead and Jed following behind the girls, who still held hands. When she reached the door to the bedroom, both girls stopped and stared. Jed lay a hand on his wife's shoulder.

"You did all this in twenty-four hours?"

"It's just a couple of new bedspreads and some pillows," she said.

But it was more than that. After a phone call, her parents delivered the white desk from her childhood bedroom and she stocked it with the art supplies she'd bought. The bookcase was full of Theo's old picture books and some other newer titles Anna contributed. There was a mobile of colorful birds hanging in one corner over two bright yellow bean bag chairs. The girls' new clothes had been washed and hung in the closet.

"This is our room?" Josie said, looking up at them.

"Yep," Jed said, smiling. He gave her a little push. "Go check it out."

Zora walked in and immediately grabbed the stuffed rabbit off one of the beds, squeezing it tightly.

"Isn't he soft?" Natalie said. Zora nodded.

Josie peered into the closet. "Whose clothes are these?"

"They're yours," Jed said. "I have some things from your apartment in the car, too, but they need to be washed. We got these for you."

Her eyes went from Jed to Natalie and back. "To keep?"

"Of course," Natalie said, "to keep." She glanced at Jed and saw his eyes cloud with memories.

"I bet you're hungry," Natalie said. "I made pizzas, we just have to put them in the oven."

On the way down the hall, Zora clutched the rabbit while Josie gazed at the array of photos on the wall. "Who's that?" She pointed to an older family photo of Jed, Natalie, and twelve-year-old Theo.

"That's our son, Theo," Jed said. "He's your cousin. He goes to college now." He pointed to the more recent high school graduation picture.

"He doesn't live here?"

"Not all the time," Natalie said. "He's twenty—a grown-up. He lives in a dorm at school. But he comes home for the weekend sometimes. I'm sure you'll meet him soon." She shot a look at Jed. They needed to call Theo and let him know what was going on.

"Let's go have some pizza, okay?" Jed said, heading for the kitchen.

The girls were amazed to see pizza that didn't come out of the freezer. Natalie got out veggies and pepperoni to let them top their own. Zora shook her head, choosing only cheese, but Josie watched Jed and made hers exactly the same, with slices of pepperoni, red and green peppers, and even onion.

After dinner, Jed let the dogs in from outside and introduced them to the girls.

"This is Finn, he's a big baby, and he'll be your best friend if you let him," he said, ruffling the yellow lab's fur. "And this is Charley. He'll eat your food and then throw up, so don't leave it lying around." That actually got a giggle from Zora, her first.

"Why's he only got three legs?" she asked.

"We think he was hit by a car," Natalie said. "Someone brought him into my dad's clinic—he's a veterinarian—an animal doctor. When no one claimed him, we took him. He gets along just fine on three legs. He's a good boy, aren't you Charley?" The beagle mix wagged his tail.

Back upstairs, Natalie gave them a tour, ending at the bathroom across the hall from their room. She showed them how the shower worked and where the towels were kept.

"I got you some toothbrushes and toothpaste. There's soap and shampoo in there and room for you girls to shower together if you want." She took a breath. "Do you need any help?"

"No, ma'am," Josie said. "We always do it by ourselves."

Natalie set down two pairs of pajamas. "Well, you girls get ready for bed, then. Just come downstairs after, okay?"

She shut the door behind her and joined Jed in the family room.

"You are amazing," he said. "Thank you."

"They look so lost," she murmured. "Did you say Zora is five? She's so tiny. I hope the clothes I got will fit."

"Yeah, the doctor said they're both behind on the growth charts, which isn't surprising."

"We should take them to Theo's pediatrician. I'll make an appointment." She bit her lip. "I know this has to bring back a lot," she said. "You okay?"

"I'm good," he said. He pulled her close and kissed the top of her head. "As long as you're here, I'm good."

****

The screaming woke them. Natalie sat up first and blinked, then stumbled out of bed, banging her shin on the bed frame. "*Shit!*" she muttered.

As she hobbled down the hall toward the source of the sound, Jed followed close behind. In the girls' bedroom they found Josie, her arms wrapped around Zora, who continued to wail.

Natalie moved toward them.

"I got this!" Josie said. "She does this sometimes." She turned her back on them and tightened her grip on her sister, whispering something in her ear. Gradually the wails faded to whimpers and Josie led Zora back to bed, tucking the blankets around her and placing the bunny in her arms. Then she looked up at them.

"She's okay now."

"How about you?" Jed said, reaching out to lay a hand on her shoulder.

Josie stiffened and backed away. "I'm sorry we woke you up."

"That's okay," Jed said. "How about some hot chocolate?"

"I should stay with her in case she wakes up. She don't like to be alone."

"I'll stay," Natalie said. "She'll be fine."

Josie's eyes narrowed. "She don't know you."

Natalie swallowed. The child wasn't wrong. "I promise I'll call for you if she wakes up," she said.

Jed smiled his thanks and offered his hand. Josie took it, and he led her down to the kitchen.

Natalie watched them leave, then sat on the edge of Zora's bed, rubbing her bruised shin and looking down at the sleeping child, wondering what the hell they'd gotten themselves into.

Chapter 13

Jed sat at his desk a week or so later, squinting at the figures on his computer screen. He yawned and stretched. "Time for more coffee," he murmured. As he grabbed his mug and pushed up out of his chair, the phone on his desk buzzed.

"We have some information on Dante Winters, the girls' father," Detective Horton said when Jed answered the call. "He was in the Army. Killed by an IED near Kunduz, Afghanistan in 2015 right before the youngest was born."

"Crap," he said. "So they were married?"

"Yes, in 2012. Evidently, she and the kids lived with his mother in Humboldt Park on the west side while he was deployed. Chelsea worked as a waitress at an Olive Garden and then at a local place called West Side Willie's. Dorthea Winters took care of the kids while Chelsea worked, but she died of breast cancer in 2016." She sighed. "Your sister certainly had a run of bad luck."

More like one tragedy after another, Jed thought. How much could one person take? "Where did you get this information?" he asked.

"On a hunch, I put his name into the military database, came up with his info, then talked to an army buddy of his—Jaden Clark. They were pretty close. After

Dante was killed, he tried to keep tabs on Chelsea and the girls, stopping in to see them whenever he was in town. But when her mother-in-law died, according to him, she just disappeared. Dante had a brother, Leo, but Jaden has no idea where he is. He and Dante weren't close."

"So we don't have much information about the last three years."

"No," she agreed. "Except that's when the arrest record starts back up. Looks like Dante and his mother were a beneficial influence, but once they were gone..."

"Chelsea went back to being Chelsea," he said. "Thanks for the information. Any leads on her whereabouts now?"

"No, but there hasn't been a Jane Doe matching her description, so that's good." He heard her pen tapping on the desk. "We haven't been able to locate the friend; Skylar Morgan either. I was thinking they might be together. Can you think of anywhere she would go?"

Jed sighed. They'd been over all this before. "We never lived anywhere but Chicago," he said. "As far as I know, she's never been out of the state."

"Alright. We'll keep at it but..."

"There are more pressing cases," he said. "I know the drill."

"How are the girls?"

"They're adjusting, I guess." Josie was still cautious and skittish with them. Zora was wetting the bed and woke up screaming every night, sometimes twice, which meant he and Natalie were up at all hours.

"My wife is going to the elementary school tomorrow to get them signed up. We wanted to get settled first."

"Probably a good idea. I hope you're getting support from social services," she said. "Sometimes when we place kids with family, they forget family needs support, too."

"They haven't been in touch," he admitted.

"I'll give them a call and have them contact you."

"Thanks."

"Also, the girls should be getting Dante's survivor benefits from the military. I'll get some information on who you need to talk to about that."

"I'd appreciate it."

"Okay then," she said. "I'll be in touch if there's anything worth sharing."

****

Jed sat up in bed and swung his feet over the side, trying not to disturb Nat, who snored softly next to him. He rubbed his eyes and tried to clear his head from the dream.

It was always the same: *He's in a building, one of the dumps they lived in after leaving Mitch's. There's a long hallway with a lot of doors. Chelsea and Noah are missing and he's looking for them. He calls their names. He hears grown-ups talking and laughing, but no one comes to help him search. He walks down the hall, throwing each door open and looking inside. Every room is empty. His heart pounds. He has to find them. He's the one responsible. If anything happens to them, it's his fault. Panic sets in and he starts to run. The building morphs into an alley full of trash and strange shadows flickering on the walls. He hears crying and knows it has to be his sister and brother, but he still can't find them. Suddenly, his mother is there. "Where are they?" she demands. "What did you do?"* That was usually the point he woke up in a cold sweat.

Jed hadn't had the dream in years, not since Theo was small. Now, since they'd taken in Josie and Zora, it was once a week, at least. He could never get back to sleep after.

In the master bath, he pulled on a t-shirt and splashed water on his face, then checked on the girls. He found them huddled together on one of the two twin beds. When he touched Zora's sheets they were dry, and he sighed with relief. In the other bed, Josie was on her stomach, one arm thrown around her sister, the other hanging off the bed, her fingers tangled in Finn's soft fur. The big yellow lab looked up at Jed.

"Good boy," he said. "Stay." Finn heaved a sigh and lowered his head. Neither girl stirred.

Downstairs in the kitchen, he poured himself a glass of milk and took it and two chocolate chip cookies from the jar on the counter into the family room. He sat on the couch, flicking through the channels until he came across *The Natural*. The movie had just started. Jed loved baseball movies, and he'd seen most of them from *Bull Durham* to *Major League* multiple times, but this was by far his favorite. Engrossed in Roy Hobb's story, he didn't hear Natalie come into the family room.

"I could never figure out why she shot him," Natalie said.

"It's an allegory."

She yawned and settled in next to him. "Couldn't sleep?"

He shrugged.

"The dream again?"

"Yeah." On the screen, Roy Hobbs swung and knocked the cover off the ball.

Natalie shifted her weight, leaning into the corner of the couch. "Maybe you should talk to someone."

He kept his eyes on the television. "I'm okay."

"Jed," she sighed. "You're not okay. You aren't sleeping."

"I said I'm alright," he looked up. "You can go back to bed."

"You could tell me about it."

"I just want to watch the movie. Maybe I'll get drowsy and fall asleep."

She pushed. "What's the dream about?"

"I've told you before... just stuff from when I was a kid. It's because of the girls and thinking about Chelsea. It brings up a lot of shit. You know."

"No, I don't," she huffed. "You never talk about when you lived with your mom. You told me once. Once. Twenty years ago... back in college. Every time I try to get you to open up about it you..."

"I've told you things."

"Bits and pieces."

He lost his patience. "What's the point? How could you possibly understand?" He sat up straighter. "You grew up *here* with parents who adored you. You didn't have the kind of life I had. You can't even imagine it."

"That's not fair," Natalie said after a moment. "I can't help that. We don't get to pick our parents."

"No, we sure as hell don't."

"It might help to talk..."

"Talk?" He gave a sharp laugh. "It was shitty, okay? I had a shitty childhood. Lots of people do, Nat—more than you'd think."

She swallowed before she spoke again. "You're the most important person in my life," she said. "I know almost everything about you. I know you floss before you brush, which is just weird, and I know you still keep all your important things in one place so you can grab them if you have to leave quickly. I know you sneak so much sugar into your coffee that it's not even coffee." She made a gagging noise.

The tension broken, he raised an eyebrow and chuckled. "Guilty."

"Yes, but I don't know the part of your life that would help explain these nightmares. They scare me, Jed. I worry about you not sleeping."

He sighed and clicked off the television, easing down and laying his head in her lap. She ran her fingers through his hair, and he relaxed a little. "I'm not sure. I mean, I don't remember them ever wandering off or anything. Chelsea used to love to play hide-and-seek, but she wasn't very good at it." He laughed. "I had to pretend I couldn't find her."

"Jed, I wish you would talk to someone. You can't go on not sleeping. There are counselors who could help. Why don't I ask Katy if she knows anyone?"

"I'll think about it," he said. He closed his eyes, concentrated on Natalie's fingers in his hair, and finally slipped into a dreamless sleep.

Chapter 14

Natalie sat on the porch swing and watched as Theo's Honda CRV pulled up in front of the house. The driver's door opened and her son's lanky frame emerged, grabbing the backpack from the passenger seat and swinging it onto his shoulder.

"Hey, Mom," he said as he came up the steps. She patted the seat beside her and he stopped, shifting his weight from one foot to the other. The pack slipped from his shoulder and he set it down. "What's going on? I thought you'd be at work," he said. "Is something wrong? Is someone sick? Is it G'ma or G'pa?"

"Oh, no, Honey," Natalie said. "It's nothing like that. I didn't mean to worry you! Just sit." She sighed. "I guess I should have listened to your father. He thought we could tell you over the phone but I..."

"Tell me what?" He sat down and his blue eyes, so like Jed's, met hers.

"Do you remember your Aunt Chelsea? She came here once when you were around four?"

"The one who stole our car? I remember you guys talking about her. I guess I kind of remember. She was blond and really skinny."

"Yes, well." Natalie twisted a strand of hair and tucked it behind her ear. Jed had taken the girls to pick up some groceries and they would be back soon. She just needed to tell Theo. Why was that so difficult?

"Is she dead or something?"

"We don't know. She's missing. But the thing is, Theo, she left her daughters behind."

"She had kids?"

Natalie nodded. "Two little girls. Josie is eight and Zora is five." She swallowed. "You remember your dad grew up in foster care, and he didn't want the girls to go through what he did, living with strangers." She rambled, her words running into each other. "When we got the call about Chelsea and learned about the girls, we took them in."

Theo's brow wrinkled. "They're living here? With us?"

"Yes," Natalie said, "We wanted you to meet them."

"How long will they be here?"

"We honestly aren't sure, sweetheart." She lay a hand on his arm. "They're really great kids, but they haven't had a lot of..." she searched for a word. "... structure. So, we're working on that."

"So you're not working?" Theo said. "What about the restaurant?"

"I'm still working. I just took this weekend off so we can all be together. I really want you to get to know the girls and it will be good for them to have us all here."

Theo bit his lip. "I can only stay tonight and part of tomorrow," he said. "I have plans tomorrow night."

"Oh, no," Natalie said. "I thought we could go to El Taco. We haven't taken the girls there yet."

"I can't change my plans."

"Okay, well..."

"Sorry, Mom." Theo said, sensing her disappointment. He stood and picked up his pack. "Can I throw a load of laundry in?"

"Of course. Your dad will be back with the girls soon."

She was still sitting on the porch when Jed pulled into the drive. The girls piled out of the backseat, each holding one of the reusable grocery bags they kept in the glove box. Jed followed with two more.

"Theo's here?" he said as she opened the door for them. "How'd it go?"

"I'm not sure, really," she said. "He says he can only stay tonight and part of tomorrow–he has plans tomorrow night. But he never mentioned that when I called him."

Jed shrugged. "He's here now. Let's work with that."

At the kitchen doorway, Zora stopped, staring up at Theo, who was drinking a can of pop from the fridge.

"Hi," he said. "I'm Theo. Are you Zora or Josie?"

After a moment she said, "I'm Zora." She pointed to her sister. "That's Josie. She's my sister."

"And Theo is your cousin," Jed said, taking the bag from her hand as Finn tried to stick his nose in, sniffing at the contents.

Theo rubbed the dog's head. "Do you girls like tacos?"

Zora nodded.

"Me, too. Maybe I can convince my parents to take us to my favorite taco place tonight. Would you like that?"

They both nodded this time.

"El-Taco?" Jed said, clapping a hand on his son's shoulder.

"El-okay-o, Dad." Theo replied.

Chapter 15

"Those girls seem sweet," Connie Dunham said. "But that little one...does she talk at all? She's five, right? When you and your brother were that age you talked a mile a minute."

"They've been through a lot, Mom," Natalie said. In the month they'd lived with them, the girls seemed to be coming around. Josie was still an enigma, but Zora talked to her and Jed more each day. She just clammed up around anyone unfamiliar, which was to be expected. The first week of school seemed to be going fairly well for both girls, although neither one said much about it.

Natalie glanced out into her parent's backyard where Josie and Zora sat in the grass blowing bubbles at Ginger, her father's latest rescue. The dog, a golden retriever mix, leapt at the bubbles, looking all around in confusion when they disappeared as she bit them. The girls giggled, watching her.

"Are you sure you want to do this, sweetheart?" Her mom said. "I know you always wanted another child, but two? Especially now that Theo is grown and the two of you could have time for yourselves. It's an awful lot to take on with the restaurant and Jed's job and..."

"Mom," Natalie kept her voice level, annoyed that her mother always seemed to be able to push her buttons. "Jed and I have considered all of that. The girls need a stable home right now, and we can provide it."

Connie took a sip of her coffee. "I suppose you're the best judge of what you can handle," she said finally.

Taking a drink from her own mug, Natalie thought back to a similar conversation with her mother just before she and Jed got married. They'd spent the morning making arrangements for the wedding and stopped at a local diner for a quick bite of lunch on the way home. As soon as the waitress took the order and left their booth, Connie started in.

"Natalie, sweetheart," she began, "you know your father and I love Jed, we really do, but..." she paused and tented her fingers. "Are you sure he's up to this? His childhood was...well, he really didn't have one, did he? He's got to be affected by that. How can he be a good father? He didn't have an example."

Despite invoking her dad, Natalie knew this worry was all her mother's.

She took a breath and tried not to sound defensive. "Mom, I love Jed. And he's going to be a great dad. He's so excited. He already read more of the parenting book than I have. I think growing up the way he did will make him an even better father. He wants his kids to have all the things he didn't."

Connie sighed, "I knew that's what you'd say."

"Because it's true."

"Because you want it to be true." She stirred her iced tea. "You don't have to be married to have this baby."

"We love each other," she said, her shoulders tensing. "We want to get married and have this baby together. It wasn't planned, and of course we were upset at first, but now we're happy. I'm happy."

"You're just like your father, always saving misfits and strays." Another sigh. "I just hope you aren't making a huge mistake marrying a man who's so damaged."

"Damaged?" Her voice rose in pitch and volume. The woman at the next table turned around to glare at them, and Natalie spoke tersely, scowling at her mother. "You think Jed is damaged? I can't believe you said that. Wait, yes, I can."

"I'm only looking out for you. It's not normal, the way he was raised. It isn't his fault but..."

"You know what?" Natalie said, slipping her purse off the back of the chair. "I'm not hungry." She stood, pressing a hand to her belly when she felt the flutter of movement. "I'm going to walk back to the apartment. I need the exercise. You enjoy your lunch."

"Natalie! You can't just run away when you don't like the conversation."

"I'm not running away. The conversation is over. There's a difference, Mom."

"Aunt Natalie?" Josie's voice brought her out of her reflections and back to the present. She turned her attention to the child.

"Zora wet her pants." Her face puckered, and she looked sideways at where Connie sat, doing the Tribune crossword puzzle. She lowered her voice to a whisper. "I'm sorry. We was having such fun with the doggie and I didn't..."

"Honey, it's not your fault," Natalie said. "Accidents happen. Where's Zora?"

"In the potty. She won't come out 'cause she's all wet."

"Okay," Natalie thought quickly. "I'm going to see if there's anything around she could wear until we go home."

"Mom," she said, "do you still collect and sort clothes for the church clothing locker?"

"Of course," Connie said. "There are three bags in the sewing room I need to get to this weekend."

"Great." Natalie headed for her old bedroom, now her mother's catch-all-slash- sewing-room, with Josie on her heels.

"Do you think Zora would like these?" After rummaging through the piles of clothing, Natalie held up a pair of pants with purple and white flowers printed on them. "They look about the right size."

Josie nodded. "She'll wear anything." Then she added, "But those are real pretty. She likes purple."

"Why don't you take them to her?" Natalie said. "Don't worry about underwear. We're heading home soon, anyway."

The little girl nodded again and took the pants, walking quietly down the hall to the bathroom. On her way back to the kitchen, Natalie heard her knock softly and say, "It's me."

"Does that happen often?" Her mother asked, not looking up from her crossword.

"What?" Natalie asked. She rinsed out both coffee cups and set them on the draining board.

"The little one–Zora–what kind of name is that, anyway? Does she wet her pants often?"

"Kids have accidents, Mom. Especially in new situations."

"At five she should know by now when she has to go," Connie tsked.

"I shouldn't have brought them here," Natalie said. "I thought you and Dad would…"

"You thought I'd what?" Russ Dunham walked into the kitchen, still wearing his blue-green scrubs from the vet clinic.

"Hi, Dad," Natalie said. She gave her father a kiss on the cheek. "I brought Jed's nieces to meet you."

"The little one wet her pants," Connie said.

"Well," said Russ, crossing the room to give his wife a kiss. "That'll be you and me soon enough."

Connie laughed and patted his hand. "Not for quite a while, I hope."

"Josie is helping her sister change. They're really sweet girls, Dad, they've just never had a chance at a normal…" She stopped talking as Josie entered the kitchen, holding her sister by the hand. She approached Natalie, giving Russ a wide berth.

"Her wet stuff is in the sink," she whispered.

"I'll take care of it," Natalie said. "No worries." She laid a hand on the girls' heads. "Dad, this is Josie and Zora. Girls, this is my father, Dr. Dunham. He's an animal doctor."

"You can call me Doc D.," Russ said. "Everybody does."

Zora's thumb went into her mouth, and her eyes slid to her sister's. Josie held out the hand not tight in Zora's. "It's nice to meet you," she said, the way Jed practiced with them. She looked at her sister. "She's shy."

Russ crouched for the handshake, Josie's tiny hand disappearing in his large one. "That's okay," he said. "This one was shy too, when she was that age." He smiled up at his daughter.

"Do you girls like cookies?" Connie rose from her chair. It always amazed Natalie how her mother's demeanor changed when her father was around, or Ian, for that matter. Natalie was the one who bore the brunt of her mother's judgement and snide remarks. Or maybe she was just the one who noticed it.

"Yes, ma'am," Josie nodded.

Connie brought Nonna's old cookie jar down from the counter and lifted the lid. "They're chocolate chip."

Josie took a cookie and turned to Zora. "You can have one, too." She said.

Zora smiled shyly and reached in.

"Thank you, ma'am," Josie said. "Zora thanks you, too, but she doesn't talk to strangers."

"You're both very welcome," Connie said.

"Hopefully we won't feel like strangers for long," Russ added. He slapped his hands on his thighs. "Now, how would you girls like to meet a pygmy goat?"

****

"That goat was funny," Zora said on the way home. "What's his name again?"

"Tattoo," Natalie said. Her father thought it was hilarious, naming the miniature goat after Mr. Roark's sidekick from *Fantasy Island*, but she knew the reference would be lost on the girls.

"That's a funny name."

"It is, isn't it?" She met Zora's eyes in the rearview mirror. Josie was quiet as she stared out the window. Both girls spent an hour running all around the barn, climbing the ladder into the loft, and being chased by her mother's chickens. It was good to see them laughing and playing.

"I'm going to draw a picture of him for Uncle Jed when we get home."

Natalie didn't have the heart to tell her niece that Jed *hated* that goat. Last summer, when her father first brought it home, Jed went to the barn to get something, startled the animal, and ended up on his butt in the mud. For a little guy, Tattoo packed a pretty good wallop.

"He'll love that," she said with a smile.

"Aunt Nat?"

"Yes?"

Zora hesitated then asked, "When is Mama coming back?"

"I don't know, Sweetie." There was still no word on Chelsea. Jed said he doubted if the police were even looking that hard anymore.

"You'd be amazed how many people go missing every year," he'd told her.

"I don't care if she ever comes back," Josie spit angrily. "She'll make us leave and I like it here."

"I'm glad you like it here," Natalie said, surprised. Her eyes flicked to the mirror again, this time focused on Josie.

"I like school and my teacher, Mrs. Kirby," she went on. "She's nice. She says I'm one of the best readers in the class."

"You are a great reader," Natalie told her. "And you're getting better with your math facts, too." Jed worked flashcard games with her every night.

"We didn't have nice books at our old school. The books were all old and some of them didn't have covers anymore. My teacher was okay, but she was old, too. Not young and pretty like Mrs. Kirby. And our principal was mean. Mrs. Murphy came in and read us a funny story yesterday. Mr. Griggs never did that." She took a breath and went on. "He was bald and he smelled funny."

"When mama comes back, maybe she can live with us!" Zora said. "She could sleep in our room. I don't mind sleeping with Josie."

Josie sighed, "Mama wouldn't stay. We never stay anywhere."

****

"I took the girls to Mom and Dad's today," Natalie said. When Jed got home, she followed him up to the bedroom to talk while he changed clothes.

"How'd that go?"

"My mother was her usual self, until Dad got home, of course." She flopped back onto the bed and put a throw pillow over her face. "Arrgh!" she screamed into it. "Why does she always have to be so irritating?"

Jed chuckled. "She can certainly push all your buttons. What did she say?"

"Oh, you know," Natalie sighed. "*Are you sure you want to do this?*" She mimicked her mother's voice. "*Isn't it a lot to take on with the restaurant? Blah, blah, blah.*"

"I'm sorry." Jed leaned on one arm over her and kissed her.

"Then Dad got home, and she was all sweetness and light and passing out cookies." She made a face as she sat up and smoothed the front of her t-shirt. "He took them out to the barn to meet Tattoo. They had fun." She pulled her phone out of her pocket and showed him the photos she took. "Zora drew a picture for you."

"Of the goat?" His nose wrinkled.

She laughed. "They loved that goat." She stood up and they walked downstairs together. "Zora asked about her mom on the way home. I told her I wasn't sure when she was coming back, and Josie said that she hopes she doesn't because she likes it here."

"Really?" Jed shook his head. "She's so sullen most of the time. I thought she hated it."

"Me, too," Natalie said. "But maybe she just doesn't want to show it."

"Or maybe she's afraid it won't last," Jed said. "I can remember feeling that way more than once."

"That could be it. Zora said that if Chelsea came back we could all live together, and Josie said her mom wouldn't stay because they never stay anywhere." She looked at him. "These poor babies."

Chapter 16

She tapped her fingers on the counter. Three weeks. It had been three weeks since she and Jed had sex. They hadn't gone that long since right after Theo was born, and even then they'd found... other ways. The restaurant, Jed's latest case, and Josie and Zora's sleeping habits – or rather the lack of them– were really putting a cramp in their style.

Natalie glanced at her watch and poured herself a glass of bourbon and another for Jed. When she heard the car in the drive, she sat on the barstool, ran her tongue over her bottom lip, and unbuttoned the top two buttons on the pale blue blouse she wore. She crossed her legs, swinging her foot, and waited for the door to open.

"Hey," Jed said, smiling as he took her in. He set his laptop bag on the chair. "For me?" He picked up the glass, took a sip.

"Um hmm," she said, meeting his gaze and sipping her own.

"Where are the girls?" He raised an eyebrow and his blue eyes twinkled.

"My brother and Katy took them to see his workshop and out for ice cream after."

He stepped closer. "So... we're alone?"

She tipped her face up to him. "Very much alone."

"Ice cream, huh? That should take a while."

One corner of her mouth turned up. "Oh, I'm pretty sure it'll take long enough."

He leaned one hand on the counter and brought his mouth to hers, softly at first, then more insistently, opening her mouth with his tongue. He tasted of whiskey. She put her arms around his neck as his other hand deftly undid the rest of the buttons on her blouse. It slipped off one shoulder and her breath quickened at his touch, but she pulled away, sliding one foot down to the floor for balance.

"Last one to the bedroom has to do *whatever* the other one wants," she said, giving him a wicked grin. She spun and made for the stairs, shedding her blouse on the way. Jed caught her in the living room, wrapping his arms around her waist from behind and lifting her off her feet.

She shrieked with laughter. "You're cheating!"

"All's fair..." he said, setting her down. She turned, kissed him and grabbed his hand, pulling him up the stairs behind her. He shrugged out of his dress shirt in the hallway and pulled his t-shirt over his head and tossed it behind him as they entered the bedroom.

Natalie turned to face him, unhooking her bra and letting it drop to the floor. She did a little shimmy out of her white jeans and underwear, kicking them aside. Naked, she fell back onto the bed and crooked a finger at him. "You're gonna need to take those pants off."

"Happy to oblige, ma'am," he said, unbuckling his belt. He dropped the pants, caught his foot stepping out of them, and stumbled onto the bed, still in his boxers.

"You're hopeless," Natalie giggled. "Do I have to do everything myself?" She tugged the boxers off and tossed them over the side of the bed.

"Can't do this yourself," he murmured, kissing down her neck and across her collarbone as he slid between her legs. Her laughter turned to soft sighs and moans of pleasure as he entered her. She wrapped her legs around him and they slowly found their rhythm.

Later, they lay entwined, face to face. "You're my favorite person," Natalie said, kissing him softly.

Jed grinned at her. "You're just saying that because I just made you..."

She laughed. "True, but..." she put a finger to his lips. "I love you."

"I love you, too." He rolled onto his back, pulling her close. Her head nestled on his shoulder. He yawned. "I don't suppose we have time for a nap?"

"I wish." She rested her hand on his chest and he covered it with his own. Drowsy, they lay together for a few minutes, their eyes closed.

"I think I just heard a car," Natalie murmured.

After another moment, the kitchen door slammed. Jed groaned and pushed up.

"Back to reality," he said, swinging his legs over the side of the bed and picking up his boxers. He stood, grabbing a pair of jeans off the hook in the closet and putting them on.

Natalie looked up at him, smiling. "I'm going to take a quick shower and I'll be right down. Maybe we can watch a movie with the girls?"

"How about Mrs. Doubtfire?"

"I love that movie! Maybe Katy and Ian will stay."

"I know." He leaned in and kissed her. "I'll ask. And I'll make popcorn."

"Popcorn and ice cream in one night?"

"The chances of spoiling them are null," he said. "Anyway, don't they deserve a little spoiling?"

****

"Time to get ready for bed." Natalie said to the girls sprawled on the living room couch. It was Monday, Sorriso was closed, and Jed was having a guy's night out, playing poker at Delgado's house.

Zora bounced right up and headed upstairs, but Josie stayed put, her eyes focused on the television.

"Did you hear me?" Natalie said. "It's time to get ready for bed."

"Why do I have to go to bed at the same time as Zora? I'm three years older."

"That's something we can talk about, but right now, I'd like you to do what I asked."

"Fine," Josie huffed, adding an eye-roll as she walked by Natalie on her way upstairs.

"Don't forget to brush your teeth."

In her own bedroom, Natalie changed into leggings and a t-shirt and padded back down the hall. The bathroom was empty. Zora's toothbrush lay in a puddle on the edge of the sink, but Josie's was in the holder, still dry. She stuck her head in the girls' room. Zora was sitting on her bed rocking the stuffed bunny. Josie was in the bean-bag chair with a book.

"Josie, you need to brush your teeth."

"Not right now."

"Yes, right now."

"I'm reading."

Natalie walked over and took the book from her hands. "Go brush your teeth, then you can have your book back."

"I hate you," Josie spat. "I wish we'd never come to live here."

Zora watched her sister stomp across the hall. "*I* love you, Aunt Nat," she said.

"I love you, too." Natalie tucked the covers around her and kissed her forehead.

Josie walked back in, much too soon to have done a decent job of brushing her teeth. Natalie let it go.

"I'm done. Can I have my book?"

"May I have my book, please," Natalie corrected. "Please pick up your clothes and put them in the hamper."

"You said you'd give it back!" Josie yelled. "Why are you lying?"

Natalie took a breath and counted to five-willing herself not to raise her voice. "I'm not lying. I didn't notice your clothes before. Please put them in the hamper so I can wash them."

Josie grabbed the pile of clothes she wore to school that day from the floor and wadded them into a ball, tossing them at Natalie.

Natalie looked down at the clothing, then back at Josie. "Pick them up, please."

"No." Josie threw herself onto the bed, crossing her arms over her chest and staring at the ceiling.

"Alright," Natalie said. "We aren't going to the library after school tomorrow. You have plenty of books here to read."

"Whatever," Josie said.

Natalie bent and picked up the clothing, tossing it into the hamper in the closet. "Goodnight, Josie."

Silence.

Jed handed her a glass of wine and sat down on the couch beside her. He reeked of cigar smoke. "You looked like you could use that."

"Thank you." She took a sip. She hesitated to tell him about her evening, but hiding it from him wouldn't do any good either.

"Josie argued with me about bedtime again. She wouldn't brush her teeth, so I took her book and wouldn't give it back until she did. She said she hated me. Then, when I asked her to pick her school clothes up and put them in the dirty-clothes basket, she threw them at me. At that point, I was afraid I'd start screaming at her, so I told her we weren't going to the library tomorrow, gave her the book and said goodnight." She blew out a breath. "I should have stuck to my guns but..."

"I'll talk to her," Jed said.

"Talking to her isn't working so far," she observed. "We might need some help with this." She reached for the piece of paper on the table. "Zora came home with this note today. I was waiting to call until I talked to you. It's in the morning, so I can go if you can't take off work."

"I thought things were going so well," he said.

"So did I."

He read over the note from Zora's pre-k teacher. "I'll go, too. This is going to take both of us."

Chapter 17

"Mr. and Mrs. Shaw," Angela Murphy, the principal of Westlake Elementary, began once they sat down in her office conference room. "This is the third incident we've had with Zora. We all understand the girls are from difficult circumstances, but she simply cannot put her hands on the other students."

"I'm not sure we're clear on what happened," Natalie said. She pressed her knee against Jed's encouraging him to let her take the lead.

"I'll let Miss Kirkland explain." Mrs. Murphy tucked a strand of dark hair behind one ear and adjusted her glasses. "Mandy?"

Zora's impossibly young pre-kindergarten teacher leaned forward in her chair. "First of all, please know that I adore Zora. Ninety percent of the time, she's a great kid. She's smart and she's beginning to come out of her shell. I've heard her whispering to several of the other little girls at recess."

"That's good to hear," Natalie said. "She's talking more at home, too."

"So," Miss Kirkland began again. "Today, at the end of snack time, the little boy who was my helper went to pick up Zora's trash and when he reached for it, she slapped him. Then she grabbed up what was left and crawled under the art table in the corner. It took me twenty minutes to get her to come out. Thank goodness our aide was there to help with the other kids."

"You are aware that Zora and Josie were often left without food, aren't you?"

"Um..." Miss Kirkland shifted in her chair and looked at the principal.

"I believe all that information was in the file I gave you," Mrs. Murphy said.

The teacher appeared flustered. "Mrs. Murphy, I got an email when Zora joined us, but never a file. I'm positive."

Mrs. Murphy rose from her desk and walked to the filing cabinet against the opposite wall. Pulling out a drawer she thumbed through several files.

"Oh," she said after a moment. "I'm so sorry." She held up a manila folder. A pink sticky-note on the front read '*copy for Kirkland*' in neat script. "It must have gotten put away before Jan had a chance to copy it for you. I'll have her do that right now. Excuse me." She ducked out of the office.

Miss Kirkland looked at Natalie. "I'm so sorry." She took a notepad and pen off the desk. "Could you fill me in a bit on Zora's history? It's always better to get information from the source, anyway."

Jed spoke up, telling the teacher about the conditions found in the apartment where Josie and Zora were living, and the information they gathered from the girls' neighbor and Josie about lack of food being a regular issue.

"I am so sorry that I didn't know this!" she said, taking down notes as she listened. "Now that I think about it, both of the other incidents happened at snack time, too."

"Is there any way you could reassure her? Make sure she has time to finish and remind her she'll get a snack and dinner at home?"

"Absolutely. She doesn't seem to have any issues at lunch." She made another note. "Zora's very bright. She's already reading our sight word books and she can add and subtract within ten."

"That's wonderful, but I'm not as concerned about her academics as I am about her behavior and emotional state," Natalie said. Jed nodded in agreement.

"Is there anyone she could talk to?" he added.

Mrs. Murphy walked back in at that moment. "We have a contract with the local counseling center. I'll have Madeline, our school nurse, put Zora on Julie's radar. It could be a week or so, but she should have time to see her."

"I really think Josie could benefit from counseling as well," Natalie said.

"She hasn't been on my radar," Mrs. Murphy noted. "Her teacher is Mrs. Kirby?

"Yes. There haven't been any issues at school, but we're having some problems at home."

Jed leaned forward. "Josie was used to being in charge before. Her mother was pretty much absent. Rules at school are familiar, but at home she has some trouble.

"I see." The principal nodded and made a note. "I'll put both their names in. Someone will call and let you know when they can see you."

Chapter 18

"What's this?" Natalie stared down at the flowered duffle Katy dropped at her feet. Stella stepped out of the office and smiled at Katy.

"Ah, you're here. Good."

Katy nodded. "She's all packed and ready to go."

"I'll take that apron," Stella said to Natalie. "The boss is cooking tonight." She winked. "I have to stay in practice."

"What? I don't understand." She looked from one woman to the other.

"You're coming with me," Jed stepped into the busy kitchen, dressed in jeans and his favorite Cubs jersey and holding a long-stemmed peach rose in his hand.

"And this," Katy said, picking up the duffle and handing it to a stunned Natalie, "is your wardrobe for the weekend. Don't worry, I packed it, not him." She hooked a thumb at Jed. "All your toiletries and make-up are in there. I know you," she reassured her friend.

"But the girls..." Natalie stammered.

"Ian and I are watching them at your house. When I found out they hadn't seen most of the *classic* Disney princess movies, well," Katy widened her eyes. "That is simply unacceptable. They must be indoctrinated." She

155

held open the top of the huge Boho bag she carried so Natalie could peer inside. *"Little Mermaid, Pocahontas –* yes, I know it's politically incorrect, but please." She rolled her eyes. *"Mulan,* and, saving the best for last, of course, *Beauty and the Beast."*

"Poor Ian," Jed murmured.

"Hey!" Katy said, punching him lightly in the arm. "You're practically a girl-dad now, so you'd better get used to it."

Jed turned to Natalie. "We had to cancel our vacation when we took the girls. The least you deserve is a weekend getaway in Chicago," he said. "I booked us a room at that boutique hotel Annie was raving about, and we have reservations at Paulo's tomorrow night. Tonight I thought we'd just hit someplace in Wrigley for burgers. The Cubs are in town and Antonio scored us two tickets." He glanced at the clock on the wall over the doorway. "We'd better get going. It's almost three and the game starts at seven."

"Um. Wow, okay," Natalie said, giving in to the ambush. "I'll grab my purse."

Katy unzipped the duffel and pulled out jeans and a faded long sleeved t-shirt that had a caricature of Harry Caray and the words *"Holy Cow!"* across the front.

"Change." She shoved Natalie in the direction of the staff restroom.

Once they were on the road, Natalie turned to Jed. "I can't remember the last time we did anything spontaneous like this," she said.

"Exactly," he reached across and took her hand. "And we aren't going to campus tomorrow to see Theo. He's fine. We're not going to be parents this weekend. We're just going to be us."

"That sounds perfect." Keeping his hand in hers, she leaned back in her seat and closed her eyes.

****

"Cubs win!" Jed yelled with the rest of the crowd and turned to Nat, giving her a high-five. She grinned and finished the rest of her beer as fireworks lit the sky.

"You still okay with meeting Antonio and Tracy at Sluggers for a nightcap?"

"Sure. We haven't seen them in ages."

"Alright, then." He grabbed her hand and they made their way through the crowd toward the exits.

The Cubby Bear was packed with happy fans and it took them a few minutes to find their friends in the crowd. Antonio had commandeered a tall, round-top table near one of the windows onto the street. There were only two stools, so after hugs all around, the ladies sat while the men stood.

"It's so good to see you," Tracy said, leaning in so Nat could hear her over the noise. "You've had a big change. I hear Jed's nieces are living with you."

"Yes," Natalie nodded. "We've had some adjustments to make. The girls just started counseling, and we're participating too, so hopefully that will make things easier on all of us."

The guys returned to the table with tumblers of bourbon for three of them and a glass of Moscato for Tracy.

Nat sipped the bourbon and looked at her friend over the rim of the glass. "I love your hair," she said.

"Thanks," Tracy said, patting her short, dark, natural curls. "It's a lot less work than straightening it. And my hair is healthier."

"I'm going to need some hair advice for the girls," Natalie said. "I have no idea what I'm doing."

"Of course you don't. Black hair is totally different," Tracy said. "I'll send you some information. Do you have Pinterest?"

"Of course."

"I'll send you some stuff and a list of products you'll want." She tapped a note into her phone.

"I would really appreciate that. Thanks."

Tracy took a sip of wine. "Antonio told me Josie is eight? That's the same age as Della. We should get them together."

"That would be awesome," Natalie said. "We could come into the city and meet you at the Shedd or the Children's Museum."

"Let's plan on it," Tracy said. "I'll text you. How are things at Sorriso?"

"It's doing really well," Natalie said. "I've cut back my evenings a bit here and there to be home for the girls, but my sous chef is a tremendous help."

"I'm glad that's working out."

"Me, too." Natalie sipped her bourbon. Kendall was doing a wonderful job. She got along with Daniel, and Natalie and Stella felt confident leaving the restaurant in her hands. Natalie still planned all the menus and the grocery order, but Kendall had taken over prep work for the next day's lunches, which took a real load off of Natalie and got her home most nights before the girls went to bed.

They ordered another drink and spent the next hour or so getting caught up with their friends. They all agreed that they needed to do this more often, but it was getting late. After Nat's third stifled yawn, Jed took notice.

"Ready, Hon?" Jed said, slipping an arm around her.

They'd dropped their things off in their room at the small hotel earlier and taken the L to Wrigley. Now they exited the bar, walking to the station with the other couple and saying their goodbyes before boarding separate trains. Fans still crowded the train, headed home after celebrating the win. Jed found a seat for Natalie and stood by her, looking out the window as the city flashed by.

The next morning, they were up early for a run along the lakefront trail. They ran from the Navy Pier all the way to the Aquarium and back, dodging bikers and other early morning runners.

"Race you," Jed said as they neared the narrow side street where their hotel stood halfway down the block. He grinned at her and picked up speed, but lighter and faster, Natalie passed him, laughing. At the entrance, they both bent over, breathing hard.

"Loser buys breakfast," she panted.

"Breakfast comes with the room."

"Oh," she said with a smile. "I guess I'll have to find another way to extract payment."

"I'm sure you'll think of something," he said, leaning in for a kiss.

After a shower *'a deux*, during which Jed more than paid his debt, they had a leisurely breakfast in the sunlit dining room.

"What do you want to do today?" he asked as they drank their second cups of coffee. "We can do anything you want."

"Don't get mad..." she began.

He chuckled. "You want to go see Theo."

Natalie shook her head. "No." She reached across the table and took his hand, linking her fingers with his. "I'd like to see where you lived. When you were with your mom." His fingers tensed in hers, but he didn't pull away. "You've seen my neighborhood, my elementary school—you've even met my third-grade teacher in the grocery store one time," she laughed. "I've loved you for twenty-two years and I want to see what you saw. I want to *know*, Jed. All of it."

He picked up his coffee and took a long swallow. "You will not let this go, will you?" When she didn't answer, he went on. "I don't even know if the places are still there."

"Let's find out."

He stared out the window and watched the leaves scatter across the sidewalk in the breeze. "Okay," he said finally. He pulled out his phone and tapped the maps app. "Some of these places are sketchy. I think we should drive rather than take the L." After typing something in, he looked up. "You ready?"

She nodded.

In the car, he drove south down Lake Shore Drive, passing Soldier's Field, the aquarium, the museum of Science and Industry. Natalie watched his hands tighten on the wheel the farther out of the city they went.

"I don't remember our dad," he said. "He left when Chelsea was a couple of months old."

"So you were what? Four?"

He shrugged. "Three or four. We lived with my grandparents in Skokie for a few years. They kicked us out when Mom got pregnant with Noah."

"They kicked you out?" Natalie said. "Why?"

"Mom fought with them all the time. They weren't kind or generous people," Jed said. "My grandfather worked at one of the steel mills and that's when they were starting to shut down. They made it clear we were a burden financially. He drank a lot and yelled at the slightest thing. We always had to be quiet. My grandmother just sat in a chair and smoked cigarettes while she watched her soap operas." He gave a sharp laugh. "That's literally the only thing I remember about her."

"Did your mom have any brothers or sisters?"

"She had an older sister, Crystal. All I know is she got married and lived somewhere in Ohio."

"Didn't they look for her when your mom..." A look from her husband silenced her mid-sentence, and she stared out the window, keeping her question to herself. Did Jed's grandparents and aunt refuse to take the kids in after his mother died? That would sure explain why he was so insistent on keeping the girls. Why had it taken him so long to share these details? Why had it taken her so long to ask?

After twenty minutes or so, they crossed a bridge. The lake shone dark blue to the left and boats bobbed at the docks in the harbor on the other side. The road veered inland, away from the water, and narrowed. They passed rundown brick buildings and empty strip malls, but glancing down the side streets, Natalie noticed well-kept bungalows.

"South Shore," Jed said. "This is where we lived with Mitch." He turned down a tree-lined street and pulled up in front of a brick apartment building. Leaning across, he pointed to a second-floor window. "That was the kitchen," he said. "Mitch wasn't a bad cook." He smiled. "Not as good as you, but a helluva lot better than Mom. She couldn't make a peanut butter sandwich."

He shifted into drive and waited for a car to pass before pulling out. Two blocks down he turned again, and came to a stop beside a weed-infested empty lot. "It's gone," he murmured.

"What?"

"The school I went to. Lincoln Douglas Elementary. Fourth grade. Mr. Chapman. Until then, I had no idea that guys could be teachers. He was great. He played kickball with us during recess. It's the only time I spent a full school year in one place until I lived with Tom and Susan."

He pointed to the back of the lot where the weeds gave way to mostly dirt. "That's where we played baseball," he said. "There were a ton of kids on this block. Boys, girls, black, white, we didn't care. We'd get together and have games and imagine being in the big leagues." He turned to her. "In my head, I was always Johnny Bench, even though I never saw him play. He was Mitch's favorite player. He talked about him all the time."

Natalie took a breath. "Have you ever looked for Mitch?"

"He could've found us if he wanted to." His blue eyes flashed and she saw his jaw tighten.

"Maybe not," she said. "You couldn't even find Chelsea because she moved around so much, and Noah was in Indiana."

"I was right here," Jed pointed out. "Not far from here, anyway."

"Maybe he tried, Honey."

"He's probably dead by now."

"How old was he when you knew him?"

Jed shrugged. "I'm not even sure how old Mom was. But she had me when she was nineteen and I was ten when we lived with Mitch, so..."

"So, he was probably around thirty. Jed, he'd only be in his 60s now. I bet he's still living." She took out her phone. "What was his last name?"

"Don't, Nat, just..."

"Alright," she sighed. She put her phone away and stared out the window at the empty lot, trying to imagine the man beside her playing baseball, young and carefree.

He pulled away from the curb and continued down the street. The residential area gave way to another strip mall, empty storefronts except for a nail salon and check cashing store. Faded *'For Rent'* signs hung in the windows of the other places.

Several blocks further, Jed pulled into the parking lot of a corner diner. A cracked plastic sign in front read *Parkview Diner* above and *Today's Special: Ro st eef & Ma h d potat es Appl ie.*

"Mom worked here waiting tables," he said. "I used to walk down after school and she'd get me a piece of pie and a glass of milk. I'd do my homework and then we'd pick up Chelsea and Noah at the sitter and go home."

"Just like you did with me when we started dating," Natalie murmured.

Jed raised his eyebrows in surprise. "You're right," he said. "I never thought of that."

Natalie got an idea. "Wait here," she said. She grabbed her wallet and got out of the car. Walking into the diner, the lingering odors of fried meat and strong coffee assaulted her. Two wizened black men sat at the counter, a deck of cards, and a glass coffee carafe between them. Empty breakfast plates and coffee cups littered two booths against the window. At the sound of the chimes on the door, a harried middle aged woman came out from the back.

"Just one?" She asked, grabbing a laminated menu from the stack.

"Could I get two slices of your apple pie and two milks to go?" Natalie asked.

"Uh, sure," the woman said. She came back with two Styrofoam boxes and two plastic cups. She put everything into a white plastic bag. "That'll be twelve even," she told her.

Natalie gave her three fives and told her to keep the change. Pleased with herself, she grinned all the way back to the car.

"What the hell were you doing?" Jed said. "I was about to come in after you. This neighborhood isn't the best."

"Didn't I see a park by the lake on our way in?" Natalie asked, stowing the bag carefully on the floor between her feet.

Jed looked at her strangely, but drove back down the main street and onto the road that led back to the city. Soon, they saw a sign for Rainbow Beach.

"There!" Natalie said. "I see some picnic tables with a view of the water."

They parked, and she grabbed the bag and walked ahead of Jed to the picnic table. She took out the contents, setting the cups on the bag to keep it from blowing away.

"Crap," she said. "She didn't give us any forks."

Jed popped the Styrofoam container open and peered inside. "Apple pie?" he said. "No fork, no problem." He winked at her, picked it up like it was a slice of pizza, and took a bite. Natalie did the same and instantly regretted it.

Jed made a grunting noise and spit his bite into the empty container. "Oh, my God. That's awful."

Natalie managed to choke her bite down, following it immediately with a long swallow of milk. "I am so sorry," she sputtered. "It's diner pie. Diner pies are legendary. I mean, how do you ruin apple pie?"

"I don't know, but they did." He drank the milk in several gulps, and choked out a laugh. "It's the worst pie I've ever tasted."

"It's horrible," Natalie agreed. "The apples are sour and the crust...ugh." She frowned. "I just wanted to bring back a childhood memory," she said. "Taste and smell are two of the strongest senses for memories."

"I have a memory that the pie used to be a lot better." Jed's shoulders shook as he continued to laugh. He looked at her face. "Aww, Nat. Don't be upset. It's funny."

"I guess..." she collected the containers and put everything into the bag. A seagull circled overhead, hovered for a moment, then flew off towards the water. Now she laughed. "Even the seagull doesn't want this pie," she said.

She tossed the bag into a trash can on the way back to the car. Jed threw an arm around her and pulled her close, and she tipped her face up for a kiss.

"Much better than pie," he murmured.

Chapter 19

Back at the hotel, Jed stretched out on the bed. Natalie was taking a soak in the garden tub before getting dressed for their reservation at Paulo's. He could hear the quiet sloshing of the water and low notes of Adele's singing.

He closed his eyes and tried to take a nap, but images from the day and Natalie's words kept him from drifting off.

"Oh, what the hell?" he muttered. Picking up his phone from the nightstand, he opened the search engine and typed in *Mitch Morrison, Chicago*.

****

The last rays of the October sunlight filtered through the etched glass windows, making the crystal lamps at each table sparkle. The wine steward made the pour into Natalie's glass and watched while she tasted it and nodded. He filled her glass and set down Jed's bourbon. "Your server will be with you shortly."

Jed raised his glass and gazed across the table at his wife. Her short blonde hair fell in soft waves around her face. She wore a deep brown sleeveless dress with a plunging v-neckline. That, and the topaz necklace and earrings that were his 20th anniversary present to her last year, set off her fading tan and her greenish brown eyes. She still took his breath away.

"What?" she said, flushing. "You're staring at me."

"Why wouldn't I?"

She smiled. "You're not so bad yourself." They clinked glasses.

The restaurant served table style with a choice of salad, starter, entrée, and dessert. Jed deferred to Natalie, and they feasted on Grilled Caesar salad, Honeycrisp octopus with a horseradish dipping sauce, and Lemon Sole with saffron. Dessert was a banana hazelnut Crème Brule.

"Thank you for today," she said after the server cleared their dessert plates. "I know it wasn't what you thought we'd be doing."

"It was okay," he said. And it was. Revisiting the places he remembered from that isolated year when things were close to normal was oddly comforting. Even though he hadn't had anything close to a storybook childhood, there were *some* happy memories. Maybe that's what sustained him. Maybe it was time to say thank you. He reached into the pocket of his jacket and took out the folded paper.

Sliding it across to her, he said, "I did a little research while you were in the tub."

Natalie took the paper and opened it. Her eyes opened wide, and she looked up at him.

"You found him!"

"I did," he said. "And I called. I was afraid it would be too late when we got back from dinner."

"Seriously? You really called him?"

"Yes." He didn't tell her that his hand shook as he punched in the number. Or that he'd almost hung up when Mitch answered. "And, if it's okay with you, we're meeting him for brunch before we head home tomorrow."

"What?" she gasped. "Oh my gosh, Honey, of course. That's awesome!" She leaned in. "What was it like to talk to him?"

"He was thrilled I called." Jed swallowed. "It sounded like he was pretty choked up." He drank the last of the bourbon.

"I can't wait to meet him."

"Yeah," Jed said. "Me, too."

******

"Jed, stop pacing." Natalie said from the bathroom the next morning. "It won't make the time pass any faster and you're making *me* nervous." There was a sigh from the other room and she heard the voice of the ESPN commentator as the TV clicked on.

She looked into the mirror and opened her eyes wide to stroke on mascara. Replacing the cap, she dropped it into her cosmetic bag. Turning back to the mirror, she ran her fingers through her hair and twisted some strands together on one side, pulling them back and securing them with a tortoiseshell barrette. She slid delicate gold hoops into her ears and smoothed the front of the blue and white striped long-sleeved t-shirt she wore with her jeans.

"Okay," she said. "I'm ready." She tucked the cosmetic case into her bag and zipped it up, then sat on the bed and put an arm around her husband. "He wants to see you," she reassured him. "I'm betting he's thought about you a lot." She squeezed his hand. "As much as you've thought about him."

******

"He said he'd be wearing his Cincinnati Reds cap," Jed said as he pulled into the parking lot at *Eggstacy,* the restaurant Mitch recommended for brunch.

"Brave man in Cubs' town." Natalie quipped, but he felt her gaze as he tapped his fingers on the steering wheel and waited for a black Mercedes to back out before swinging into a parking place.

There was a chill in the air, but the sun was warm and the restaurant's small patio was full. Glancing around, they saw no one in a baseball cap, so he held the door for her as they walked inside. Natalie's eyes swept the room, landing on a table by the windows near the back of the main dining area. She nudged him.

"Two?" The hostess approached, menus in hand.

"We're meeting someone," Jed said. "I think he's back there."

"Oh, yes," she said. "He told me. Follow me."

Mitch took off the hat and rose from his chair as they approached. The strong jaw was looser, the sandy brown hair faded to gray and receding, brushed back from his face. But the smile was the same. That lopsided smile hit Jed in the solar plexus like a punch, and he was ten years old again.

"Jedi," Mitch said. "You grew up."

Jedi. Jed swallowed. How could he have forgotten that nickname? Mitch put out his hand and Jed took it, but avoided his eyes. He had to hold it together. "This is my wife, Natalie," he said.

Mitch's gaze lifted to her, and Jed could breathe.

"Natalie," he said. "It's so nice to meet you."

"You, too," she murmured, taking his hand. "I've heard so much about you."

Jed pulled out her chair and they all sat.

"The food is great here," Mitch said. "I hear you're a chef."

"Yes," Natalie said, smiling. "It's a small restaurant in our hometown."

"Still, quite an accomplishment."

"I love what I do. Thank you."

The waitress approached their table. "Coffee?" she asked.

Mitch raised his cup for a refill. Jed and Natalie turned their cups over and the waitress filled them. "Cream or sugar?"

"Cream, please," Natalie said, then to Mitch. "What's good here?"

"All of it," he laughed, patting his slight pot belly. "But I've always loved breakfast."

"Pancakes," Jed said, remembering. "You used to make us blueberry pancakes." He didn't realize he'd spoken out loud until Mitch replied.

"They were your mom's favorite," he said. "I really loved her, you know."

Jed looked up.

"I loved all of you."

Silence descended until the waitress interrupted. They gave their orders, although Jed was sure he wouldn't be able to eat a bite.

"I kept in touch with Teri–that's what I called her–through a mutual friend after she left," Mitch said, once the waitress was gone. "I called once or twice a week, and she'd call back about half the time. I tried to get her to go to a meeting with me, but she wasn't having it."

Jed looked up, puzzled.

"You wouldn't know how your mom and I met," Mitch said. "She didn't have custody back yet. We met at a meeting." He waited for Jed to comprehend.

"AA?"

"Yeah, she'd come to AA when she couldn't find a narcotics meeting. We're told not to get involved with anyone who's less than a year sober, but..." he smiled and shook his head. "Your mother was something."

"You're an alcoholic? I never knew that."

"Why would you? You were a kid." He blinked and rubbed his chin. "I looked for you," he said. "I called protective services so often I think they had me marked down as some nutcase."

"But I gave our social worker your number," Jed said. "Darlene was her name. She promised me she'd check it out and let you know what happened."

"Oh, they let me know Theresa was dead," Mitch said. A shadow passed across his face. "But they wouldn't tell me anything else." He sipped his coffee. Jed did the same and felt Natalie's shoulder bump against his. He reached for her hand under the table and squeezed.

"They told me I had no legal right to know, not where you were, how you were doing, nothing. They wouldn't even give you a message from me."

"That must've been hard," Natalie said.

Mitch nodded. "It was. I was a mess for a while."

Their food arrived and as they started to eat, Natalie brought the conversation back to the present. "This omelet is amazing." She held out a forkful for Jed to taste.

"Mmm," he said. "What's in that?"

"Arugula, blue cheese, and wild mushrooms," Natalie said. "And bacon, of course."

"Of course, she loves bacon," Jed told Mitch.

"You two have any kids?" Mitch asked, taking a forkful of his pancakes.

"A son. Theo is twenty," Natalie said. She pulled up a picture on her phone.

"Handsome young man," Mitch said. "I see both of you in him."

"He's a sophomore at Northwestern," Jed added. "Dean's list."

Mitch smiled. "Smart like his father." He pointed with his fork. "And his mother; I'm sure."

"Jed graduated from Northwestern, too," Natalie said. "That's where we met." She took a bite of toast and swallowed. "Theo was a surprise, so I dropped out, and we got married. I took some culinary classes when he went to kindergarten, but I got most of my experience on the job, working for a caterer."

Mitch nodded slowly, watching Jed. "Are you going to eat or just move that around on your plate?"

Jed kept it simple with a smoked ham and cheese omelet and toast. Now, he glanced at the food cooling on his plate. To his surprise, he *was* hungry. He took a bite.

"Jed played baseball in college," Natalie said, continuing to fill in his history for Mitch. Jed was happy to let her.

"You did?" Mitch grinned. "What position?"

"Catcher," Jed said, then took another bite of eggs.

"Catcher. Just like Johnny Bench. Alright. Alright. That's perfect." The man's eyes shone with something like pride.

"They made the Big Ten finals when he was a junior," she said.

"That was more because of Antonio's pitching than anything else," Jed interjected before she could make him the hero.

"It goes hand in hand," Mitch said. "I've always believed the relationship between the pitcher and catcher is the true heart of a good baseball team." He gestured, bringing his hands together.

Natalie finished her omelet and leaned back in her chair. "I am absolutely stuffed," she groaned. "But I couldn't possibly leave one bite on the plate. It was delicious."

"Told you," Mitch said. "How are Chelsea and Noah?"

Natalie glanced at Jed, and he knew this question was his to answer.

"Noah is good," Jed said. "Did you know he had a different father? Anyway, his paternal grandparents adopted him. He grew up in Indiana and he's an accountant. Married, just had a baby."

"They separated you?" Mitch said. "Damn it. I'm sorry. Did they at least keep you and Chelsea together?"

Jed shook his head.

"Well, shit," Mitch muttered, then glanced at Natalie. "Sorry."

"No," she smiled. "You should hear me in the kitchen."

He laughed. "How is she? Chelsea?"

"She's...out of touch right now," Jed sighed. "She's never been in touch, really." He filled Mitch in on his attempts to communicate with his sister after he went to live with the Whites and what he knew of her life as an adult. "So, after she snuck out on us, I didn't know where she went. I didn't even know she had kids."

"And now her girls are living with you?" He pushed his plate away, leaving the last pancake uneaten. "Is she an addict? I worried the most about her, you know. She was so much like Teri, even then."

Jed frowned. "I don't know for certain that she's an addict, but she's following in Mom's footsteps in other ways. Putting her girls through the same shit we went through. I'd like to shake some sense into her."

The waitress dropped the check on the table and Jed won the battle for it. Natalie plucked it from his hand and said, "I'll pay. I need to use the restroom before we head home, anyway. You two keep catching up."

"She's great," Mitch said as Natalie walked away. "Kind, smart, and beautiful, the total package."

"Yeah, yeah, she is. I got lucky."

"You did get lucky, in a lot of ways," Mitch said, nodding slowly. "Chelsea wasn't as lucky, was she? Sounds like every time she grabbed onto something, it slipped away. Maybe she just needs a little luck now. A little support from her big brother."

"And maybe that won't matter at all," Jed said. "Mom had you and look at all the good that did."

Mitch had no answer for that.

"I'm sorry," Jed said. "I shouldn't have said that."

Mitch's eyes clouded and he looked down. "Why not? It's true."

The older man reached into his jacket pocket and pulled out a fat envelope, sliding it across the table to Jed. "I kept these. Had copies made for you."

Jed lifted the flap and took out the stack of photographs. The one on top showed his mom holding Noah. Jed stood in front of her with Chelsea leaning against him. They were all smiling. They looked like a normal family. He'd never seen this picture before.

"You don't have to look at them all now," Mitch said. "I just thought you might like to have them. Figured you don't have many photographs of your childhood."

"I don't have any," Jed said. "Theo's never even seen a picture of his grandmother." He looked back down at the photograph. "Thank you."

"She wasn't all bad, Jed." He sipped his coffee. "Do you remember your grandparents at all?"

Jed shrugged. Two walks down memory lane in two days were wearing on him. "Not much."

"Let's just say Teri's childhood wasn't much better than yours. Plus, there's a thread of addiction running through it all. I hope you're careful about that."

"What's this?" Natalie slipped past her husband and sat back down. "Oh my gosh!" She picked up the photograph. "Is that your mom? Is that you? What were you? Around ten or eleven? Theo looked just like you at that age!"

"Yeah," Jed said. "Uh, I think I'd like to wait and look at the rest of these later."

"Okay," she said. "Thank you, Mitch. This is a wonderful gift."

They stood and made their way out of the restaurant. In the parking lot, Mitch cleared his throat. "I was hoping we could stay in touch."

"I'd like that," Jed said, and Mitch's face lit up in relief.

Natalie smiled. "You should come to Westlake sometime. I'll cook for you."

"We'll get Theo to come home," Jed added. "I'd like him to get to know you."

"That'd be great," Mitch said. He leaned in and kissed Natalie on the cheek. "It was really lovely to meet you."

"You, too." She gave Mitch a quick hug. "Why don't you let me drive?" she said to her husband. After a beat, Jed handed her the keys. "I'm going to call Katy to check on the girls." As she got into the car, she glanced back in time to see Mitch wrap Jed in a hug.

Chapter 20

Natalie stole sideways glances at her husband as she navigated the light traffic out of the city. He was pensive, his face turned toward the window, the envelope of photographs in one hand occasionally slapping against his leg in time to whatever song was playing. She knew well enough to leave him alone with his thoughts, even though she had a thousand questions.

At home, they found the girls in the living room acting out their favorite scenes from the weekend's Disney marathon while Katy and Ian looked on.

"Man, am I glad to see you," her brother said to Jed. "I'm outnumbered."

"We're still outnumbered," Jed observed.

"Yeah, but misery loves company," Ian said with a laugh.

"Maybe misery should have a beer and a cigar," Jed said.

"Excellent idea." Ian pushed up from the couch and kissed Katy on top of the head.

The men headed to the kitchen for beers and then outside to the deck with their cigars.

Natalie watched the two girls wrap scarves around themselves, pretending to be mermaids. "Looks like the indoctrination was a success," she said.

"It was so much fun watching with them!" Katy gushed. "We ended up getting *The Princess and the Frog*, too." She smiled sheepishly. "We might have stayed up a little late last night."

Natalie looked around at the mess in the living room. Pillows and blankets were piled on the couch. They'd draped a sheet over one chair, and there were scarves and clothes everywhere. "Where did all this stuff come from?"

"The girls wanted to put on a show, so we were looking for props and costumes. Ian remembered your mom asked him to take some clothes and stuff to the clearinghouse. The bags were still in his trunk. We got the wands and glitter at Dollar Tree."

"Glitter?"

"Pixie dust!" Zora cried, leaping into the air.

"Peter Pan, too?" Natalie raised an eyebrow at Katy, who flushed and nodded.

"We watched SIX movies, Aunt Nat," Josie said. "I can't wait to see Layla at school tomorrow and tell her! I bet she's never watched six movies in one weekend." At that moment, she twirled and tripped on the end of the scarf. She fell into Zora, who collapsed onto the floor. The girls lay there giggling until they lost their breath.

Natalie sighed. The mess in her living room—even the glitter that would be in the carpet forever—was a small price to pay to see them acting like happy, normal little girls.

"Thanks," she said to Katy. "I can see you had a great time."

"How about you?" Katy's eyes went wide. "Did you and Jed...reconnect?" She grinned.

"We did," Natalie said, smiling back. "Several times."

Both women laughed, then Natalie brought her friend up to speed, telling her about their breakfast with Mitch.

"Wow," Katy said. "I've never thought about that. Jed has nothing from his past. No heirlooms, not even a baby book or a photo album."

Natalie nodded. "I know. There are a lot of gaps for him. Theo, too. We don't know much about Jed's side of the family." She turned to the girls. "Let's get this cleaned up, okay?"

She bent to pick up a shirt, folding it and placing it on the couch. Katy and the girls joined her in straightening up.

"At least now Jed can show Theo what his grandmother looked like. She's the girls' grandmother, too," she added, as it dawned on her.

"Was that the only photo?"

"No, there are more, but Jed hasn't looked at them yet."

"I would have gone through them right away."

"Me, too," Natalie said. "But I'm sure he'll do it when he's ready."

"Aren't you curious?" Katy's gaze went to the envelope Jed left on the coffee table.

"Sure, but they aren't mine to look at."

She fingered the envelope and looked at Natalie. "Not even a peek?"

"I'll wait for Jed."

"You're a more patient woman than I am," Katy said, shaking her head.

******

Later that evening, after the girls were in bed, Natalie found Jed on the couch, the envelope in his hand. Slowly, he opened it and slipped out the family photo she'd seen earlier, laying it on the coffee table. The next one showed him, about the same age, holding up a fish he'd caught, his grin wide and genuine.

"I can't get over how much you look like Theo at that age," she said. "I knew he looked more like you, but... wow."

The next few photos seemed to be from the same day; Jed and Chelsea ankle deep in the blue-gray water of Lake Michigan, Noah sitting in the sand with a shovel, Chelsea holding a tiny frog in her hand, her face a mixture of disgust and fascination.

"I wish I could remember this day," Jed said.

"That's why we take pictures." She rubbed his neck as he slipped the next picture out of the envelope. This one showed Mitch and Jed's mother. Mitch was turned to her, his mouth open as if he'd just said something, and Teri's head was thrown back laughing. The photo was slightly out of focus, the edges of the profiles blurred.

"I must have taken this," he murmured.

There were several more pictures of the kids at the beach, then the color photos gave way to black and white. The first of these showed a square brick house with a 'sold' sign in the yard. Beside the sign stood a woman in a beehive hairdo and a man in an ill-fitting suit. Two young girls in matching plaid dresses with Peter Pan collars stood in front of the couple.

"I think that's my grandparent's house," Jed said. "So that must be them, with Mom and Crystal."

"Crystal was older?"

"Yeah, two or three years, I think."

There were several other pictures of the house from different angles, and one more of the family, this time in the small backyard.

"That's it," Jed said.

Natalie took the photos, looking through them again. As she slipped them back into the envelope, she picked at the edge of one.

"There's another photo stuck to this one," she said, "Give me a sec." He followed her to the kitchen. "I read about this the other day." She put some water in a bowl and lay the photos in it. "Water won't hurt old photos, because it was part of the developing process."

After about twenty minutes, Natalie took the pictures from the water and carefully peeled them apart. "Voila!" she said, laying them on a paper towel.

In the faded color print photo that had been on the bottom, Teri beamed into the camera, a chubby baby in a blue and white sailor suit held tight in her arms. A young man stood beside her, one arm around her, his face in profile, looking down at the baby. Ballpoint script in the white frame read *Jed, August 1977.*

"You were three months old," Natalie said.

"That's my father," Jed murmured. "It has to be."

Her fingers stroked his neck again, and he leaned into her. "I've never seen a picture of him. I didn't remember what he looked like."

"Does he look familiar?"

"Not really." He shrugged and tossed the photo on the counter. "I'm happy to have the pictures of Mom, but I couldn't care less about him. Mitch was more of a father to me than he ever was."

Chapter 21

The counselor's office was in an old Victorian house close to the vet clinic. Natalie glanced at her watch as she pulled up in front and parked.

"Whew," she glanced in the rearview mirror and spoke to the girls in the backseat, "I thought we were going to be late, but we're right on time."

Josie hauled her backpack onto her shoulder and reached for the door.

"Josie, please leave that stuff in the car, okay?"

"But I have homework."

"Which you can do when we get *home,*" Natalie struggled to keep the irritation out of her voice. Any request or instruction to Josie continued to be a struggle. Fortunately, she was compliant at school, but at home, she was obstinate and contrary, talking back to Natalie and Jed and arguing about everything. They weren't sure yet if or how they should punish her behavior. Hopefully, Julie, their counselor, would have some suggestions.

Jed came to the first session before their weekend in Chicago, but an unexpected development in a case he was working on made it impossible for him to get here today, so Natalie was on her own. Zora unbuckled her booster seat and hopped out of the car, reaching for Natalie's hand. Josie refused a booster, and they had decided not to fight it at this point. Avoiding a screaming hissy fit anytime they went anywhere was worth the ticket if they got pulled over.

Once they were inside, Leslie, one of the interns, took the girls to the playroom and directed Natalie into the therapist's office. Last time, she and Jed talked with Julie first, then they all played a bit with the girls. Julie led them as they talked through some issues they were having at home.

"Hey," Julie said as Natalie came in and sat on the faux leather couch under the window. "So how did this week go?" The slim, pony-tailed woman took the chair across from the couch, pad and pen in hand.

Natalie tucked a strand of hair behind her ear and leaned forward. "Zora is doing really well," she began. "She's adjusted to our routine and to school. She's invited to a birthday party on Saturday for one of her classmates."

"That's great," Julie smiled. "No more issues at snack time?" She made some notes.

"The teacher is making sure she has plenty of time to finish," she said. "I also started packing an extra snack in her lunch like you suggested, so she knows she has something else if she's hungry."

"Good. So, Zora is doing well. How about Josie?"

"Bedtime is just a nightmare." Natalie wrapped her hands together to keep them still. "She talks back, refuses to brush her teeth or pick up her clothes...," she sighed. "It's the same in the morning when we're getting ready for school. Everything is a battle. The only time she listens to me is when I let her help with dinner."

"Tell me about that."

"Um... well, I really just wanted to give Jed some time with Zora, since she hangs on me a lot, so the other night he took her to walk the dogs, and I asked Josie to help me make the salad. I was really surprised when she didn't throw a fit."

"What did you have her do?"

"She tore the lettuce and divided it into the bowls. Same with the veggies after I chopped them."

Julie tapped her notebook with the pen. "So she seemed to enjoy that?"

Natalie nodded. "She did. She told Jed she helped."

"Maybe you could start giving her a task every day? Some way to participate in making dinner or packing lunches? It might be a way for you two to connect. That may help with the defiance."

"I could do that." She swallowed. "What about punishment? What do we do when she defies us?"

"Let's call it consequences rather than punishment. You have other children, right?"

"Yes, a son, but Theo is twenty, so it's been a while since we've dealt with this kind of thing."

"Okay. So, growing up, he was a pretty good kid?"

"Sure. I mean, we had our moments–like anyone, but he understood the rules and usually followed them."

"And when he didn't?"

"He knew what would happen...oh," she said, realizing.

"Yeah, so Josie and Zora haven't had anything like that at home. Home was chaos. They seem to understand the rules at school, because those are familiar, but having someone telling them what to do at home is new, especially for Josie. She probably told Zora what to do. She's used to being 'in charge'. It doesn't matter that she never should have been, it's what she knows, and she's going to instinctively fight any changes to that." Julie leaned forward. "Try not to take it personally. It isn't *you*. She would do this to anyone." Julie jotted some notes.

"So you and Jed have some homework for this week. You need to decide on two or three behaviors that are important to you and the consequences for the girls if they don't comply. Talk to Josie and Zora about them, write them down and post them somewhere where they can see them."

"Okay. Can you help us with that?"

"What did you do with your son if he misbehaved?"

Natalie thought. "We would restrict television or electronics, but the girls aren't as into that as he was. Josie loves to read, but I don't want to take that away."

"No, you shouldn't."

"I did take her book away until she did what I asked the other night," Natalie admitted, "but I gave it back."

Julie nodded. "How did she react to that?"

"Not well," Natalie sighed. "I thought of 'no dessert', but was afraid to make food a consequence."

"Depriving them of dessert is not starving them. They're allowed to eat as much as they want at meals, right?"

"Of course."

"Then saying 'you can't have ice cream tonight because you argued with me about brushing your teeth' isn't abuse. It's a consequence. As long as they understand that it's a consequence, you're doing fine." She smiled. "Why don't you talk to Jed about it, then email me what you come up with. I'll take a look and get back to you before our next appointment."

"Sounds good."

"Let's go see what the girls are doing."

****

In the playroom, Zora and Leslie were engaged, playing with the baby dolls. Josie was sitting on the floor crisscross-applesauce watching them, her face blank. Julie plopped down beside her, and Natalie followed, sitting on the other side.

"What are they playing?" Natalie asked Josie.

"House, I guess." the girl shrugged.

Julie spoke next. "You don't want to play?"

"It's boring."

"Why is it boring?" Julie said.

Josie stole a glance at Natalie and chewed her lip. "It ain't real. It's *not* real." she corrected herself.

"Well, make-believe isn't real, that's true." Julie looked back at Zora who was rocking the doll baby in her arms. "Would you rather draw a picture? I have some paper and markers, crayons, anything you want over here."

Josie shrugged, then got to her feet. "I guess," she said.

Julie moved with her, but motioned for Natalie to stay with Zora and Leslie.

Josie sat at the table and picked up a pencil, quickly sketching out the frame of a house. She tacked on what Julie assumed was a porch, sticking out in front. Biting her lip, she continued, putting in windows and a door.

"Who's house is this?" Julie asked.

"Where we used to live."

"Was your apartment in a house?"

"No." Josie looked at her. "This is my grandma's house. We lived there first."

"What color was it?"

Josie closed her eyes. "White," she said. "But those things on the windows..."

"Shutters?" Julie said.

"Yeah. They were blue."

Julie picked up a light blue crayon. "Like this?"

"No. Darker." Josie's eyes scanned the pile. "Like this one."

"What was your grandma like?"

Josie shrugged. "She was nice. She got sick."

"How did that make you feel?"

"Sad, I guess. She couldn't play with us anymore or cook or anything. Mama had to stop working and stay home to take care of her. Zora was just a baby, and I had to help Mama with her."

"That sounds hard."

The child's shoulders lifted and fell again.

The hour was almost up. "Maybe next time we can talk a little more about your grandma."

"I don't remember much. Mama made a book of pictures for us, so we'd remember her and Daddy. But I don't know where it is now."

As they got ready to go, Julie pulled Natalie aside. "Josie mentioned a book her mother made. It sounded like a scrapbook of some kind. Did you find anything like that in the apartment?"

"The landlord packed things up. Jed put the boxes in the garage, except for a few things we salvaged for the girls."

"You might want to look through it. It could be helpful."

"Okay, I'll look. Thanks."

"See you next week. Work on those rules and consequences."

Chapter 22

"Ow!" Zora cried as Natalie gathered the other side of her hair and started wrapping the band around it.

"Sorry." She glanced again at the picture in the link Tracy sent for a website called *Hairstyle Hub*. Using the pick, she fluffed Zora's curls into two puffy balls on each side of her head.

"What do you think?" Natalie smiled and held up a mirror so the child could see. "We could tie some ribbons on to match your outfit."

Zora's eyes widened, and she patted one puff. "It's pretty," she said. "I like it."

"Do you want to try another style?"

Zora shook her head. "I want to wear it this way. Can we do it this way for school? With ribbons?"

"I think I can manage that," Natalie said, happy Zora hadn't chosen one of the more elaborate styles.

"Josie? Did you see anything you'd like to try?"

The older girl kept her face in her book, feigning disinterest, as Zora continued to admire herself in the mirror. Now she looked up.

"I like my hair the way it is."

Natalie took a breath and bit her lip. Josie's hair was a tangled mess that she brushed and pulled into a ponytail when the child would let her. It was clean, at least. Natalie had gotten a shampoo Tracy recommended, and they insisted Josie wash her hair once a week.

She tried again. "I thought you might like something different."

"You always wear your hair the same way," Josie said, not looking up.

"Sometimes I put clips in it, or pull the front back."

"It always looks the same."

"Well, I like it. It's easy," Natalie said. "No fuss."

"I like this one," Zora piped up, looking at Natalie's iPad. She pointed to a picture of a girl with six thick braids and held it up to show her sister. Josie shrugged, but watched as Zora scrolled to the next photo. In this one, the girl's hair hung to her shoulders in loose coils. Josie took the iPad and looked at it, then up at Natalie.

"Could we do this?"

Natalie looked at the instructions. "I'd need to get you some conditioner to relax your curls a bit. Then, from what it says, I guess we just let it dry naturally. We could try it on Saturday."

"Okay." Her eyes drifted back to her book.

Natalie smiled. "Good. It will be nice to have different ways to wear your hair. Maybe we can go to

Tracy's salon in the city sometime and get your hair braided. Would you like that?"

"Yes!" Zora said. "Moria in my class has a thousand braids with beads on them."

"No one has a thousand braids," Josie said, rolling her eyes.

"Moria does," Zora insisted.

"We'll get you braids with beads if that's what you want," Natalie said. "But probably not a thousand." She put an arm around the child.

"Now it's time for you to get ready for bed. Josie, you can read for fifteen minutes, then you need to get ready too, okay?"

Josie looked up, her mouth open to protest, but then her eyes drifted to the chalkboard hanging above the desk; a list of three rules and the consequences for breaking them. *No arguing* was number one.

She sighed. "Okay, Aunt Natalie."

Natalie *might* have done a fist pump as she exited the room.

Later, after she tucked them in for the night, and Jed was watching the Bears' game, Natalie walked out into the garage and turned on the light. The boxes from Chelsea's apartment were not on the shelves with their Christmas decorations or on top of the cupboard with

Theo's elementary and middle school memorabilia. Squeezing through to the other side of Jed's Blazer, she found them stacked against the wall. She stood on tip-toe and took the first box off the top, set it on the hood of the SUV and opened it. It was full of clothing, mostly jeans, t-shirts, and sweatshirts. There were a few dresses and skimpy camisole tops, obviously Chelsea's. Setting that box aside, she pulled out the next one. This one was full of pots and pans, some with traces of burned food still stuck to them. She put those on top of the garbage can to be thrown out. The bottom box held books, so she took them out one by one, piling them to the side. Chelsea was evidently a fan of cheap romance novels.

At the bottom of the box, Natalie found several kids' books, and under that, wrapped in a baby quilt that looked to be handmade, was the photo album. She replaced the rest of the books in the box and tucked the wrapped photo album under her arm as she came back into the house.

In the laundry room, she unwrapped the album and tossed the quilt into the washer. She walked into the living room and sat next to Jed, the album on her lap.

"What's that?" he asked, as the game went to a commercial.

"Josie mentioned a photo album at therapy this week. I thought it might be in those boxes in the garage and I just found it."

"Huh."

Natalie opened the cover. The first picture was of Chelsea and a handsome, round-faced black man with close cropped hair and a neat moustache. His eyes were warm and kind; Zora's eyes.

"That must be Dante," she said.

"Look at her," Jed said, his finger tracing his sister's face. "She looks so happy."

"She really does." Natalie turned the page.

There was Josie, swaddled tightly, looking up from her father's arms. Dante's smile split his face as he gazed at his daughter.

More pictures of Josie filled the next few pages. They showed the baby naked in the bath, in the arms of an older woman with graying curls and red-framed eyeglasses, or sitting on Chelsea's lap. There was one of her in a white sleeper with bunny ears on her head.

"She was such a pretty baby," Natalie gushed.

"I can't get over Chelsea. She looks like a different person."

The next page was a formal wedding portrait from the courthouse. Chelsea wore a simple white sundress and held Josie in her arms. Dante stood beside her in his dress uniform, one arm around her. The judge was behind them, and another black man, taller and with sharper features than Dante, stood by his side. Dorthea, on the other side of Chelsea, was the only one not smiling.

"She looks formidable," Jed commented.

Natalie agreed. "Definitely."

The album continued as Josie grew, crawling, walking, playing with wrapping paper on Christmas morning, in a pool with Dante dangling her feet in the water.

Natalie turned past the last few empty pages and an envelope and two newspaper clippings slipped out onto the floor. Jed retrieved them.

The envelope was from the United States Army and they could imagine what the letter inside said. The newspaper clippings were the obituaries for both Dante and Dorthea, just six months apart.

There were no pictures of Zora.

Chapter 23

Jed sat at the bar drinking his coffee and reading the Tribune. Natalie came in, feet bare, her hair still damp from the shower. She brushed a hand on his shoulder as she walked by.

"Morning," she said, leaning in for a kiss. He caught the mint of her toothpaste lingering on her lips.

"Morning."

She poured herself some coffee and sat down across from him. He automatically handed her the food and dining section from the paper.

"Thanks, hon."

"Sure. Hey, I've been thinking," he said, keeping his voice light. "It worked really well when you did lunch at Sorriso when Theo was younger. Maybe you could do that again? Just for a little while until the girls get settled? You said Kendall was doing a great job, right?"

He folded the paper and laid it on the counter.

Natalie sat up straighter and ran a hand through her hair, tucking one side behind her ear. He knew she was choosing her words carefully.

"I'm at a different place in my career than I was then, Jed," she said. "I'm responsible for ordering, planning the menu and specials, developing new recipes...I have a reputation – a good one. I can't just back off and leave Stella in the lurch."

"But you wouldn't be," Jed said. "You've trained Kendall. You said she…"

"Kendall is wonderful, but she isn't ready to be in charge of the dinner service every night, and I'm not ready to let her. I've worked hard, and I love what I do, Jed. I thought you knew that."

"I do!" He reached for her hand, and she let him take it. "I know you love it." He gave her hand a squeeze. "And I'm very proud of you, but…"

"But you want me to give it up."

"I never said that. Maybe just scale back a little for now."

She pulled her hand away, folding her arms over her chest. "Scale back? So that I can deal with school and counseling and friends and…" she huffed out another breath. "What does 'for now' mean? How long is 'for now'?"

He shrugged. "A few months? A year? I don't know."

"A year?" Natalie's voice grew shrill.

"The counseling seems to be helping, but what if they don't find Chelsea, Nat? Have you thought about that? Or if she's…" He dipped his head and pressed his forehead with a finger and thumb. "What if she's dead? What happens then?"

Her gaze softened. "They'll find her. And we'll make sure she gets the help she needs."

"Yeah," he snorted. "That worked out so well for our mom."

"Chelsea isn't your mom. Maybe if your mother had family support things could have been different."

"So it's a 'no' to scaling back?" Jed wasn't going to drop the subject. It was too important.

"I think the girls have been doing just fine the way it is. Josie seems to be doing much better now that our expectations are clear. We're going to keep up the counseling, too."

"But with fall and Christmas coming, the restaurant will be busier. It will be hard to be consistent. You know how it is during the holidays. How will you get them to counseling appointments when you have back-to-back luncheons plus a full house for dinner?"

"Maybe *you* could scale back," she countered.

The laugh came out before he could stop it.

"You're laughing about this?" She grabbed the dishrag and picked up his empty cereal bowl before wiping down the counter and scrubbing at imaginary spots. "It's not funny, Jed. Of course you make more money than I do, but that's just insulting."

"I carry the health insurance, too," he said. "Good insurance. Which we'll need for them." He sighed, "I understand you're upset, but you have to admit it would make things easier around here if you weren't so busy."

"Easier for who?"

"For you, for the girls, for all of us."

"You aren't listening to me. I don't want to give up my job." She bit her lip and blinked back tears. "Damn it! I can't talk about this anymore right now. I have to meet the liquor supplier at ten. I'm going to go."

She picked up her purse and left without kissing him goodbye.

"Goddamn it!" he muttered.

****

"You okay?" Stella said once the dinner rush had passed that evening. "I'm only asking because that's the second order you've messed up, and you *never* mess up orders."

"I'm..." Natalie started, then her face crumpled.

"Kendra, you're in charge," Stella said. She took Natalie gently by the arm and led her into the office, closing the door behind them.

"Tell me what's going on." Stella sat in the leather desk chair, crossing her legs and leaning forward. "Sit."

Natalie sat in the other chair and used her apron to wipe her face. "Jed and I had a fight, a huge one. I left without kissing him goodbye. I never do that."

"I'm sorry. I know you don't fight often."

"We have disagreements, just like everyone, but this was...different. I just wasn't expecting it. He's being so damn stubborn. He's not listening to me at all." She sniffed again and Stella held out a box of tissues.

"The girls?"

Natalie nodded. "Jed is worried about them. He wants me to 'scale back' here to be home more."

"And you don't want to do that."

Natalie stared past her boss for a moment. "I love those girls, I really do. And I'm aware they're needy and starved for love and attention. The counseling is going well, and right now we're making my schedule work, but he's right." She wiped away more tears. "If something has happened to Chelsea, I couldn't do this job and raise those girls. Not the way we raised Theo."

"Well, of course not," Stella said. "You have an entirely different life than you did when Theo was that age. Lots of mothers work. They have people who help them. There's more than one way to raise children."

"But...the girls have been through so much. Jed expects me to..."

"He'll come around. Anyway, giving up your job will not make the right impression on those girls. They need to see that doing what you love and what makes you happy is important."

"I hadn't considered that." Stella seemed so sure of her opinion. Natalie wished some of that confidence would rub off on her.

The older woman reached over and squeezed her hand. "Why don't you head home early?"

"I'd rather finish the night," Natalie said. "Really."

"Okay." Stella rose from the chair. "Back to work then." She glanced at her watch. "It's almost eight. There's only two tables that haven't been served. I'll tell Daniel he's in charge of cleanup. When you're done cooking and the list is up for tomorrow, you can head home. Or, you can come to my house for a drink if you want to talk."

"Thanks. I'll let you know."

****

Jed was quiet as they got ready for bed. Natalie felt an apology on the tip of her tongue more than once, but she swallowed it every time. She had nothing to apologize for. She loved her job. She'd worked hard to get it, and she was *good* at it. People loved her food. They came to Sorriso for *her*. She was *not* going to apologize for wanting to keep doing what she loved. Stella was right. The girls needed a good example.

She washed her face and took her time with her nightly routine, hoping that Jed would be asleep by the time she got into bed, but he turned to her immediately.

"Goodnight," she said, giving him a soft peck on the lips.

"Hey," he said.

"We were busy tonight," she said, rolling away from him. "I'm exhausted."

"This is about this morning, isn't it? About the girls? You know I'm right. They need more of your time."

"Jed, can we not do this now? Please?"

He huffed out a breath. "I'm not asking you to do anything I wouldn't do. I gave up a dream for our family once, too."

"What?" She sat up. "What did you just say?"

"I was going to go to law school, remember? That was our plan until..."

"Until what, Jed?"

"Natalie..."

"That was our dream until *I* got pregnant. That's what you were going to say, isn't it?" Natalie swung her legs out of bed. "I didn't exactly do it by myself!"

"Shhh! The girls will hear you." He was out of bed now, too, moving toward her. "And that's not what I meant."

"Well, it's what you said." She pulled her nightgown off and grabbed sweatpants and a t-shirt off the hook on the door.

"What are you doing?" He reached for her but she pulled away.

"I'm going to Stella's. She invited me over for a drink after work and I turned her down, but now I'd really like one. Maybe two." Slipping her feet into tennis shoes, she walked down to the kitchen, Jed trailing behind.

"Natalie... come on..."

"No. Jed, the answer is no. I don't want to be a full-time, stay-at-home mom again. I don't. And I shouldn't have to give up what *I* love while you just go waltzing into work every day."

"Dammit! Can't we just talk about this?"

"No. I'm not changing my mind. I'm not giving up Sorriso."

He leaned on the counter, arms crossed over his chest. "And I'm not changing mine about what I believe is best for the girls. So where does that leave us?"

She shook her head. "I don't know."

****

Twenty-four hours later, Natalie stared into the fire pit on Stella's patio, her eyes heavy. It had been another busy night at the restaurant, and she'd had too much to drink the night before, sitting up talking to her boss past midnight. As comfortable as Stella's spare room was, she hadn't slept well without the warmth of Jed next to her.

She wanted to go home, but she didn't know how to apologize when she wasn't sorry. Jed had *always* supported her dream. She couldn't believe he wanted her to give it up *now*. Still, she'd never gone this long without talking to Jed. She missed him. The flames blurred as a tear rolled down her cheek. The patio door opened, and she wiped it away quickly.

"You have a visitor," Stella said. "But I'll send him away if you don't want to see him."

"No. It's fine."

Footsteps came toward the fire pit, and her voice caught in her throat. "Who's with the girls?" She didn't look up.

"Mitch," Jed said. "I called to talk, and he came all the way here." He squatted in front of her. "I'm an asshole," he said.

"Yep, you are." She bit her lip. "But I was a bitch, so maybe we deserve each other."

"God," he said, his mouth turning up at one corner. "I hope so."

She leaned forward, and he wrapped his arms around her, burying his face in the curve of her neck.

"I can't do this without you," he murmured.

"You don't have to," she said, stroking his hair. "We'll figure it out. We always have."

He pulled away, those clear blue eyes searching hers. "Come home?"

She nodded and let the tears fall as he pulled her back into his arms.

******

"Thank you," Natalie said, giving Mitch a kiss on the cheek.

"You're welcome. They're sweet girls. They brushed their teeth, and I read them a story. It was no big deal."

She met his gaze. "That's not what I meant."

Mitch dipped his head. "I may be an old bachelor, but I recognize something special when I see it. I just reminded him that not everyone gets the relationship you two have."

Natalie nodded, knowing he was talking about himself.

Jed came in with Mitch's jacket. "You sure you won't stay?"

"I'm not that old, Jedi. I can drive back to the city after dark just fine."

Jed grinned. "Okay, but we're on for Thanksgiving, right? You're coming?"

"I would not miss it for anything," Mitch said.

Natalie looked in on the girls while Jed let Finn and Charley out, locking up and turning out the lights after the dogs came in. Both animals trotted upstairs, settling in next to the girls' beds.

"We've been abandoned," Jed remarked as they made their way to the bedroom.

"Greener pastures," Natalie said. "I'm pretty sure Zora still squirrels away food."

"I think they just know where they're needed."

Natalie washed her face and threw her dirty clothes into the hamper, slipping into her nightgown before walking into the bedroom. Jed's back was to her, and she pressed against him, resting her cheek between his shoulder blades and wrapping her arms around him. He took her hand and kissed the back of it, then turned around.

"There's nothing I want more right now that to throw you on that bed and make love to you," he began. "But..."

She put a finger on his lips. "I'm exhausted. I don't think I slept a wink last night, and the restaurant was jammed all evening. I'll be plating fettucine in my dreams."

"I didn't sleep either. I missed you." He kissed her softly. "Tomorrow," he whispered.

"I'll hold you to that. Now let's go to bed."

Early the next morning, Natalie used the bathroom and slid back into bed, tossing one leg over Jed's and laying her head on his shoulder.

"Ummm," he said. His eyes stayed closed, but he stroked her hip and his lips curved into a smile. "You don't have any clothes on."

"You *did* say 'tomorrow'." She ran her hand down his chest and stomach and kissed behind his ear. "It's tomorrow," she whispered.

He opened one eye. "Indeed, it is. Com'ere." He pulled her on top of him and captured her mouth with his.

After, in a tangle of sheets and limbs, Natalie wove their fingers together. "If we're creative, and willing to do this differently than we did with Theo, we can make it work."

"That's kind of what Mitch made me consider."

"Stella said that giving up my job wouldn't be a good example for the girls."

"She's probably right," he admitted. "They wondered where you were."

"Oh!" she said, flushing. "I didn't even think about that. I was so angry. Are they okay?"

"Yeah, I told them you were helping a friend, and you'd be home soon." He kissed her forehead. "The bed was way too empty last night. I ended up on the couch and I couldn't even find a good baseball movie."

Natalie smiled. "I got drunk on Stella's expensive wine and woke up with a screaming headache."

"Have we learned our lesson?"

"I'd bet on it."

"So we can talk about this? Come up with a plan?"

"Yes, maybe the counselor can help us," Natalie said. She pushed up onto one elbow, looking down at him. "The plan needs to include me continuing at Sorriso."

He nodded. "I agree."

"But..." she said. "I'm willing to do some rearranging of responsibilities if Stella will let me. Kendall is probably ready to handle some of the ordering and menu planning. We'll have to work that out, see what it looks like. I'm not giving up the dinner service entirely, but maybe I can turn Wednesdays over to her."

Jed stared up at the ceiling. "I'm going to talk to Tom and see if there's a way to work from home one or two days a week. So much of what I do is on the computer anyway, maybe that would be possible." He shrugged. "I'm not sure."

"See," Natalie said. "Look at us being creative problem solvers."

"I've got another problem for you to solve," he said, moving her hand.

Her eyes widened and she laughed, "I like this problem." She raised an eyebrow. "What do you suggest I do about it?"

"Let's be creative," he said with a wink

Chapter 24

Jed slipped in the back door of Sorriso. For a moment, it took him back to the early days of their relationship, as he saw Natalie at work. It had been too long since he'd really watched her. There were three pans on the stove. Peppers and onions sizzled in one, tomato sauce bubbled in another. She adjusted the flame under the last pan as she swirled butter and added a pile of sliced mushrooms from the cutting board on the counter. As she turned for the salt and pepper, she saw him and smiled.

"Give me just a minute," she said.

Daniel stepped over. "I've got this, Chef," he said, shooing her toward her husband.

"Thanks. Don't let the peppers burn." she kissed Jed. "Hi. What're you doing here in the middle of the lunch rush?"

His smile faded, and he motioned to Stella's office. "They found Chelsea," he said, once they had some privacy.

Natalie gasped and her hand flew to her mouth.

"She's been arrested. The police raided a drug house on the west side, and she was there with a bunch of other people."

"At least she's alive," Natalie said.

"Yeah, yeah, I know." They'd both been afraid that wouldn't be the case.

"Maybe she can get some help now." Natalie looked up at him. "How did you find out?"

"Detective Horton called me as soon as she got word. They're holding her at the Metropolitan Correctional Center, and she'll be arraigned tomorrow. I'm going to go talk to her. Tom gave me the name of an attorney he knows. This guy's son died of an overdose, and now he does pro-bono work for people on drug charges. He tries to get them court-ordered rehab rather than jail. I'm going to call him, see if he can meet me there. I know you're working tonight, but..."

"It's okay," she said. "I'll get ahold of Mom and Dad and have them pick up the girls. They can take them to their place. Zora will be thrilled. She loves that goat."

Jed rolled his eyes and laughed. "Can I get one of your chicken parm sandwiches for the road?"

"Sure. Give me five minutes."

Ten minutes later, Jed pulled onto the interstate, headed into Chicago. The mid-afternoon traffic was light, and he ate his sandwich as he drove, one hand on the wheel. The Metropolitan Correctional Center, MCC, was in downtown. Jed drove through traffic, past the building he would always think of as the Sears Tower, to a parking garage where he paid an excessive amount to park for two hours. It was fortunate that the attorney was there today to meet with another client and could see Jed after. He told him to wait in the third floor lobby.

The building rose in front of him, a triangle of concrete with rectangular slits of windows dotting its surface. He showed his DCI badge to the security at the door and passed through the metal detector. Following the guard's directions, he found the elevators and made his way to the third floor.

Jed was pacing in front of the double safety glass windows, checking email on his phone when a short, older man with shaggy graying hair approached him. Alan Edwards had heavy dark eyebrows over sad eyes. He wore a well-tailored gray suit, white shirt, and boldly patterned necktie. He held out a hand and the two men shook.

"Jed Shaw? Alan Edwards," he said. "I've already checked on the charges. Let's have a seat and go over a few things."

****

Chelsea sat on the thin mattress atop the concrete bunk, her eyes barely registering the bleak holding cell or the other women sitting on benches and lying on other bunks or on the floor. Their moans and curses hardly penetrated the fog in her brain.

Her entire body ached. She twisted her hands in her lap, knitting her fingers together to stop the shaking. Her heart pounded in her chest. Every breath seemed to be more challenging. She couldn't suck enough air into her lungs. It made her sleepy, but she'd tried lying down and it brought no relief. Her mind started racing as soon as her head hit the pillow.

This was hell. She needed a fix, and Cody was going to be furious. She had to get out of here.

****

Jed sat with his hands braced on his knees and listened to the lawyer explain the intricacies of the judicial system. As law enforcement, Jed already knew most of it, but not from this side. For once, he was more concerned about the offender than the offense.

"So you'll be at the arraignment tomorrow?"

"Yes," Edwards said. "It's scheduled for 11 a.m., but there's a full docket, so it may not happen until afternoon. It depends."

"Will there be bail?"

"I'll ask for a screening investigation. That means they'll evaluate her to determine if she is in control of her actions or if her addictions make her unable to control herself. Once the police and addiction specialists make that determination, there will be a hearing. I might have you testify to the history of addiction in your family. Then the judge will decide."

"So she stays in jail until then?"

"Right now, unless we could get an emergency order, it's the best place for her. She's going to be withdrawing from whatever she's been on–some kind of opioids most likely–and here at least they will monitor her."

"In the infirmary?"

Edwards shook his head. "No. She'll be in a cell. If she's having a hard time, they might put her in solitary – she would be under more surveillance there. Usually withdrawal only lasts a week or ten days, the worst of it anyway."

"Should I come to the arraignment?"

"Up to you, but you might end up sitting there for a long time. If it means burning a vacation day, I'd save it for when she really needs you. Now, normally there aren't any family visits today, but since you're here and I'm her lawyer, they're going to let us go in together." He stood. "You ready?"

"Yeah." Jed rose to his feet. He was ready to get this over with.

****

Natalie stroked the back of Jed's neck gently, letting her fingers curl against his hair as they sat together on the couch. "How was she?"

"Not good," he sighed. "She was shaking and sweating, and I thought she was going to throw up." He shook his head. "She wouldn't look at me and she didn't even ask about the girls until I brought them up, and *then* she started crying."

Nat chewed on her lip as she thought about what to say next. She knew how hard this was for her husband. It brought back memories of his mother that he would much rather keep buried in the back of his mind. "What did the lawyer say?"

Jed closed his eyes, pressing them with his thumb and forefinger. "He thinks he'll be able to get her rehab rather than jail time, but it's not a sure thing because she has prior offenses. He's going to argue that she should have gotten a chance at rehab before this. Maybe it will work; who knows?"

"What are we going to tell the girls?"

"Nothing for now. Let's wait until we know what's going to happen. I talked with the social worker in charge of the girls' case. If Chelsea goes to rehab, they'll try to set up some kind of supervised visitation and go from there."

Chapter 25

Alan Edward's argument worked. The judge sent Chelsea to a 90-day program at Gateway, a rehab center in a town about twenty miles from Westlake. That was two weeks ago. Today was the first scheduled visit for the girls, and Jed took off work to bring them. Now, Zora clutched his hand as they walked through the lobby. Josie walked several paces behind, head down, hands stuffed in the pockets of her light blue jacket.

"Will you stay with us?" Zora looked up at him.

"I don't know," he said. "I'm not sure how this works, either. But it will be okay. If you want me to stay, I'll try. I promise."

The receptionist at the front desk directed them down a hallway. "It's the last door right at the end. Just knock, and someone will let you into the visitation room," she said.

"Hannah is supposed to meet us here–the caseworker from CPS?" Jed couldn't recall her last name.

"She's not here yet. You can wait down there. They won't send the parent in until she arrives."

The visitation room was bright and cheerful. The walls were pale yellow and potted plants lined the windowsill behind an overstuffed couch. They'd scattered

large pillows and beanbag chairs around on the floor.
There were shelves of books, toys, and board games, and
even an outdated gaming system hooked up to a small
television in the corner.

"This is nice. There are lots of things to play with,"
Jed said, trying to get the girls comfortable.

"My stomach hurts," Josie said. "Maybe I'm sick.
Maybe we should go home."

The door opened, and there was a crash. All three
heads turned to see a thin man with blond hair and wire-
rimmed glasses stooping to pick up a thermal mug, its dark
brown contents spilling in a growing pool on the floor.

"Nuts!" He said. He went to a nearby cabinet and
pulled out a roll of paper towels. He cleaned up the mess,
tossed the towels in a trash can, and continued toward
them.

"Lance Shelby," he said, extending his hand. "I'm
your sister's counselor."

Jed shook the man's hand. "Where's Hannah? She's
our caseworker."

"Oh," Shelby said. "Hannah Wilkes? Protective
services called me. She quit. It's a high-stress job, so that
happens a lot." He squatted in front of the girls. "I'm
guessing you're Zora and you are Josie," he said, pointing
to each. "Am I right?"

Zora nodded. Josie stayed frozen to the spot.

"Your mom is probably excited to see you. Why don't you girls sit on the couch, or find something to play with? I'll be right back with Mom."

Zora still held tight to Jed's hand.

"Should I stay?" He asked.

Lance looked down at the folder he carried. "This is the first visit, right?"

"Yes."

"They'll probably be more comfortable if you stay." He held up his empty cup. "I'm going to find some coffee, and then grab their mom."

****

Jed's eyes drifted to the rearview mirror, watching the girls in the backseat. Neither had said much since they'd gotten back in the car. After a few miles, he saw a sign for *Caravelle's Dairy Bar,* and took the exit, and pulling up in front of the ice cream shop.

"I'm sorry your mom wasn't feeling well enough to see you," he said, taking a breath. The only customers this time of day, they sat at one of the faded wooden picnic tables beside the drive in. Zora stared at her chocolate vanilla twist cone, while Josie sucked the chocolate fudge off the spoon from her sundae.

"I'm not sure how much you understand, but your mom is an addict. She has a disease. It's not your fault, and you didn't make her sick."

Lance had said almost the same thing to them when he came back without Chelsea. Jed hoped hearing it again from him carried more weight. He took a sip of his banana cream pie milkshake. It was delicious. He'd have to bring Natalie here sometime.

"Can they give her medicine to make her better?" Zora asked. Ice cream dripped from the cone onto her hand and she licked it off, then finally started eating.

"There isn't really any medicine for it," Jed said. "But she's talking to doctors and working at getting better. It's hard work, and I'm sure it makes her tired."

"She just didn't want to see us," Josie said as she stirred her sundae into a muddy-looking mess.

"I don't think that's true," Jed said. "But it could be she didn't want *you* to see *her*."

"Why?" Zora's huge brown eyes filled with tears.

Jed reached across the table, dabbing her eyes with the corner of his napkin. "Remember when Finn chewed up your new tennis shoe?"

"He hid in the closet."

"Yep. He knew we were upset, and he was afraid we'd always be mad at him." Jed glanced at Josie, glad to see she was listening. "I think that's how your mom feels. She thinks we're all mad at her and doesn't want to see that right now."

"Maybe we should tell her we aren't mad," Zora said.

Josie looked at her sister, then back at what was left of her ice-cream. She pushed it away.

"If you *are* upset with her, that's okay." He pressed his lips together and blinked before continuing. "Your grandmother—my mom, who was your mother's mom, too—used to leave us alone. I had to take care of your mom and Noah when I wasn't much older than Josie. Sometimes I got really angry with her, which was confusing because I loved her, too. I know this is hard, but I can understand how you girls feel. You can always talk to me about it."

****

At the girls' next therapy session, Jed explained what happened, and Julie suggested they draw pictures for their mother. Zora started right away, drawing a house, yellow like Jed and Natalie's, with four stick figures standing out in front. Natalie helped her label the people and drew clothes on for her to color, and after that, Zora added a heart and her name and declared she was finished.

Josie's paper stayed blank for a long time. Finally, she drew some characters from the Disney movies they'd watched with Katy and wrote *Arielle is my favorite* in her best handwriting.

"Do you want to say anything else to your mom?" Julie asked.

Josie shook her head. "No."

"Okay, I'll get an envelope, and we'll address this and get it in the mail so she'll have it before your next visit."

Chapter 26

In her room at the rehab center, Chelsea opened the envelope and unfolded the papers, looking at the pictures her daughters had drawn. Zora's was on top. She stared at the names printed beneath each stick person. *Uncle Jed, Aunt Natalie, Josie, me.* Chelsea swallowed the lump in her throat and slipped the second picture out from behind. Josie's drawing was more detailed, and the writing was neater, but who the hell was Arielle?

She set the papers on the flimsy bedside table and flopped back against the pillow. Some women just weren't meant to be mothers. What if she was one of them? When Josie was born and the nurse handed her over, Chelsea immediately passed the baby to Dante. He'd held their daughter close, bending over so she could see the baby's tiny face. Those big brown eyes staring at her were the most terrifying thing she had ever seen.

Chelsea refused any drugs during labor, worried about her history of addiction. Dante thought she was being brave. He didn't know that piece of her past, and she needed to keep it that way. His mother, Dorthea, already disapproved of her. She didn't need another reason.

"Hey," he'd said in that deep, resonant voice of his that always sounded almost like singing. "We've got ourselves a gorgeous baby girl."

He kissed Chelsea's forehead and placed the baby back in her arms. Her eyes filled with tears. She had no idea what to do next. It was a relief when the nurse took the baby to clean her up. Chelsea's eyes slid to Dante's. Pretty soon he was going to find out what his mother already knew. Chelsea was damaged, maybe beyond repair.

But Dante didn't live long enough to figure it out. He died in Afghanistan when she was eight months pregnant with Zora. He wasn't there to hold their second daughter when she was born. By then, the breast-cancer her mother-in-law thought she'd beaten was back. The death of her son took all the fight out of Dorthea, and despite an aggressive course of chemotherapy, she went downhill fast.

Chelsea quit waitressing to care for the girls and her mother-in-law. As the medicine cabinet became filled with more and more powerful pain medications, she told herself it was fine just to take one or two so that she could sleep. One or two at night, maybe another during the day, to take the edge off. By the time Dorthea passed away, Chelsea was spiraling back into addiction.

She was supposed to turn the leftover medication back in to the hospice after Dorthea died, but Chelsea packed up the girls and took off before they could come back for it. It lasted her three weeks. Once those pills ran out, everything, even her girls, took a backseat to finding a fix.

Now she stared at the ceiling of her room, clenching and unclenching her fists. She'd been clean before and blown it. How was this time going to be any different?

****

Jed and Natalie both went with the girls to the second scheduled visitation. This time, Lance Shelby convinced Chelsea to join them. She came into the room uncertainly, shuffling her feet as she made her way to the corner of the couch, curling her legs up and avoiding their eyes.

After a moment, Zora crawled up beside her mother, leaning against her with her thumb in her mouth. "Hi, Mama," she said.

Chelsea's hand came up to stroke her daughter's hair, plaited into four neat braids, but she remained silent, her face blank.

233

Jed kept an eye on Josie as the older girl took in the scene. It had been a tough morning. Josie didn't want to come, and Natalie could only talk her into it by promising she could leave any time she wanted. He cleared his throat.

"You look good, Chels," he said.

Chelsea bit her lip and dropped her hands into her lap, twisting her fingers together.

He told himself she did look a little better. She was clean, for one thing, and her skin wasn't as sallow, the bones of her face less prominent. She wore jeans and a plain navy-blue sweatshirt, her feet in white, rubber-soled slip-ons.

"How are you feeling?" Jed tried again.

She met his eyes and one shoulder lifted and fell.

"I'm not mad at you, Mama," Zora said, gazing up at her.

For the first time, an emotion flashed on Chelsea's face, but it was gone in an instant, too quickly for Jed to even identify it before it was replaced by the mask of indifference.

"Do you want something to eat? There are snacks here in the cupboard," Lance said. He sat at the counter, typing away on his laptop. He'd clarified that this was a visit, not a counseling session, and he was an observer, nothing more.

"I'm not really hungry," Chelsea's voice sounded rough, as if she hadn't used it yet that day.

"I have to go to the bathroom," Josie said.

Natalie rose from the chair by the window. "I'll take you. I saw them on the way in."

"Why don't you go, too," Jed suggested to Zora. She hopped down from the couch and followed.

Jed took her spot, putting a hand on Chelsea's shoulder. "Can't you just talk to them?"

"What am I supposed to say?"

Jed squeezed his eyes shut and tipped his head back, taking a deep breath before answering. "Ask them about school or their friends, or anything." He swept a hand out in front of him. "They just want to talk to you. That's why we're here."

"Josie doesn't want to talk to me," Chelsea said. "I can tell."

"Then talk to Zora. Josie will warm up. She's got a lot going on. She doesn't communicate with us as much as we'd like, either."

"I just don't have the energy to deal with this, Jed."

He sprang to his feet. "They're your kids, for God's sake!"

"It doesn't feel like it."

"Maybe it would if you'd act like you want to spend time with them. Smile. Make an effort. It's like you don't care about them at all." He struggled to keep his voice low.

Chelsea sank further into the couch, wrapping her arms around her knees.

"Come on. Dammit. Don't do this."

Jed felt someone behind him.

"Why don't you back off a bit." Lance said. "Give her some space."

Jed turned to him. "Why are we even here? This is a waste of time."

The door opened, and Natalie and the girls came back in, walking up to Jed. Lance was on the couch, murmuring quietly to Chelsea.

"What's going on?" Natalie asked.

Jed shook his head. "I don't know. She's just..."

"Alright," the counselor walked up, interrupting them. "I think that's all for today. Next time, I think you should drop the girls off and wait outside. Chelsea needs time alone with them. I thought it might be better to have you here the first few visits, but the dynamic between you and your sister is pretty negative."

Jed's jaw tightened and he blinked. "If she'd take some responsibility and start acting like she's their mother, our *dynamic* would be better."

Lance Shelby didn't flinch at the sarcasm in Jed's voice. "I'd like you to come to our session for family members tomorrow night," he said. "It starts at 6:30."

"I don't know," Jed said.

"I think it will help you to hear from people going through the same thing. You aren't alone."

Chapter 27

"That wasn't bad," Natalie said as Jed pulled his seatbelt across and snapped it in. Her husband didn't answer at first, shifting into reverse and turning his head to back out of the parking space.

"It was okay, I guess." He pulled out into traffic and eased on to the highway. "You feel like a milkshake?"

"Sure." She smiled. "You've been talking up this place for weeks."

Once they sat down at the picnic tables with their shakes, banana cream pie for him and peanut butter and jelly for Natalie, he shook his head. "All of those stories," he said. "That one mother; Sophia? Her son has been to rehab four times."

"And she still has hope." Natalie spooned some of the thick shake into her mouth.

"I don't know if I would," Jed admitted.

"I think it might be different if it was Theo," Natalie said. "You've always had a good, solid relationship with him. Everything with your sister is complicated."

"Am I wrong to think that this is all going to blow up in our face? She just doesn't seem invested in it."

"I'm not sure she would show us if she was."

The family session at Gateway was a roundtable discussion. No one had to speak unless they wanted to, and Natalie and Jed chose to listen this first time out. The stories were familiar and yet each one was unique.

Sophia's son was an athlete prescribed pain meds after knee surgery. Once he became addicted, he turned to heroin because it was cheaper. The last time he OD'd, it took two doses of Narcan to bring him back.

Dan and his wife had three children. Before her addiction, Annette was head of the PTA at their school and a respected event planner in their community. Since then, she'd been arrested three times for prostitution to support her habit.

Jenni's father was in his mid-fifties when he became addicted after being overprescribed meds for a back injury he acquired while working at a home improvement store. They fired him for stealing money to support his habit.

It went on and on.

"Lance said the most important thing after the addict wanting help is a support system, right?" Natalie said, watching Jed's reaction.

He nodded, then sighed. "I want to support her. But what can we do? I don't think she would want to move in with us, even if we wanted her to."

"I have an idea," Natalie said.

****

Chelsea waited in Gateway's lobby, watching out the window for her sister-in-law's bright blue Honda SUV to pull up. She glanced at her reflection in the glass. The olive green parka she found at Goodwill on a group shopping trip made her skin sallow and the dark shadows around her eyes stand out, but it was too damn cold to go without a jacket and besides, it covered up the shapeless sweater she wore with her jeans. She'd tried to do something with her hair. Allie, one of the other residents, was a stylist in another life and cut it into a shorter bob for her, but it was still dull and lifeless. She told Chelsea it would take a while for it to get back to normal. Chelsea didn't even remember what normal was.

The car pulled in, and she hitched her purse onto her shoulder before pushing the door open. A sharp icy wind hit her face as she came outside. When she grabbed for the door handle, it was locked, and she watched Natalie fumble for the unlock button.

"I'm so sorry!" she said as Chelsea fastened her seatbelt. "I thought it was unlocked."

"No problem."

"Brrr. It's cold for November! I hope this isn't a sign of a bad winter coming." She pushed a button and turned the heat up. "Your seat is heated, too, if you push that button." She pointed.

"I'm fine."

"Okay," Natalie said. "Let's go show you the apartment."

As they pulled into traffic, Chelsea let her prattle on, telling her about living in this same apartment when she and Jed were first married and Theo was a baby. Chelsea looked her over. Natalie's blond hair was tucked behind her ears and she wore a thick brown sweater with fall leaves stitched into it under a puffy orange vest, faded jeans, and boots. By comparison, Chelsea knew she looked like a street person in her thrift store coat and scuffed sneakers. She sighed and plucked at a loose thread on the jacket.

In Westlake, her sister-in-law pointed out the elementary school where Josie and Zora were in class and two blocks later turned onto a tree-lined side street. She pulled the car into a narrow parking lot next to a two-story house, white with yellow trim and a wrap-around porch. A sign in the yard read: *Russ Dunham Veterinary Clinic– Walk-ins Welcome*

Chelsea followed Natalie up the steps and inside. The smell of bleach and animal piss assaulted her senses, but the waiting room was empty, except for a huge fish tank built into one wall filled with colorful tropical fish.

"Hi Gwyn," her sister-in-law said to the woman in pink scrubs behind the counter. "Is Dad in?"

"Back in his office," she said. She opened a half-door beside the counter and Chelsea followed Natalie through and down a long hall lined with cabinets full of bottles, syringes, and other medical supplies. Russ Dunham stood when they entered the office, and Natalie kissed his cheek.

Chelsea had been trying to think of who the man reminded her of ever since meeting him when he brought the girls to one of their supervised visits. The other night, watching reruns on the communal television at Gateway, she'd figured it out. Natalie's father looked like that guy on M*A*S*H. Not the smart-alecky dark-haired guy, but the other doctor, the scruffy one. A.J? B.J.? Whatever. He looked just like him, especially in his green scrubs.

"Thanks for letting us look at the apartment," Natalie said.

"No problem." He turned to her. "It's nice to see you again, Chelsea," he said. "I hear you want a place close by."

"Yes," she said. In another month, she would be out of rehab. Then there would be two weeks in a halfway house, giving her time to adjust and find a job. She needed an apartment, too, and it had to be in Westlake, since she would have to go to meetings, not to mention prove to Lance Shelby that she could take care of her girls on her own. Just thinking about it made her tired.

Dr. Dunham reached into the desk drawer and took out a plastic key ring shaped like a dog bone. He handed the keys to his daughter. "Here you go," he said. "Hopefully it will work for you. It would be nice to have someone up there again. It's been awhile. The girls could come down and help with the animals who are boarding anytime they'd like, too."

"I'll drop the key off later," Natalie said.

He waved a hand. "Keep it. She might want a second look."

"Alright." Natalie turned. "The stairs are around the back."

Outside, they took another set of steps off the porch onto a paved walkway that wound around the side of the clinic. A staircase led up to the second-floor apartment. Natalie started up. "We put this stairway in when we lived here. The entrance used to be through the clinic, and that got old pretty quick."

Chelsea followed up the stairs and watched as she wiggled the key in the lock.

"It's always been tricky," she said.

Finally, the door gave and she opened it into a small entrance way with hooks on the wall and a coat tree in one corner. Another doorway led them into the kitchen. The walls were painted a bright yellow with a wallpaper border of chickens and roosters running along the top edge near the ceiling. There was a stove and refrigerator next to each other against the far wall and the other wall held a window over the double sink and a small dishwasher. They'd recently painted the cupboards a clean white, but the hardwood floor was dented and scratched from years of wear.

"It's small, but there's room in that corner for a table and chairs," Natalie said, pointing. "We have a set in storage that you're welcome to."

Chelsea stuffed her hands in the pockets of her parka and nodded. Charity. All her life she'd depended on it. How did Jed ever make it out? This was nicer than any place she'd ever lived, except for the short time at her mother-in-law's, and it had been his starter home. It wasn't fair.

The kitchen opened up into a living room that stretched across the front of the house, giving a view of the street below through two large windows. Beige carpeting covered the floors, trampled down in spots.

"Theo took his first steps in this living room," Natalie said. Her face softened.

"Why didn't you have more kids?" Chelsea asked. She'd put the question to Jed once when they talked, but he'd acted like he hadn't heard. That had only made her more curious.

"Oh." Natalie's eyes clouded over. "There was a problem when Theo was born and... I couldn't."

"I'm sorry," Chelsea said, secretly glad that her brother's entire life wasn't as charmed as it seemed.

"It was disappointing, sure, but we were grateful to have Theo. He was an easy kid, and we tried hard not to spoil him, knowing from the start that he would be an only child."

Chelsea envied her the 'we'. She'd been part of something like that for just long enough to miss it when she lost Dante. Again, not fair.

"Okay," Natalie said. "The bedrooms are back here. There are only two – one is quite a bit smaller, but has a great view of the park on the next street over." She opened the door.

The room *was* small, but the window made it bright and she could see the playground in the park. She could sit here and watch the girls play. She tried to imagine it, but the image refused to come into focus.

"The girls seem to enjoy sharing a bedroom," Natalie said. "If you like this one, the other one could work for them." She walked down the hall, and once again Chelsea followed. "The bathroom is right across the hall. Dad just had it redone a few years ago. It's all updated.

Chelsea peeked in. "There's no bathtub. How will the girls take a bath?"

Natalie bit her lip. "They've gotten used to showers at our house. The only tub we have is the big one in the master bath."

"I don't have any furniture," Chelsea said. "Landlord put it on the curb after social services took the girls."

The truth was, she'd been three months behind on the rent and the landlord only extended it because he was trying to get her to sleep with him. She probably would have, to keep a roof over their heads, but thank God it hadn't come to that. The furniture hadn't really amounted to much, anyway.

"We have a great Habitat store," Natalie said. "The prices are very reasonable, and we have some other stuff in storage, too. There's a double bed and a loveseat besides the table and chairs."

"Why are you helping me? Jed hates me."

Natalie's brown eyes widened. "You're his sister! He doesn't *hate* you."

"Well, he thinks I'm a lousy mother. I can feel his disapproval every time we're in the same room. He doesn't understand. He thinks we lived the same life, but we didn't. He got placed in a decent family. I got shoved into one group home after another."

"I'm sorry that happened to you," her sister-in-law said. "Jed is, too. On some level he feels responsible."

She barked out a laugh. "He thinks he's responsible for everything. But maybe he's right about that."

"What? Do you really think he could have stopped you from being separated? You know, Jed has a dream – a nightmare, really. It's always the same. He can't find you or Noah, and he's panicking. Did anything like that ever happen?"

"Not that I remember." Chelsea shrugged. "I used to hide from him, but that was just joking around."

"Jed probably didn't see it that way. He felt responsible for you. He *was* responsible for you."

"He was always telling me what to do. I hated that."

Natalie studied her sister-in-law. "There wasn't anyone else. Someone had to be the adult. If your mother or father…"

"You were your daddy's little princess, I'm sure," Chelsea spat angrily. She knew how she sounded, but she couldn't stop herself. Waves of jealousy washed over her for the life this woman had growing up and the life she had now, too.

Natalie lowered herself to the carpet, hugging her knees to her chest. "I won't deny that my parents love me," she said. "And my dad and I were–are–close. I've had this conversation with your brother more than once. Every family has their own stuff to deal with. Having a normal family doesn't mean my life was perfect."

Chelsea leaned against the wall and slid down. "Compared to mine?"

"There's no comparison," Natalie said. "I wish no one ever had to go through what you and Jed went through."

"Like I said, from what he's told me, it seems like he got a pretty sweet deal with the Smiths or whoever he went to."

"The Whites," Natalie corrected. "It wasn't bad, but..."

"Did he sleep with a kitchen knife under his pillow in case one of the other kids attacked him during the night?"

Natalie shook her head. "I'm..."

"I know. I know." She rolled her eyes. "You're sorry. That and a dollar will buy me a Coke."

****

"How did it go with Chelsea today?" Jed asked as he slipped out of his sport coat and tie, tossing them onto the back of a chair. He ran a hand over his hair and looked at her, waiting for an answer.

"It was fine," Natalie said, too brightly. "I think she liked the apartment. We had a... good talk."

"About what?"

She turned back to the stove, adding the chopped carrots to the pot and replacing the lid. "Just... stuff. She's really struggling, Jed. I can feel it. There's so much anger there."

"Anger about what?"

She kept her eyes on the potato she was cutting.

"Honestly, I think she's jealous of where you ended up, in a good home, while she...didn't."

"I hate it, too. But I can't do anything about the past."

Natalie saw her husband ball his hands into fists at his sides and his eyes slid away from hers.

She took a breath and let it out slowly before speaking. "I got the name of a counselor from Katy. It's on the fridge. Maybe you should call him."

Chapter 28

"Jed Shaw?" The man held out his hand. "Mark Fletcher. It's nice to meet you." The counselor was tall and thin, with graying hair and a salt-and-pepper beard. He wore wired-framed glasses, and his smile was welcoming. "Come on in and have a seat."

Jed stepped uncertainly into the office. It was full of natural light from a set of windows high on the wall. A leather couch sat against the same wall, with a table and two overstuffed chairs across from it. After an awkward moment of hesitation, he took a seat on the couch, rubbing his hands down the legs of his jeans.

Mark Fletcher picked up a clipboard and pen from the desk in the corner and took the chair across from Jed, crossing one long leg over the other. "So, the referral says you're having trouble sleeping?"

"A bit," Jed said. "It's better now, but my wife is concerned."

"Why don't you tell me about it? What seems to be keeping you awake?"

Jed sighed. He was doing this for Natalie, not for himself. She seemed to think that talking to someone would help him *and* Chelsea. There wasn't much else he could do to help his sister at this point, so why not? *This* was why not. God, he was uncomfortable telling a stranger all about his life.

Mark didn't say anything. He just sat quietly and waited.

"I fall asleep fine, but I have this dream," Jed said. "After, I can't get back to sleep."

"So this is a recurring dream?" Mark made a note. "It's always the same?"

"Yes, well, mostly. I guess sometimes there are differences, but it's basically the same."

"And what's the dream?"

Jed described it, filling in bits and pieces so that Mark had some background. "Anyway, that's it. I never find them and my mother blames me."

Mark nodded. "I take it there were family issues when you were growing up?"

"My mom had issues, yeah. Our father wasn't around. We lived with my grandparents for a few months, but mostly we were on our own."

"You're the oldest?"

"Yeah, Chelsea is four years younger than I am, and I was seven when Noah was born. He has a different father, but he didn't stick around either."

"Were you in charge of them?"

Jed nodded.

"What age would you say you were when that became normal to you?"

Jed paused, wiping a hand over his mouth. "I can't think of a time after Chelsea was born that I didn't feel responsible for her. And then for Noah."

"Wow. That's a lot for a kid." Again, the counselor sat quietly, letting Jed absorb his words. "How did you feel about that?"

"I don't remember feeling any particular way," Jed said with a shrug. "It was just the way it was. We went into foster care when I was eight," he continued. "For almost two years. Then Mom got us back and it was okay, even pretty good for a little while."

"What made it better?"

"Mom's boyfriend, Mitch, was a great guy. We had a nice apartment, clean clothes, enough to eat."

"That didn't last?"

He shook his head. "She couldn't stay sober, and Mitch kicked her out. We lived with him for a while. I think he would have kept us, but she came back for us. It got bad after that, worse than before."

"How so?"

Jed shrugged.

"What was worse?"

"The places we lived in. The people we lived with. Mom couldn't hold a job. I don't know what she did to keep a roof over our heads. There was never enough food or clean clothes. She wasn't around much."

"So you were basically parenting your younger sister and brother."

"Yes, and then...," Jed stopped.

"What happened?"

"She died."

"Your mother?"

Jed nodded.

"That must have been hard."

Another shrug. "It wasn't much different. She was never there anyway." Jed ran a hand through his hair and leaned forward, elbows on his knees. "We went back into foster care, and they separated us."

"All of you?"

"Noah's grandparents claimed him, took him back to Indiana with them. Chelsea and I got separated. She had... she was difficult."

"Difficult?"

"She had mood swings; screaming fits. She could be violent... hitting... throwing stuff. She pulled a knife on one foster mom. So the two of us were in and out of three or four placements before they gave up and sent her to a group home for troubled girls."

"And you?"

"I was lucky. I got good foster parents. They were decent people."

"How did you feel about that?"

"About what?"

"About being in a good home while they warehoused your sister."

Jed paused, the word *warehoused* echoing in his head. His first instinct, despite the case he was working on and his personal experience, was to defend the system, but he resisted.

"I asked the Whites, my foster parents, if they would take her," he said. "They were willing to try, but they already had two younger foster kids, and CPS wouldn't place Chelsea with them because of that. I tried to stay in touch with her. But they worried about it."

"The Whites?"

Jed nodded.

"How so?"

"They thought it was taking too much out of me. They made me see a counselor for a while."

"How did that go?"

Jed shrugged again. "I did what they wanted. I stopped looking for her." His chest tightened, and he looked away from Mark at a painting on the far wall.

"When did you see her again?"

"She found me when I was a senior at Northwestern. She came to my apartment asking for money."

"And?"

"I offered to take her shopping, but she threw a fit and ran off. She was with some guy, so I called CPS, and they sent her back to the group home."

"I have a feeling there's more, but I want to stop you here, because I think I have an idea of what may be going on."

"Okay." Jed waited.

"Guilt is a very powerful emotion," Mark said, tenting his fingers. "When we feel responsible for someone and believe we failed them, well, it can be traumatic on many levels. You've obviously gone through some trauma, and the dream may be your mind's way of trying to resolve that." He tapped his pen on the paper. "I'd like you to try something for me."

Jed waited.

"Can you say out loud 'I was a kid, and I did the best I could'?"

"Uh, okay," Jed said. He swallowed and managed

not to roll his eyes. "I was a kid, and I did the best I could." He felt silly.

Mark chuckled. "I know it feels strange, but say it again."

"I was a kid, and I did the best I could."

"A bit less strange?"

"Maybe," he admitted.

"So," Mark said. "When you have this dream and wake up, I want you to say that, out loud, and see if it helps you go back to sleep. Will you try that?"

"Sure, yeah," Jed said. He took a breath. "I think my sister might be angry with me for not keeping us together."

"You aren't responsible for her anger, any more than you were responsible for what happened when you were a child."

"But I need to find a way to deal with her now," he said. "We have to work together for her daughters' sakes."

Mark Fletcher looked at his watch. "You're my last appointment. I can spare a few more minutes. Tell me what's going on."

Jed told him about the girls and his sister's arrest and time in rehab. To his surprise, he was fighting back tears by the time he was finished. Fletcher handed him a box of tissues.

"I just... I don't know what to do to help her. She reminds me of our mother, and I don't want her to end up the same way."

"And you love her," Mark finished.

"Yes," he said.

"The girls are getting counseling, I hope," he said, as Jed blew his nose and composed himself.

"Yes, through the school. They're doing pretty well, considering everything."

"Good. I'd like to see you again, Jed. I'm pretty sure I can help. Can we make another appointment?"

"Yeah," Jed nodded. "That's a good idea."

******

"So," Jed said when they were lying in bed a few nights later. "I was thinking about inviting Chelsea to Thanksgiving. What do you think?"

Natalie rolled over to face him. "She's allowed a 48-hour pass at this point in the program. If she came for Thanksgiving, I could take her shopping the next day and get some things for the apartment."

"What if she doesn't want to come?"

"Then that's on her. Just don't say anything to the girls until you know for sure. They'd be disappointed if it didn't work out. At least Zora would be." Josie still barely interacted with her mother during visits.

"It would give me a chance to talk to her," Jed said. "Maybe get some things out in the open. I know she blames me on some level for us being separated."

Natalie considered this. "Maybe that's something you should talk about together with a counselor."

"Why?"

"Well," she said. "It might be good to have someone there who is impartial."

"True. She'd probably just argue with me if I brought it up."

"I think she knows on some level that you couldn't do anything. She just needs someone to blame."

"If she'd just been different, willing to cooperate and behave herself..."

"Sounds to me like *you* need someone to blame, too."

"Huh." Jed looked at her. "Maybe so."

Chapter 29

As they pulled out of the parking lot of the halfway house Thanksgiving morning, Chelsea felt her brother's eyes on her.

"I'm glad you're coming," he said. "The girls are excited."

"Me, too."

The silence grew heavy as he drove through the quiet streets, and finally Jed spoke again.

"It's been a long time since we've celebrated a holiday together."

She was thinking of how to answer, but then Jed pulled to a stop in front of a pale yellow house with a low-pitched roof that came out over a wide front porch supported by four square columns. There was a porch swing and two cushioned chairs clustered at one end. The second story jutted out above like two triangles stacked on top of each other, with two square windows under the roofline. A brick walkway led from the front sidewalk to the porch. Hydrangeas and lavender lined the fence up to the gate into the backyard.

"Well," he said to her, "This is it. Remember?"

"You're kidding me, right?" She stared at him. "You actually have a white picket fence? Seriously, big brother?

You've really bought into the whole All-American dad thing, haven't you?" She laughed.

Jed sighed and leaned back against the headrest. "Look, it's Thanksgiving. Your girls are in there waiting for you. We can actually have a day together as a family. But if you'd rather sit out here and make fun of my life, I can take you right back to the halfway house."

Chelsea flipped down the visor to look in the mirror. She ran a hand through her hair; not that it did much good. It was dry and brittle and broke off so easily she was tempted to shave it all off and start over. She'd put on makeup for the first time in forever, and the face staring back at her looked like a little girl playing at being a grown-up.

"No," she said. "I want to see them." She glanced toward the house. "Who else is here?"

"Just Connie, that's Nat's mom and Theo. Her dad, Ian, Katy, and Stella are coming later."

Chelsea wove her hands together in her lap. Her nails, as brittle as her hair, were broken or bitten down to the fingertips. Why had she let him talk her into this?

"That's a lot of people," she said. "Maybe this isn't a good idea. Maybe I should see the girls another time."

"Chels, I told you how excited they are. Zora changed clothes three times before I left." He shifted in the seat. "And there's someone else coming. Someone who wants to see you."

She looked at him. "Who?"

"Mitch."

"*Our* Mitch?"

"Yeah," he nodded.

"How...?" Her head spun with disconnected memories of that long ago year when she was seven; blueberry pancakes, pizza, dance class, her mother laughing, happy for once. She blinked back tears.

"I looked him up when Natalie and I were in Chicago back in September. It was great to see him. He looked for us, Chels."

"He did?"

"Yes, after Mom died. Anyway, we've stayed in touch. We talk once a week or so. He's been here a few times, and I invited him for Thanksgiving."

"He's not married or has kids or anything?"

"Nope. He never got married. He's looking forward to seeing you."

"You know I'm supposed to avoid triggers like shocks and surprises," she said. "I wish you'd told me."

Jed nodded. "Yeah, I probably should have."

"You thought I'd back out."

"Might have crossed my mind after what happened before. Look, just come in and see the girls. If you decide it's too much and you don't want to stay overnight, I'll take you back whenever you want, okay?"

"Okay." She flipped the visor back up and picked up her purse and duffle from the floor of Jed's Bronco and swung them onto her shoulder.

At the door, two dogs greeted them, one big and white, tongue hanging out as he lifted his front paws off the floor. The smaller dog gave several high-pitched barks and wagged his tail. As Jed bent and grabbed both by the collar, a tall young man with wavy dark blonde hair came down the stairs.

"I've got 'em, Dad," he said. Then blue eyes met hers. "I'm Theo and this is Finn and Charlie. They have no manners. You must be my aunt."

"Chelsea," she said. "Yes." She'd forgotten she was an aunt. She had a nephew. She had family. It felt... weird.

Suddenly, little feet pounded on the stairs. "Mama! Mama!" Chelsea turned, and Zora hurled herself off the steps into her arms.

"Oh, baby," she said as Zora's arms went around her neck. "I missed you." She put her down and looked around. "Where's Josie?"

Theo hooked a thumb over his shoulder. "She's in the kitchen helping Mom and G-ma."

"Josie really enjoys cooking," Jed said. "Nat's been teaching her."

"I'll show you Mama, come on!" Zora pulled at her hand.

Choking back her jealousy, she let her daughter lead her through the tastefully decorated living room and down a short hallway to the open, airy kitchen. It was different. The table in the corner was gone, and an island sat in the center of the room with four barstools. There was a small fridge built into the bottom, and Chelsea could see wine bottles stacked inside. She couldn't quite picture what the kitchen looked like before, but this was like something out of a magazine.

Her daughter's back was to them. Josie stood on a stool that brought her up to the butcher block counter. Her dense curls were in perfect cornrows, ending in braids that hung to her shoulders. Chelsea briefly wondered how Jed's wife had done that. Dante's mother Dorthea always had a way with the girls' hair, but whenever she tried to do it herself, Chelsea ended up with a mess, so she usually just made ponytails.

She continued to watch as Natalie placed her own hand over the child's, steadying it as Josie chopped something Chelsea couldn't see.

"That's it," Natalie said. "Nice and even. You're doing such a good job!" She planted a kiss on top of Josie's head.

"Josie!" Zora cried. "Look! Mama's here."

Jed's wife turned her head and wiped her hands on a dishtowel tucked into her jeans before holding one out.

"Chelsea," she smiled warmly. "I'm so glad you're here." Then, "Josie, your mom is here."

"I'm busy," Josie said. Chelsea's stomach clenched. Her older daughter made it obvious at every visit that she wanted nothing to do with her.

Natalie bit her lip and leaned in, whispering something in the child's ear. Josie's shoulders drooped, but she stepped down from the stool and walked over to Chelsea.

"Hi, Mama," she said. She accepted a hug, but pulled away quickly. "I gotta finish chopping the cel-ry. We're making sausage stuffing." Her eyes sought Natalie's, and the woman nodded.

"It's my Nonna's—grandmother's-recipe," Natalie said. "We have it every Thanksgiving."

"I've never heard of sausage in stuffing," Chelsea said.

"It's not that much different from plain," Natalie assured her. "It's good."

"Aunt Natalie is a chef," Josie said. "Everything she makes is good."

The words hit Chelsea like a slap. This was a mistake. She felt stupid, standing here in this beautiful kitchen. She didn't even know what half the appliances on the counters did.

"Do you want a cup of coffee?" Natalie asked, reaching into the cupboard before she could answer.

"Sure," at least it would give her something to do with her hands.

"Cream or sugar?" Natalie asked, setting a large white mug on the counter.

"Sugar, please."

Natalie laughed, "Just like your brother."

After the cup was full, Chelsea picked it up, wrapping both hands around it. Zora tugged on the hem of Natalie's shirt.

"Can I show Mama our room?"

"Sure, Honey. Josie, do you want to go, too? I can finish this."

"No," Josie said. "That's okay. You show her, Zora."

Chelsea fought two impulses at the same time. The first was to grab her girls and get as far away from here as she could. The second was to smack Josie's face. Instead, she took her younger daughter's hand and said.

"Let's go see your room."

****

Late autumn sunshine shone through the window, making the room bright and cheery. Two single beds, each covered with a yellow bedspread splashed with daisies, sat in an L shape against one corner of the room. Zora ran over and jumped onto one of the two beds.

"This is mine," she said. She patted a fat stuffed bunny. "Mr. BunBun and I sleep here and Josie sleeps right there." She pointed to the other bed. A stuffed unicorn with a rainbow horn lay on the pillow. "Sometimes we sleep together," Zora added. "If I get scared."

"It's very nice," Chelsea said, swallowing hard.

At the foot of each bed, a flowered backpack hung on the bedpost. Now Zora jumped up and pulled hers down. "I can read, Mama. Do you want to read a book?"

Chelsea nodded, which was all she could manage. Zora sat on the bed and pulled a plastic bag out of the backpack. Reaching in, she took out a book and patted a spot beside her. Chelsea set her mug of coffee on top of the dresser and sat down, awkwardly putting an arm around her daughter.

"This book is about a duck," Zora said. "See?" She pointed to the picture. She read the book, which only had a word or two on each page, haltingly, but without missing a word. Chelsea didn't realize she was crying until a drop splashed on the page.

"Mama? Are you sad?"

"No, Honey," she said. "Mama just missed you."

"Are you better now?" Zora's brown eyes looked up at her full of questions. Trouble was, Chelsea didn't have any answers, for her daughter, or herself.

Chapter 30

Jed watched his sister as he took the extra leaf for the dining room table out of the closet. She sat in one of the overstuffed chairs in the family room, Zora on her lap. The Thanksgiving Day parade was on the flat screen television, and the child was enthralled as characters from The Lion King danced across the screen. Chelsea's eyes, however, darted over the room, taking everything in as if she couldn't quite grasp where she was. Her shoulders were tight, her entire body thrummed with a tension he could sense from across the room. And Jed remembered.

The first time he went home with Natalie, the trappings of middle class life overwhelmed him. Even at the White's or at friends' houses in high school, he'd never been as completely immersed in it as he was at Russ and Connie's farm. It wasn't a farm really, just an ordinary two-story house on a double lot at the edge of suburbia, with a small barn where Russ kept whatever stray animals he had collected, and Ian kept the Camaro he was restoring.

The house itself had a lived-in quality, not unlike the White's. There were no fancy furnishings or overly expensive electronics. What there was in abundance in the home Natalie grew up in was history; family memories. A concept totally foreign to Jed. An antique grandfather clock passed down generations stood in the entryway. Family photographs, old and new, graced the mantle and lined the hall into the kitchen; vacations, weddings, babies, aunts and uncles, cousins, grandparents and great-grandparents on both sides. In the kitchen, several of her great-grandmother's handwritten recipes were framed and hanging on the wall. Without Natalie as an anchor, Jed would have drowned in all the memories. As it was, even with his almost instantaneous inclusion into her family, he could still sometimes feel like an outsider who didn't know the story about Great Uncle Leo and his dog, Skipper.

"Hey," he said to his sister now. "Help me with something?"

She stood, sliding Zora off her lap.

"Finn and Charley need a walk around the block before everyone gets here or they'll be nuts all day." He took the leashes down from the hook by the door. Both dogs came running at the sound, skittering to a stop in front of them, tongues out, tails wagging.

"Can I go, too?" Zora said, suddenly there by her mother's side, unwilling to let her out of her sight.

"Sure, Kiddo," Jed grinned at her. "Get your scooter."

"She has a scooter?"

"Yeah, well, I may be spoiling them a little."

270

Chelsea gave a snort, but felt a twinge of affection for her brother. His love for the girls was obvious. He handed her Charley's leash. The beagle was slower and easier to manage than the two-year-old lab.

Zora put on her helmet and raced ahead of them on the pink scooter, occasionally glancing back to make sure they were still there, or calling out "Mama! Watch me!"

The lab stopped to sniff a hydrant, and Jed turned to Chelsea. "I get that this is a lot to take in," he said. "All the 'stuff' and the space and..."

"You have a *really* nice house."

"Yeah, I do, *we* do," he corrected. "But we started out in that apartment above Russ's clinic. This house was smaller when we first got it, too. We've added on since you were here."

"Everything is so clean and new and..." Chelsea stopped to let Charley pee against a bush. "Wow, Jed. I've just never even imagined living in a place like this."

"It didn't come all at once," he said, although when they were first married, Natalie's parents had always made sure they had everything they needed. "We got pregnant my senior year of college," he told her. "So we got married and..."

"That's my brother," Chelsea said, rolling her eyes. "Mr. Do-the-Right-Thing."

"Hey!" he said, loud enough that the dogs startled and looked up at him. "It wasn't about doing the right thing. I was in love with Nat. We've always loved each other. We had plans to get married eventually, anyway. Theo is... the best thing that ever happened to us. The point is," he said. "Life threw us a curveball, something we weren't expecting. But with people to help us, we made it work."

"Good for you, but you really have no idea what my life has been like, Jed. No idea."

"Why didn't you get in touch with us when your husband... when Dante died?" he asked. We would have been there for you and the girls. Maybe we could have avoided all of this."

"And by all of this you mean me going off the deep end?" Chelsea shook her head. "You know, I never thought I could have kids. I wasn't exactly careful when I was younger, and yet I never got pregnant. But I met Dante and BOOM! Josie. We got married when she was a year old. They adored each other." She smiled, remembering. "He was just finishing his second tour in Afghanistan and then he was going to get out. When he came home on leave, I got pregnant with Zora. We decided he should reenlist because it paid more than anything he'd be able to find, and the insurance was good. I went along with it, and then he got himself blown up."

She stopped walking and stared into space. "Dorthea, Dante's mom, blamed me, I think. She wasn't too keen on us getting married in the first place. But she loved the girls, so after he died, she let us stay." Chelsea turned and looked at him. "I held down two jobs when she got sick. I worked hard to stay sober."

"Good for you," Jed said. "And I truly mean that. But it doesn't answer the question. Why didn't you call me?"

Chelsea leaned on one leg and blew out a breath. "The last time I saw you, I stole your car. I didn't think you... or your wife... would want anything to do with me. With us. Besides," she continued. "Dante knew nothing about that part of my life. He knew I grew up in foster care, but that was it. I never told him about you or Noah or about being in prison. I didn't want his mom to know. It would have been one more strike against me."

"Well, it would have been nice to know you were okay, that I had nieces, that Theo had cousins."

"I'm sorry," she said. "I just didn't have it in me to reach out."

"Even after your mother-in-law died?"

"I never thought of it."

Jed stepped back as if she'd slapped him, but he met her eyes. "That's in the past, Chels. I don't know about addiction," he paused. "But I know about feeling alone and disconnected. You aren't alone. We're here for you. You have *family* to help you. You can do this."

"Do what?" Chelsea gazed at him for a moment, her face impassive. "Live a life like yours, here in suburbia?"

Jed stiffened. "You might like it if you gave it a chance." His blue eyes fixed on her and she felt judged.

"What if I don't want to?" She gave the leash a jerk and walked away from him, Charley in tow.

Chapter 31

Mitch cupped his hand around the cigarette and lit it, inhaling deeply and holding it, before exhaling into the dusky backyard.

"Thank God," he heard a voice say from behind him. "I hate it when I'm the only smoker."

He turned around. The woman, Natalie's boss... Sophia? No. Sylvia? Crap. What was her name? Stella! That was it. Mitch was never good with names. He usually gave people nicknames for that reason. It made the names stick somehow. Now he looked at Stella as she held out her cigarette for a light. She had her long silver-white hair pulled back into a twisted braid that hung over one shoulder. The hand not holding the cigarette grasped the edges of a burnt orange cardigan she wore with skinny jeans and short brown boots.

He gave her a light, and she inhaled and blew out a plume of smoke. "Oh. That's good," she said. "I only allow myself three a day, and this is number two."

Mitch chuckled. "You have more self-control than me," he said. "I was never a smoker until AA. Just traded one addiction for another, I'm afraid."

Mitch always slipped his status as an alcoholic into conversations this way. It was something his first sponsor suggested years ago to take the pressure off. He had nothing to hide, and he was proud of his almost forty-year sobriety.

Stella cocked her head to one side, her gray-blue eyes settling on his. "Good for you," she said. "My ex-husband is an alcoholic. He's never managed to kick it though."

"Is that why he's your ex?"

She smiled. "I loved him, so I might have put up with that, but there were other... issues."

"Didn't mean to pry," Mitch said. He leaned against the deck railing and looked back into the house through the French doors. He could see Josie carefully putting a folded napkin at each place.

"Oh," Stella waved a hand. "I know. I didn't mean to be touchy. Holidays." She shook her head.

"You have kids?"

Another shake. "No, that never happened for us. Probably for the best, the way it turned out. Sorriso is my baby." She took a deep pull on the cigarette. "Have you ever been married?"

"Might have once," he said.

"Jed's mom?"

He nodded, stubbing out his cigarette. He dropped it into a nearby planter and scraped some dirt around it.

"Burying the evidence?" Stella laughed. He liked the sound of it, low and melodic. "Natalie said you probably saved Jed's life–or at least saved him from going down a different path."

Mitch let out a breath. "That boy was nine going on twenty-nine when I met him. He would have been fine without me."

"She says you allowed him to be a kid. That's huge. Don't underestimate it." She took another long drag. "He's a good man; a good husband. They really have it all."

"You and Nat are close." It wasn't a question.

"We are," she nodded. "Connie –Nat's mother–can be difficult, with Natalie anyway. I think I mother her in a less judgmental way, at least career-wise."

"Aren't you a little young to be a mother figure for her?"

She raised a perfectly groomed eyebrow. "How old do you think I am?"

"Oh, no," he grinned and shook his head. "I am not going there."

"Smart man." Stella stubbed out her own cigarette and copied Mitch, burying it in the planter. "I'm sixty-three," she said. "So I could easily be Natalie's mother."

Mitch gave a low whistle. "I wouldn't have guessed that."

"Even with the hair?" Stella brushed a loose silver-gray lock behind one ear.

"Your hair is striking," Mitch said. "It suits you."

She blushed. "Thanks. I started going gray in my late twenties. By the time I was forty, I was tired of fighting it." Shifting her feet, she put her hands in the pockets of her sweater. "I'd say you're..." she paused, looking him over. "Sixty," she said. "Give or take a year."

"Sixty-two," Mitch said.

"It's nice to talk to a contemporary," she said. "All of my employees are Natalie's age or younger, except one bartender, who started not long after my father opened the place. I think Glen is close to eighty, but I'd never ask. He can work as long as he wants to."

"How many employees do you have?"

Stella moved to lean against the rail beside him. "Fourteen full time and six part-time at the moment. It can vary depending on the season. When the patio is open, we add several more servers and busboys."

"Your father started the restaurant?"

"My parents, yes. My grandparents came over from Campania, on the western coast of Italy, just after World War I. They moved here to Westlake when it wasn't much more than farms and opened a grocery. My mother and father started the restaurant after they got married in 1952; it was called *Napoli* then. I was born five years later."

"Amazing to have something that's been in your family so long."

"After my father passed away, I updated and changed the name for him."

"How so?"

"Everyone who came to Dad's service remarked how he always had a smile for them anytime they saw him. Sorriso means *smile* in Italian. My favorite picture of him hangs above the bar."

"That's a lovely way to honor him," Mitch said. "Natalie's been trying to get me there, just haven't made it yet."

"I hope you come soon. Natalie's fall menu has been wonderful. This has been our best month yet."

"Hey you two," Natalie called from the kitchen window she'd opened to let in some cool air. "We're almost ready to sit down to eat."

At the same time, Jed came out the French doors. "There you are," he said. "I was looking for you."

"We were having a lovely conversation," Stella said.

"And a smoke," Mitch added with a grin.

They followed Jed back into the house to the dining room. The table was laid out with a feast. There was the traditional turkey, mashed potatoes, Josie's sage and sausage stuffing, and homemade cornbread. But there were also Natalie's touches; pumpkin gnocchi with gorgonzola, ricotta stuffed mushrooms, stuffed and fried green olives, and roasted beets with sweet onions. Candles glowed in hollowed out gourds scattered across the table.

Mitch was pleased to find himself sitting catty-corner across from Stella. Chelsea was to his right, and Jed sat at the head of the table to his left.

"Let's all join hands," Natalie said, reaching for her husband's and Stella's. "Dad, would you say the blessing?" Chelsea stiffened, but after a moment, she took Mitch's hand on one side and Zora's on the other. Josie sat across from her mother, between Stella and Theo.

Russ smiled at his daughter. "Lord, thank you for family and friends." He looked directly at Chelsea and continued. "Please let everyone here feel loved and welcomed as a part of this family. Thank you for this wonderful meal and the hands, large and small, that prepared it. Bless us all in your grace. Amen."

'Amens' echoed around the table.

"Now let's eat," Jed said.

After dinner, while her girls helped Natalie and Connie clear the table, Chelsea pocketed Mitch's phone and made her way out to the deck. The others gathered in the living room, watching the overtime of the Bears/Cowboys game. She'd known better than to ask Jed for a phone; he would have been suspicious or aware of Gateway's rules about phone calls being logged and monitored. Mitch harbored no such prejudices—or he believed her when she said she just wanted to look something up online. He was happy to lend her his phone, even telling her his password so she could unlock it.

Outside, she hesitated. Cody was probably angry with her. She hadn't been able to call him. There were strict rules at rehab, and she could only call people on an approved list. He was not on her list, for a whole lot of reasons. She stared at Mitch's phone. His screensaver was a recent photo of him with Jed. She bit her lip, punched in the number she knew by heart, and waited for Cody to answer. Finally, just as she was sure voicemail was about to pick up, he answered.

"Who is this?"

"Cody? It's me."

"Chelsea? This isn't your number."

"Yeah. I had to borrow a phone."

"Where the hell are you? Where have you been? Skylar said..."

She told him the entire story–leaving the girls, her binge, being arrested, and the time in court-ordered rehab.

"So now I'm at my brother's on a 48-hour furlough for Thanksgiving." She rolled her eyes even though he wasn't there to see and took a deep drag on the cigarette she'd bummed from Mitch. "He has, like, this perfect family. I don't belong here."

"Then leave. I'll pick you up."

"I'm not leaving without my girls."

"So bring 'em."

This surprised her because Cody didn't like being around Josie and Zora. He acted like he wanted her all to himself. That's why she left them with Skylar so often. Maybe missing her had changed his mind.

She stared out into the backyard, past the garden and the leafless oaks, past the white picket fence, as if she could see to the city beyond. She missed the city. The noise and chaos were familiar and numbing. Here, there was too much time to think.

"Chels? You still there?"

"I'm here," she said. "You'd really come get us?"

"I could be there by midnight."

She considered it. "Midnight might be too early," she said. "I'd want to make sure everyone was asleep."

"Name your time, Babe, and I'm there," he said. "I've missed you."

"I've missed you, too," she said. "How about around two? It should be quiet by then." She rattled off Jed's address. "The bedrooms are in the front of the house, so turn your lights off if you pull into the driveway. And no loud radio," she added.

"I'll be there," he said. "I'm glad you called."

"Me, too."

She clicked off and held the cigarette between her lips as she scrolled to recent calls on Mitch's phone and deleted Cody's number. Leaning on the deck railing, she inhaled deeply and blew smoke out into the evening air. Rehab was a waste of time. She felt good knowing she wasn't going back. No amount of talking to her counselor or group sessions with the other losers chanting mantras was going to make her feel any better, or make her more ready to take her girls back. She was their mother. They belonged with her.

Zora wouldn't be a problem. That child had been her shadow ever since she got here. She would do whatever her mother asked her to do. Josie was another story. Her oldest had always had a mind of her own, and from what she'd seen Josie was way too attached to Jed and Natalie. Chelsea thought for a moment about taking Zora and leaving Josie, but that seemed too much like letting Josie– or Jed and his wife–win something.

She finished the cigarette and stubbed it out on the railing, tossing the butt into the grass below. A plan formed in her mind. There was an air mattress on the floor in the girls' room, made up for her to sleep tonight. She could pack some things in their backpacks, even put them down by the door or on the front porch, ready to go when Cody got here. Maybe Josie would be drowsy enough that she wouldn't put up a fuss.

She felt better now that she had a plan. Walking back into the kitchen, she took a dish towel from the counter and started helping dry the glasses and other items that they couldn't pack into the dishwasher.

"Mitch was so happy to see you," Natalie said, beaming at her.

"It was good to see him, too," Chelsea said, being truthful. "Those are some of the happiest memories I have."

"It's the same for Jed. Oh!" she added. "Did he show you the photographs?"

"Photographs? No."

"I'll remind him," Natalie said. "Mitch gave him some photographs of you all from when you were kids." She lowered her voice to a whisper. "I'm going to get a couple of them blown up and framed for him for Christmas."

Once the game was over, Jed put in a DVD of *Christmas Vacation* – evidently it was some kind of family tradition. Chelsea found herself drawn in, laughing at the silliness along with everyone else. It almost made her regret deciding to leave. Almost.

Chapter 32

When the movie was over, Connie and Russ were the first to leave. Jed carried Zora, who'd fallen asleep, upstairs to bed while Josie got into her pajamas.

After putting on his coat, Mitch approached Chelsea. "It's good to see you."

"You, too," she said.

He bent and kissed her cheek. "I hope we can do it again, soon. Maybe dinner? Just you and the girls?"

Chelsea nodded. "Sure. That'd be great."

As Stella rose from the couch, Mitch noticed her weave a bit before catching her balance.

"I guess I shouldn't have had that last glass of wine," she said, laughing.

"I'm ready to take off," Mitch said. "You shouldn't drive. I'd be happy to take you home."

"I suppose that's the wise thing to do," she said. "Thank you."

"It's not a problem," he assured her.

They said their goodbyes and Stella left her keys so that Jed could move her car into the driveway overnight. She was quiet on the way, speaking only to tell Mitch where to turn.

"I don't usually drink that much," she said. "I don't know what I was thinking." He could sense her embarrassment.

"Please don't apologize for having a few glasses of wine," he said. "I'm the alcoholic, not you and I never want you to feel awkward enjoying a drink around me."

"This is it," Stella said. "Turn left here."

Mitch gave a low whistle as she directed him into the circular driveway. "Nice digs," he said, thinking about his own older duplex in Chicago.

"It was my one splurge with the money my father left me," Stella said. "Everything else went right back into the restaurant."

The mid-century modern house was set back from the road, framed in the front by several large oak trees and a stunning blue spruce. The garage roof extended to shade the front door, bisecting a roof-to-ground window and ending at the brick chimney.

Mitch pulled to a stop in the drive, and Stella clicked the opener. "I can give you the ten-cent tour before you head back to the city," she said.

"Sure," he said. "I'd like that."

They entered through the garage door into an open kitchen. There was an oven built into the wall with gas burners on the countertop below. Light oak cabinets rose almost to the ceiling, their glass doors revealing dishes, stemware, and, on the higher shelves, brightly colored Italian pottery.

"The kitchen is the only place I completely redid," Stella said. "I wanted to display my mother's dishes and some things I've collected over the years. But I tried to stay true to the house."

She walked down a stone step into the large sunken living room. "Careful," she said as he moved to follow.

She had decorated the room in warm shades of brown and buttery yellow. Bright pillows accented the leather couch and loveseat, picking up the colors in the area rug covering the hardwood floor. The focus of the room was the natural stone fireplace and the painting above it.

The oil painting showed a young woman in profile gazing out a window at a city skyline. Her dark hair was swept up in a low chignon, her posture perfect. She wore a red dress with cap sleeves and a square neckline. One hand rested against the glass while the other rested on a strand of pearls at her neck.

"My mother," Stella said. "She posed for it when she was twenty-one. My father bought the portrait from the artist's estate when I was just a little girl."

"It's a beautiful painting," Mitch said. "I can see a resemblance."

"Oh," Stella smiled. "Thank you. I hope so."

"Now for my favorite space." She moved to the French doors and opened them, showing him the empty brick patio. "I hate putting everything away, but even with the fire pit it isn't warm enough out here in the winter."

They moved from the living room down a hall and she showed him the bathroom, a spare bedroom she used as an office, and the master bedroom. "There are two other bedrooms down there." She pointed to an open stairway leading to another level, partially below ground. "One was my mother's room when she lived with me. She passed away six years ago. Now it's a guest room. The other room is pretty small. It just collects things," she laughed.

"I think everyone has a room or closet like that," Mitch said.

"Would you like a cup of coffee before you go? I have decaf. I also have tea. That's what I prefer."

"Tea sounds fine," he said, following her into the kitchen.

Stella filled a teapot and placed it over the gas flame. Reaching into the cupboard, she took down several canisters of loose tea. "Oolong is my favorite. Is that alright?"

"No preference here," he said. She gestured, and he sat in one of the high-backed oak and cane chairs at the table against the wall and watched her. Her movements were sure and graceful, even in something as simple as spooning tea into the strainer and lowering it into the teapot.

"We'll let that brew for a bit," she said, taking the chair across from him. She leaned her elbows on the table and cupped her chin in one hand. "So where in the city do you live?"

"I live in Norwood Park," Mitch said. "Big Oaks, to be specific. I have half a duplex. It's an older house. The owner is a cop, and he lives on the other side, so it's pretty safe," he chuckled. "It's a pleasant neighborhood and I enjoy being able to go into the city whenever I want, although that's less than it used to be. And," he continued. "I'm only fifteen minutes from Wrigley, which is a bonus."

"Ah, you're a Cubs' fan." Stella smiled.

"Of course. Is there another team in Chicago?"

Stella's warm laugh rang out in the kitchen just as the teapot whistled. "My father never completely gave up the Yankees," she said as she poured the tea. "I used to watch games with him. Steven, my ex had season tickets to the Bears, but he wasn't much of a baseball fan."

"So you've never been to Wrigley?"

"I watch the games on television." Stella set a cup in front of him and sat, shaking her head. "But, no, I've never been to Wrigley."

"Well, we need to remedy that in the spring. There's nothing like it."

She stirred sugar into her tea. "I think I would enjoy that," she said.

"I hope we don't have to wait until spring to see each other again." He cleared his throat. "If you're ever in the city and would like to meet up, I'd love to take you to lunch...or dinner." Heat came to his face, and it wasn't from the steam rising from the cup in his hand.

Stella dipped her head. "Actually," she said. "I'm planning on doing some Christmas shopping in the city soon. I usually get a hotel room and spend the night. Meeting up would be lovely."

"Let's plan on it," he said, excited that she shared his interest in doing something together.

"So," she said, sipping her tea and looking at him over the brim of her cup. "You're retired?"

"Yes," Mitch nodded, setting his own cup down. "Thirty-three years at the post office. I carried mail twenty-five years, all over the city."

"That must have been interesting," Stella said.

"Oh, it was. Some days more than others," he chuckled. "One of the houses on my last route had a mail slot in the door. Most days I had no problem, but every once in a while, I'd try to stick the mail in and a cat's paw would come out of the slot and swipe at me. No matter how I tried to jam it in, the cat would bat it back out."

Stella laughed. "What did you do?"

"The first couple of times I went on, then doubled back and tried again. Finally, I saw the owner one day and told her what was happening. She put up a mailbox the next week."

"What do you do with your time now that you're retired? I can't quite imagine it for myself."

"I work part-time for a florist making deliveries," he said. "And I volunteer at the community garden and the animal shelter. I love dogs, but my landlord doesn't allow pets." He drank the last of his tea. "I'm busier now than when I was working."

"More?" Stella reached for the teapot.

"No, if I drink any more I'd have to stop on the way home." He glanced at the clock, surprised to see that it was after midnight. "It's later than I thought. I'd better get going," he said.

"It is awfully late to be driving all alone," Stella said. "You're more than welcome to my guest room."

"I wouldn't want to impose."

"You would not be imposing. In fact, I would sleep better knowing that you aren't heading back to the city so very late all because you had to help me get home."

"Well," he said. "If it's really no bother..."

"It isn't, so that's settled."

They talked a bit longer until Stella stifled a yawn.

"Why don't you show me the spare room, and we'll both get some sleep," Mitch said. "I'll take you out for breakfast in the morning as a thank you."

"Totally unnecessary," she said as she led the way downstairs. "But I love breakfast so I'll allow it."

She turned on the light and showed Mitch where the towels were kept in the small bathroom across the hall. In the bedroom, she took an extra blanket from the closet shelf and laid it on the bed.

"Thank you," he said.

"You're welcome," she said from the doorway. "Goodnight."

"Good night," Mitch hesitated, then stepped forward and kissed her cheek. "I enjoy talking with you."

"Same," she said, blushing. "I'll see you in the morning."

Chapter 33

Chelsea opened the front door as a dark shape pulled into the driveway. She stepped quietly onto the porch, holding a finger to her lips. Cody mounted the steps and took her by the shoulders, pulling her in and kissing her hard on the mouth.

"You ready, Babe?"

"Put the backpacks in the trunk," she said, pointing to where the girls' bags leaned against the railing. "I'll go get the girls. I didn't want to wake them until the last minute."

He picked up the backpacks and moved toward the car. "Your brother got any beer? I could use a drink."

"In the fridge in the kitchen, but be quiet, okay?"

Upstairs, she lifted Zora without waking her and gently shook Josie. The child looked up at her through heavy-lidded eyes.

"Come on," Chelsea said. "Get up."

"Why?" Josie buried her face in the pillow. "It's not morning."

"We're going for a ride," she told her. "Mama's friend is here."

Josie stared up at her, awake now. "I don't want to go anywhere with you."

"Fine," Chelsea said. "But you'll never see your sister again."

****

Jed awoke to Finn's whining at the side of the bed. "What's up, Bud?" he said. Lately, neither dog hardly ever left the girls' room until morning. "You gotta go out?"

He figured with all the guests and all the food, Finn got into something he shouldn't have. They were probably lucky he wasn't throwing up.

As he headed down the hallway, he heard a noise from downstairs. Finn stopped, too, looking up at him with a low growl.

"You trying to tell me something?" he whispered. "Stay."

Jed crept down the stairs as quietly as he could. At the bottom, he glanced toward the front door and saw his sister with Zora in her arms, shoving Josie out onto the porch.

"What the hell do you think you're doing?" he yelled. "You can leave if you want, but you aren't taking those girls!" He crossed the room in three bounds, grabbing hold of Chelsea's arm.

"Let go!" she cried. "You're hurting me."

"They're her kids," said a voice from behind him. "And we're leaving."

"Cody!" Chelsea cried. "No!"

Jed turned just as the man raised the gun and fired. A hot white pain shot through his shoulder, and he dropped to his knees on the hardwood floor. Footsteps ran past. Josie screamed and a door slammed. He rolled onto his back and opened his mouth to yell for help. Then he passed out.

****

"You shot my brother!" Chelsea yelled as the car careened around the corner and down the main street toward the highway. "What the hell, Cody?"

"Did you want to get out of there or not?"

"You didn't have to shoot him!"

"Just calm down, okay? I didn't kill him."

"You don't know that!"

"I shot him in the damn shoulder for God's sake!"

In the backseat, Josie sobbed while Zora, awake now, stared straight ahead, her eyes wide.

"Mama?" she said. "Where are we going? Where's BunBun? I want BunBun."

Oh crap, thought Chelsea. That damn stuffed rabbit.

"Can't you shut them up?" Cody said. "I'm trying to drive here." He took a swig of beer from the can in his hand.

She swiveled around in her seat. "Shut up!" she said. "We'll get you another rabbit."

Zora began to cry. "I don't want a new rabbit. I want BunBun!" Josie scooted over and wrapped her arms around her sister.

"I *hate* you!" Josie snarled at her mother. "I wish *you* were dead."

Chelsea reached over the seat and slapped Josie hard on the side of the face. "I said shut up. And shut your sister up, too." She turned back around, and Cody reached for her hand, squeezing it tightly.

"It'll be fine when we get to where we're going. I have a place we can stay for a while until things settle down." He brought her fingers to his lips and kissed them. "I really have missed you."

Chelsea didn't respond. She just stared out at the road in front of them, trying not to hear the muffled crying from the backseat.

****

Natalie sat on one of couches in the surgical waiting room, knees pulled up to her chest, arms around her legs. Her feet were bare. She sat perfectly still except for her eyes, which flicked from the swinging doors they'd wheeled Jed through, to her son, who was pacing in front of the bank of windows on the other end of the room, talking on his cellphone. Maybe if she didn't move, this wouldn't be happening. She would wake up, Jed snoring beside her, and it would all be some awful dream.

She counted her breaths, in and out, not daring to look at her phone to see how long it had been since they took her husband into surgery. Her pajama pants were stained with his blood. There was so much of it. She bit her lip as tears threatened again.

At the sound of the gunshot, she and Theo had come running at the same time. Theo called 9-1-1 while she grabbed the linen tablecloth from the dining room, pressing it to Jed's shoulder to staunch the bleeding, talking to him the whole time. "You stay here. You stay right here. Don't you dare leave me."

He looked up at her, his blue eyes wide with shock. He sucked in a breath and tried to say something, but only a moan came out.

298

"The ambulance is on its way," Theo said. "Let me do that. This is going to hurt, Dad."

He'd taken over applying pressure while she sat, pulling Jed's head into her lap, continuing to talk to him. "It's going to be okay. You're going to be fine," she repeated, over and over.

Just before the ambulance arrived, his eyes flickered open. "Josie..." he croaked. "Zora..."

"Shhh," Natalie murmured. "They're fine."

"No." He shook his head. "No. She took them. And he..." His eyes closed.

The sirens stopped in front of the house, and Theo rose to let the paramedics in. As they took over, Natalie ran upstairs, throwing open the door to the girls' bedroom. In her shock, it hadn't even occurred to her that Chelsea should have been woken up by the shot, too. The beds were rumpled, the room empty.

The *ding* of the elevator and the sound of voices brought her back to the present. Mitch and Stella rushed into the lounge, still wearing the same clothes from dinner earlier. Stella sat and wrapped her arms around Natalie.

"Sweetheart," she murmured. "I'm so sorry."

"How long has he been in surgery?" Mitch asked.

"Only about forty-five minutes," Theo said. "But it seems like forever."

"There was so much blood," Natalie said. "I tried to stop it..." Safe in Stella's embrace, she began to sob.

An hour later, in clean scrubs Stella had scrounged up from one of the nurses, Natalie took a sip of the coffee Mitch placed in her hands. Theo sat beside her, hands wrapped around his own cup, eyes fixed on the surgical doors, willing them to open.

Jed's boss, Tom Delgado, sat across from them.

"He's a tough guy," he said. "He's going to pull through this." He took out his phone. "Did either of you see anything?"

Natalie shook her head. "I woke up when I heard the shot."

"Me, too," Theo said. "I heard a car back out of the drive, but I didn't look. Dammit. Why didn't I look?"

"You probably wouldn't have seen anything in the dark anyway," Delgado said. "I gave the description of Chelsea and the pictures of the girls you texted me to the local cops and DCI. We're all coordinating on this. State Police are on the lookout. We'll find them."

"Where did the car come from?" Natalie said. "Where did she get the gun? I can't imagine her shooting Jed, but who else could it have been?"

"Dad started to say 'he' something, right before the ambulance got there. Maybe there was someone else." Theo speculated.

"She asked to use my phone after dinner." Mitch ran a hand over his thinning hair. "She said she wanted to look something up online. I didn't worry about it, but now I'm thinking she called someone. Maybe they picked her up." He handed the phone to Delgado.

"There's nothing in my recent calls. But she could've erased it. I'm sure you have people who can find that kind of stuff."

"Do we ever," Tom said, slipping the phone into his jacket pocket. "Thanks. I'm going to get this to Cleo right now. Nat," he bent and placed a hand on her shoulder. "You've got my number. Call if you need anything... anything at all. I'll be back as soon as I can."

Natalie nodded her thanks and took another sip of coffee. As she lowered the cup from her lips, the doors opened and the trauma surgeon approached them. Natalie and Theo stood, grasping at each other's hands.

"He'll have some rough recovery to get through," the surgeon said. "But your husband is going to be fine." He glanced down at the chart he carried, flipped a sheet of paper over. "He's lucky. The bullet nicked the subclavian artery. The pressure you applied before the paramedics got there went a long way toward saving his arm, and probably his life."

"Can I... can we see him?" Natalie asked, wiping away tears of relief.

"He's in recovery, but I can take one of you in."

"You go, Mom," Theo said, his fingers closing around hers and releasing.

She followed the surgeon, who continued to explain. "There's no nerve damage I can see. With physical therapy, he should have full use of his arm. We'll know more when he wakes up here in a bit. I put a pin in to stabilize the collarbone and repaired the artery. He'll be in a sling for four to six weeks, and there will be therapy after that."

He pushed open the door, and there was Jed, his chest bare, his right arm and shoulder wrapped in bandages. Monitors beeped and fluids dripped into his other arm from two different IV bags.

"We're giving him antibiotics and pain medication," the doctor explained. "They'll be moving him to the surgical ICU in just a bit. You're welcome to stay."

Natalie thanked him and sat in the chair, scooting it closer to take Jed's hand in hers, careful to not disturb the IV.

"I'm here," she whispered. "I'm right here."

Chapter 34

Natalie's face was the first thing Jed saw when he opened his eyes. She smiled at him through tears, but his tongue was thick and his eyelids were *so* heavy. He felt her hand close around his and tried to squeeze back, not sure if he succeeded before the fog took over, and he slipped under. The next time he forced his eyes open, it was Mitch sitting beside the bed, a book opened on his lap, his head drooped in sleep. Jed managed a guttural noise, and Mitch sat up.

"Jedi," he said. "Welcome back."

"Nat?" His tongue was still so slow it came out *"Naahhd",* but Mitch understood.

"She was here all night. Stella made her go home to shower and change, but I'm sure she'll be back soon." He took a cup from the bedside table and shook it to loosen the ice chips. "Bet you're thirsty."

Jed nodded and Mitch spooned some ice chips into his mouth. Jed sucked and swallowed. He looked over at his right shoulder, wrapped in gauze, then back at Mitch, who offered the ice again.

After a second swallow, he found his voice. "He shot me."

"Yep. Doc says you were lucky. No nerve damage. Your collarbone is broken so you're gonna have to wear that sling for a while."

Jed flexed the muscles in that arm and grimaced. Mitch held out the cup again and he took more ice.

"Josie and Zora?"

"Nothing yet," Mitch shook his head. "Your boss was here. There are a lot of people looking for them. Do you remember anything?"

"Chelsea called him Cody," he said. "She yelled 'Cody don't' or something like that right before he fired the gun."

"That's good. Now we have a name. The police will want to talk to you, but first I'd better let the nurse know you're awake."

****

Jed came home on Sunday, his arm in a sling, his head still a bit woozy from painkillers. Natalie made a cozy nest on the couch with a pillow to support his arm and settled in next to him on the other side, handing him the remote.

He put his good arm around her and leaned over for a kiss. He looked at the remote in his hand and chuckled. "You must have really missed me."

"We are so blessed," Natalie said, cupping his chin in one hand and looking into his eyes. "I could have lost you."

"You won't lose me for a long time," Jed said, kissing her again.

"Still..." she shivered and reached behind him, pulling the afghan off the back of the sofa and tucking it around them.

"I'm really worried about the girls," he said. Even the drugs hadn't been able to keep that particular pain away. "I can't stop thinking about them."

"I know. Me, too." Natalie bit her lip. "She wouldn't hurt them, though, would she?"

"Not on purpose, I don't think," Jed said. "Which means nothing. But Cody?"

"I just wish the police would find them."

The police had no leads, beyond discovering that Cody's last name was Whitlock, and he was a low-level drug dealer in one of the Chicago organizations with an extensive rap sheet, including several assault charges and an eight-year stint in state prison for drug trafficking. They'd tried his last known address, but had found nothing there that would tell them where he might be now. They brought Chelsea's friend, Skylar, in for questioning, but she clammed up and told them nothing. Thinking she might lead them to Chelsea and the girls, the police put a tail on her, but the only places she went between Friday and Sunday were work, the grocery store, and home. A judge denied their request to examine her phone records, citing lack of evidence.

They were able to access Cody's phone records, but they showed no activity since Thanksgiving. Tom Delgado figured he was using burner phones at this point.

"We'll find them," he assured Jed. "They're going to have to surface at some point."

But they didn't. Two weeks passed, then three. Jed was beginning physical therapy, pushing himself to recover quickly. He wanted to help in the search. Natalie was busy at Sorriso with the rush of holiday get-togethers and parties. Theo came back to the restaurant to help out and earn some extra money while he was home on break.

A little over a week before Christmas, Theo poked his head into the kitchen just as the dinner rush began. "Mom!" he said. "Phone call for you."

Natalie turned to Kendall. "It's probably the seafood supplier. I left several unhappy messages earlier today about the salmon in that last order. I'll be right back."

Stepping into Stella's office, she picked up the phone. "Hello, this is Natalie Shaw."

A faint buzzing came over the line. "Hello?" she said again.

The voice was a whisper. "Aunt Nat?"

Natalie's heart started pounding. "Josie? Josie! Oh, sweetie! Where are you? Are you okay?"

"I... we're... okay." She sniffled. "I don't know where we are. We're locked in. Is Uncle Jed alright?"

"Yes, he's fine. He's fine. Think, Josie... is there anything you notice about where you are?"

"I hear trains. Like I did at our old apartment."

"Are you in Chicago? How far did you drive the night you left?"

"I don't know. I fell asleep."

"Okay, Josie, is there a window? Can you look out and tell me what you see?"

"I'm not supposed to."

"I bet you aren't supposed to use the phone, either, but you did. Why did you call me here?"

Josie's voice broke. "I couldn't remember your number or Uncle Jed's, but I remembered the name of the restaurant so I Googled it on Mama's phone."

"You are such a smart girl."

"Mama will be back in a minute. She's not supposed to leave us. Cody will be mad if he finds out."

"Just take a quick look, Josie. Are you in Chicago?"

"I think so." There was a pause. "I can see the building across the street. It's all boarded up and there's a big crane there. It says R-E-A-R-D-O-N on it."

Natalie wrote the word down on a scrap of paper. "Good! Do you see anything else? A street sign maybe?"

"Maybe a store? There's a sign. It looks like..." she stopped. "Someone's coming. I gotta go. I miss you and Uncle Jed."

The phone went dead.

****

Tom Delgado sat at the bar at Sorriso, typing into his phone. "Tell me again about the crane," he said.

Natalie closed her eyes and repeated what she'd written down and now knew by heart. "The building is boarded up and there's a crane with REARDON written on it."

"Is that a construction company?" Jed asked.

Stella came over with a bottle of bourbon and four glasses. She added a solid square ice cube into each glass and poured the bourbon over it. Jed took a sip immediately. Sorriso had closed an hour ago, and he arrived with Delgado and a technician shortly after that. The restaurant's line was being wired so they could trace it if Josie called again.

"Did you eat?" Natalie asked Jed. "You have to eat with those pain meds. Not to mention the bourbon you shouldn't be having."

"Uh..."

She shook her head at him. "I'm taking that as a 'no'. Tom, would you like something?"

"Sure. I can always eat your food." Tom and his wife were frequent patrons.

Natalie took her glass of bourbon with her into the kitchen, returning in ten minutes with an empty glass, two plates of the simple chicken pasta with asparagus she'd done for the night's special, and a loaf of focaccia, warm from the oven.

Tom was reading from his phone. "Reardon Construction LLC has a contract with the city of Chicago. They're taking down 'eyesore' buildings, or buildings condemned by the fire department or the city planner."

He stuffed a forkful of pasta into his mouth and continued talking around it. "There are nineteen buildings scheduled for demolition scattered across the city. Eleven of them are pretty close to an 'L'."

"So we need to check all of those out," Jed said. "I can help with that." He started eating, too, breaking off a piece of bread and swirling it through the olive oil Natalie poured onto a plate.

"You aren't supposed to drive yet," she pointed out.

"I have a lot more mobility since I started therapy. I think I can manage to get to the city, then I bet Mitch could drive me around," he said.

"I'd feel better if we hooked you up with someone from CPD," Delgado said. "Let me make a few calls first thing tomorrow."

******

Natalie sat down beside him, and Jed looked up from his computer. "This is interesting," he said. He moved the screen so she could see it. "Do you notice anything about the years Cody was in prison?"

She studied the dates. "He was arrested in 2009," she said, "pled guilty to possession with intent to distribute and got eight years." She looked at Jed. "So?"

"Those eight years are when Chelsea met Dante and got straight."

310

"And Cody was released right around the time she lost her husband and her mother-in-law." Her eyes widened. "Do you think she was with Cody before?"

"Who knows? He could even be who she was running from when she came here all those years ago."

"Why would she go back to him?"

Jed shrugged. "Why does she do anything? Because of what we – what she – went through, I'd imagine."

"If only Dante hadn't been killed," Natalie said. "Or if her mother-in-law hadn't gotten sick. It seems like she's had nothing but the worst kind of luck." She bit her lip. "It's just not fair."

Jed nodded. "I know."

Chapter 35

"Why is your sling off?" Natalie set down the bag she carried on the kitchen counter and stood looking at her husband with her hands on her hips.

"The PT told me to take it off sometimes," Jed said.

"For how long?"

He shrugged his good shoulder. "It feels fine."

"It feels fine now, but how is it going to feel later if you've overdone it?"

"Okay, okay," he said. He picked up the sling by one strap. "A little help here?"

Natalie came over, helping him slip the strap over his neck and secure it, then leaning in and giving him a soft kiss.

"I brought dinner home," she said, pointing to the bag on the counter. "We had lasagna and salad left over from the city council Christmas luncheon. Sound good?"

"Sounds great. I'll open that second bottle of the Jordan Cabernet Stella brought on Thanksgiving."

"Speaking of Stella," Natalie said. "Theo mentioned something the other night that has me thinking." She unpacked the food and began dividing it up onto two plates.

"What's that?" Jed reached into the wine rack and pulled out the bottle of Cab, setting it on the counter and taking two Bordeaux wineglasses out of the cupboard.

"The night you were shot, they got to the hospital at the same time."

"Huh," he said.

"And, they were wearing the same clothes they had on at dinner." She bumped her husband with her hip as she reached for the salad bowls.

"O-kay," he said, breaking the word into its syllables. "I guess that's weird." He placed the wine-opener on the bottle and pressed the button. Ejecting the cork, he poured the wine into the glasses and set them, one at a time, on the bar.

"Yeah. I thought you told me Mitch was going back to the city, didn't you?"

"That's what he said," Jed nodded. "I asked him if he wanted to stay over, since it was pretty late, but he said he had some stuff to do on Friday. He did drive Stella home, remember? She'd had too much to drink."

"Yes, but they left the house around 10:30. It was close to three in the morning when they got to the hospital. What were they doing all that time?" Natalie said, raising an eyebrow. She set the plates and bowls on the bar and got silverware out of the drawer, then unwrapped a loaf of warm focaccia baked with sundried tomatoes and olives.

"Who called them?"

"Theo called Stella. She said she would 'get' Mitch."

"Maybe he turned around and came back?"

"Not enough time." Natalie shook her head. "I think he stayed with her."

"Like *overnight?*" Jed's forehead wrinkled. "Mitch and Stella? But they just met."

"I know, right?" She speared the salad with her fork. "I mean, Stella has had gentleman friends before, but she hasn't mentioned anyone for a while."

"I have no idea about Mitch," Jed admitted in between bites of lasagna. "He's never mentioned anyone either, but maybe that would be awkward for him to talk about with me."

"They're close to the same age, I bet." Natalie swirled the wine in her glass and took a sip.

"What's Stella? Sixty?"

"Sixty-three."

"Mitch is sixty-two."

Natalie took a bite of lasagna. "I guess I could see it."

He took a drink of wine. "They're so different though, I mean, Stella is so cultured and elegant and Mitch..."

"Mitch isn't exactly a Neanderthal," Natalie laughed. "He appreciates good food and he and Dad talked for a good hour about the history of Chicago since the fire."

"Mitch was a mail carrier for over twenty-five years," Jed said. "He had different routes all over the city, so he absorbed a lot of history."

"Stella loves the city. She goes there whenever she can find an excuse. I think she might live there if it wasn't for Sorriso."

"Hey, maybe they were just enjoying each other's company. It's really none of our business, right?"

"I guess," Natalie said, not sounding convinced.

His phone vibrated and Jed glanced at it, then at Natalie. "It's Detective Grant," he said. "The one on the girls' case." He clicked the button. "Hello?"

****

Stella's phone buzzed on the nightstand and she glanced at it, smiling as she read Mitch's name on the screen. "Well, hello," she said. "Are we making this a nightly thing?" He'd called the last two nights, once, to ask her about a restaurant for a possible gift certificate for Natalie, and last night to confirm his choice. She suspected these were only convenient excuses.

"I kind of like talking to you before I go to sleep," he admitted.

She laughed softly. "I like talking to you, too. How was your day?"

"It was good. I helped at the animal shelter."

"What do you do there?" She stretched out, pulling the extra blanket over her feet against the chill.

"Oh, anything they need me to. Today I took some of the dogs for a walk around the neighborhood. They like getting out of the kennels. It also sometimes gets them noticed. What did you do today?"

"Well," Stella said, "I had to fire one of our waiters for stealing liquor from the bar."

"I'm sorry. That has to be one of the worst parts of owning a business."

"Not my favorite thing," Stella said. "Fortunately, it doesn't happen that often. Natalie handles the kitchen staff. She doesn't like it any more than I do. But sometimes it has to be done."

"I hope the rest of your day was better."

"It was, actually. I had a lovely lunch with a friend and got a bit of Christmas shopping done. I like to do as much as I can locally." She paused, considering her next words. "I do need to come into the city next week, though. Any chance we could meet for dinner like we talked about?"

"I have the perfect place in mind," he said. "Let me know what day and I'll make a reservation."

She smiled, thinking about how nice it would be to see him. "How about if *I* call *you* tomorrow night and we can firm up our plans?"

"I will look forward to it," he said. "Goodnight, Stella."

"Goodnight, Mitch. I'll talk to you tomorrow."

Chapter 36

"California?" Natalie punched the pillow and propped it up behind her, leaning back against it and looking at her husband. Immediately after hanging up from Detective Grant, Jed called his own boss and disappeared into the downstairs office.

"That's what he said." He pulled on a clean t-shirt with his boxers and slid under the covers, leaning up on one elbow to face her. "They talked to some guy who they with Cody last time; he said he talked to him a week ago and Cody told him he was headed to California. The assumption is Chelsea and the girls are with him."

"But we don't know that for sure," Natalie said. "I wonder..."

"What?"

"Do you think they found out Josie called me? Could that be the reason for them taking off; going so far away?" She chewed her bottom lip. "How will we ever find them?"

"This might actually be good news," Jed said. "Delgado thinks if they cross state lines, then the feds might get involved. He has a contact at the Bureau and he's going to call him tomorrow. I really thought we'd have them back by Christmas," he said, flopping onto his back with a sigh.

"Me, too." Natalie put down her book and snuggled in beside him, her head on his chest. They both lay awake for a long time.

****

The next night, Jed poked the fire and tossed on another log, then joined Natalie on the couch. Theo sat on the floor, leaning against a chair, his long legs stretched out in front of him. He reached for a slice of pizza.

Natalie sipped her beer and picked the cheese and toppings off her slice, nibbling at them.

"You're quiet," Jed said. He tapped her temple. "What's going on in there?"

She looked toward the living room, where the tree sparkled, gifts piled underneath.

"I wrapped the girls' presents today," she said. "I couldn't *not* wrap them." Even though Christmas was less than a week away and there was no sign of them, it seemed too sad to leave the toys and clothing they'd gotten for Josie and Zora just sitting there unwrapped.

"So they'll open them when they come home," he said. "We'll have Christmas in January...or April...whenever."

"This is their home, isn't it?" Natalie said. "If we get them back, we'll make it work somehow."

"**When** we get them back," Jed said, pulling her closer.

Theo got to his feet. "I'm not hungry," he said. "And I'm not into this movie. I'm going over to Jeremy's."

Jed started to say something, but Natalie elbowed him and her eyes slid to his. *Is he jealous?* She mouthed.

Theo clomped up the stairs, came down with his keys jangling in his hand, and left without another word, slamming the door behind him. Jed grabbed the pizza box and dirty paper plates and headed to the kitchen. Natalie followed.

"He *is* jealous!" she said.

"Well, he's had our undivided attention for twenty years. Wouldn't you be a little jealous?"

"What do we do?" Natalie got herself another Blue Moon from the fridge and popped the cap.

"We don't need to 'do' anything.," Jed said. He grabbed a beer for himself. "Theo is a grown man. He'll adjust. He was great with the girls over break. They adored him."

"That's when he thought this was temporary. What about now that it might not be?"

"Nat," Jed kissed her. "He'll be fine. We've loved him his whole life. At some point, he's bound to realize that the girls deserve that, too, and he'll love them as much as we do."

Natalie bit her lip. As much as she hated to admit it, Theo was still her baby boy, and she hated that he might feel slighted.

"You know," she said. "He's been wanting us to turn the basement into a bedroom suite for him since he was about twelve. What if we did it now, as one of his Christmas presents?"

"Which of the twenty or so gifts you already got for him are you going to take back?" he teased.

"It wouldn't cost that much," she continued, ignoring the jab. "The one room needs painted and we could replace the shower, but the carpet just needs cleaned. Mom and Dad would be happy to get rid of some of the furniture they have in the barn and I'm sure Stella would help me paint."

"Mitch and your dad would probably help me redo the shower," Jed mused.

"And then," Natalie said, clinking her bottle against his and winking at him. "We could observe Stella and Mitch together ourselves."

The next morning, Jed and Natalie sat at the bar drinking their coffee. "What's on your agenda today?" Natalie asked.

"I've got an interview for this case I'm working, but we're doing it on Zoom since the guy works somewhere in California now, so I can work from home."

"Kendall is handling lunch today, so I'm not going in until later."

"Morning," Theo came into the kitchen in gym shorts and a t-shirt, brushing the hair out of his face. He took a mug from the cupboard and poured himself some coffee.

"You're up early," Jed observed.

"Yeah, I, uh, wanted to talk to you guys." He took a long drink from the mug. "Sorry about last night. I like Josie and Zora. I really do. It's just weird sometimes, you know?"

"I get that, honey." Natalie reached out and stroked his arm.

"And," he took a breath. "I've been doing a lot of thinking lately, too. Trying to figure some things out."

"Is everything alright?" she asked.

"Yeah, it's fine. Just school."

Jed spoke up. "What's up with school? Are your classes rough?"

Theo shook his head. "No. Classes are fine. But I'm thinking about transferring back here to Delphi."

"Delphi? I thought you were happy at Northwestern." Jed said.

"I have been, but since I've been working at Sorriso, I discovered I really like the restaurant business." Theo sat on one of the bar stools, cupping his hands around his coffee mug, "Delphi has a great business program with a specialty in restaurant management."

Natalie caught Jed's eyes and then her son's. "What is it you like about the restaurant business?" She knew he wasn't that interested in the kitchen.

"I was talking to Stella the other night while I was on break. I had a couple of ideas and she really listened. She said I have good instincts."

"What were your ideas?"

"Well," he said, leaning in, "I had heard her talking about how slow it is in January and February, so I suggested doing a weekly special with two dinners, wine, and dessert for a certain price. You could bundle the cheaper pasta dinners with a more expensive wine and change it up each week."

Natalie nodded. "That *is* a good idea."

"I also suggested adding a takeout option for dinner during the week. Weekends are too busy, but during the week it would be pretty easy, and you usually end up with food left over, don't you?"

"Yes, we do. Another good idea."

"About that leftover food," he said. "I know there are health regulations, and I'd have to look into it more, but in the city, some restaurants are pairing up with shelters. They give them their leftovers and sometimes get people into jobs as bussers or dishwashers, things like that. If you contact local media, you can get some great publicity."

"These are all great ideas, Theo," she said. "You've put a lot of thought into this. I'm really impressed."

"But you could take business at Northwestern," Jed said, drinking the last of his coffee.

"I could," Theo agreed, "but if I live here, work at *Sorriso* and go to Delphi, I could save a lot of money. Maybe enough to buy into a restaurant once I graduate." He looked at them both. "What do you think? If I'm here, I could help with the girls, too-when they come home-I mean, if you guys don't mind me living here."

Natalie rose and walked over, wrapping her arms around him. "Mind? I would love having you home," she said. "You know that."

"Absolutely," Jed agreed. "Actually, if your mom doesn't care, we could tell you about one of your Christmas presents now."

Theo raised an eyebrow. "Yeah, uh, what's that?"

"How about the basement apartment you've always wanted?" Natalie said.

His eyes lit up. "Really?"

"Your dad and I were just talking about it last night. I don't think it will take much to get it ready. You'd have your own entrance from the garage, just turn right down the stairs instead of left into the kitchen."

"This is awesome! I'm going to put in my transfer papers today."

Chapter 37

They spent the next three days working on the basement apartment. Theo, Jed and Mitch, with some help from Russ and Ian, enclosed the bathroom area, upgraded the shower stall, and put in a pedestal sink.

Everyone pitched in to get it ready. Stella painted walls the first day and Connie used a slipcover to update an old couch. Ian stained a coffee table from Jed and Natalie's first apartment. Katy brought art posters to hang on the walls. Trips to Target and IKEA brought a chair, lamps, pillows, and a funky striped rug for the floor.

Natalie and Stella left Kendall in charge at Sorriso and came home early the next night, calling their favorite Chinese restaurant for takeout. While Theo and Jed showered and Mitch went to pick up their order, Natalie poured wine for Stella and herself.

"So," she said, leaning her elbows on the bar and looking at her friend over the rim of her wineglass. "Mitch. Spill."

Stella blushed and took a long swallow of the Italian white. She closed her eyes for a moment. When she opened them, they sparkled and she smiled.

"He is the sweetest man," she said. "You know that I've been perfectly happy with my life. I haven't dated anyone in a while and I was fine with that."

Natalie nodded, sipping her own wine.

"But talking to him on Thanksgiving was such a nice change. I didn't realize how much I missed connecting with someone my own age."

"Not to mention a handsome man your own age," Natalie said with a grin.

"He is pretty handsome, isn't he?" Stella said, then waved a hand in front of her face as if brushing the words away. "I'm not making any more of it than it is. We are enjoying each other's company."

"I'm glad," Natalie said. "He's a great guy, and from what he's shared with us, it's been a long time since he's had anyone special in his life."

"I think you're right." Stella settled back in her chair, becoming more comfortable in the conversation.

"He's told me quite a bit about Teri—that's Jed's mom, right?"

"Yes."

Her face clouded. "I think he blamed himself for not being able to keep her sober and then not being able to find the kids."

"At least *he* stayed sober through all of that," Natalie mused. "I'm sure it wasn't easy."

"He credits his sponsor for that. He told me that without Jim, he never would have made it. He was his sponsor for almost thirty years. He got sick and passed away last year."

"Oh! I'm sure that was hard on Mitch."

"It was. But he is so thrilled to have Jed back in his life now. You know, he thinks of him as a son."

Natalie nodded slowly. "I'm pretty sure the feeling is mutual. I know they talk once or twice a week at least. Jed needed that. He gets along with my dad fine, but it's not the same."

"Mitch is a connection to his past," Stella observed.

"Yes. He was hoping he would be the same for Chelsea, but..."

"Still no word on the girls?"

Natalie blinked away tears and shook her head.

"You really miss them, don't you?"

"I do," she said. "Don't worry, I haven't changed my mind about working I just hate that it's Christmas and God only knows where they are or what's happening to them."

"I completely understand that. I saw the gifts for them under the tree. I have gifts for them, too."

"Bring them over. We'll save them for when they come home."

When Mitch arrived with the food, they ate family style, sharing egg rolls and plates of cashew chicken, Kung Pao shrimp, moo goo gai pan, and fried rice.

"I think I'll head to campus and pack up my things tomorrow. I can't wait to get the TV and my gaming system hooked up downstairs. Can I have a few guys over after Christmas to show off?"

Jed laughed. "Sure. It's your place."

'Thanks, guys." Theo grinned. "This is awesome."

Chapter 38

"And..." Stella said, locking the door behind the last of the evening's customers. "We are closed."

Christmas was in two days, and Sorriso would be closed until New Year's Eve. She moved to the center of the room and raised her glass of champagne.

"Merry Christmas everyone!"

There were hugs and toasts all around as Natalie brought plates of antipasti and appetizers out of the kitchen, setting them on the wide bar. Leaning back into the kitchen through the open door, she motioned to Trevor and Dakota, the two dishwashers, to join everyone else in the dining area. The two young men, students at the local vocational school, glanced at each other before shyly slipping past her.

Stella made her annual speech to the staff, listing all of Sorriso's accomplishments during the year; the updates to the kitchen and expansion of the outdoor dining area, Maddy's introduction of a weekly Italian inspired cocktail, and Natalie's successful fall menu. She applauded everyone's efforts and passed out gifts to each of them—gift certificates to local businesses and modest bonus checks.

Then the party began. With a little help from Theo, Natalie handled the music, an eclectic mix of everything from Led Zeppelin to Lady Gaga. Glenn and Maddy gave generous pours of whatever anyone wanted to drink, and Stella promised Uber rides home for anybody who needed one.

Natalie approached Kendall with a small, silver wrapped package. "I never could have made it through these past few months without you. You run the kitchen perfectly and I never worry about leaving it to you. Merry Christmas."

"You didn't have to..."

"I know. I wanted to."

Kendall tore off the wrapping and lifted the lid to the box. Inside, nestled on a pillow of blue silk, lay a delicate chain with a silver charm shaped like a spatula. "Oh!" she said. "It's just like yours."

"A spatula instead of the whisk," Natalie said, fingering the charm around her own neck, a gift from Jed last Christmas. "But yes, the same artist. I hope you like it."

"I love it." The usually stoic younger woman gave Natalie an unexpected hug. "Thank you."

"You're welcome. Merry Christmas."

"You, too." She raised her chin and her dark eyes flashed. "I hope you find the girls and bring them home."

"Thank you," Natalie said. "So do I."

The staff mingled and talked and ate and drank for over an hour. Close to eleven. Stella approached Natalie, keys in hand. "I'll leave you to lock up," she said. "I'm heading home." She paused, then added, "I noticed Theo hanging near the bar helping Maddy tonight."

"Yes," Natalie said. She had noticed too, and wondered if the pretty bartender could be part of why Theo wanted to stay in town.

"Don't worry," Stella said, seeing Natalie's frown. "She's a smart girl. She's working her way through school."

"She is?"

"Yes. She's in Delphi's nursing program. The nights she isn't here she's working at the hospital, getting her hours in."

"Well, good for her," Natalie said, seeing the young woman with the tattoos and multiple piercings in a new light.

Stella yawned. "Alright. I really am leaving now."

"We'll see you tomorrow night."

Stella blushed and nodded. "Thanks for the invite."

Natalie drew her into a hug. "We couldn't leave out Mitch's girlfriend," she whispered into her boss's ear.

Her face flushed even more and Stella shook her head. "I'm a little old to be anyone's girlfriend."

"Mitch obviously doesn't think so."

"Oh!" Stella said. "I forgot to tell you. We are officially completely booked for New Year's Eve. Last seating is at 9:30. Everyone is very intrigued by the special menu."

Natalie spent weeks planning the NYE menu, a 'Tour of Italy', in six courses. She was pleased the community was responding and even more pleased that it would make the evening much easier on the kitchen staff. With only six items to prepare, they could work together and manage the chaos that was New Year's Eve in the restaurant business. She knew that Jed and Mitch had already booked a table for the last seating, along with Tom Delgado and his wife, Jenni.

The party wound down after Stella left. Natalie watched Theo walk Maddy to an Uber and kiss her cheek before heading to his car. She walked through the dining room, picking up random glasses, plates, and silverware and putting them into the dishwasher in the kitchen. When everything was reasonably clean, she gathered her own things and glanced around, double checking that everything was turned off. The last thing she did was turn out the basement light someone had left on before letting herself out the backdoor and locking it behind her.

At home, she found Jed and Theo in the family room, a football game on the television. She flopped onto the couch and swung her feet into her husband's lap, leaning back and closing her eyes. He rubbed one foot, deeply stroking the arch with his thumb. Natalie moaned with pleasure.

"Should I be watching this?" Theo said, smirking.

"Watch and learn, my son," Jed replied. "The way to a woman's heart..."

"...is through her feet after a long day," Natalie finished. Then she yawned.

"I'm going to pick up Jeremy and head over to Bender's for a little while," Theo said. "Maybe shoot some pool. Some of the guys who are home will be there."

"Okay," his dad said. "If you..."

"I know. I know. If I drink anything, call you. Will do." His keys jangled as he left.

Later, when she heard Jed's phone, Natalie's first thought was that Theo needed a ride. She felt her husband sit up and heard the indistinct murmur of his voice on the phone. Then he shook her gently.

"Nat," he said. "Nat, honey, wake up."

She blinked and looked up into worried eyes.

"That was Stella. Sorriso is on fire."

Chapter 39

They dressed quickly, and Jed drove downtown. Two engines and a tank truck blocked Culver Avenue, where Sorriso was, so Jed parked the Blazer against the curb. He grabbed Natalie's hand, and they walked down the block. Halfway there, she looked up and gasped. Flames were shooting up into the air above the wrought iron grating that framed the roof, turning the winter sky into a kaleidoscope of yellow, orange, and red.

"Oh no!" She said, burying her face in her hands. She felt Jed's arm around her and leaned in.

"Come on," he said. "I think I see Stella."

The crowd of gawkers parted for them and soon they came up beside Stella. Her long silver hair, usually pinned up or braided, hung in loose waves down her back and she still wore her pajamas under a winter jacket. She had her arms wrapped around herself, but when she saw Jed and Natalie, she reached for them.

"Sorriso," she said. "I can't believe it." She blinked, bringing a hand to her mouth.

"I checked everything before I left. I know I did!" Natalie's voice cracked, and she shook her head.

"I'm sure you did," her boss said, patting her arm. "You always do. And you've trained everyone else to do it, too." Her eyes never left the scene in front of them.

A fireman came out the front door and shouted. "Captain! You need to see this."

A uniformed man standing by the tanker put on more gear and followed the first fireman back in.

"What's going on?" Jed said. "How did it start?"

"I don't know." Stella shrugged. "They won't tell me anything."

Jed pulled his state police badge out of his pocket. "I'll see what I can find out."

Natalie stood, holding Stella's hand, both of them watching firemen going in and out and all around the restaurant. There were no more flames, just rolling smoke and the smell of burnt wood and plastic. As far as Natalie could see, it looked like the fire spared the front dining area and side patio much damage. She could still see white tablecloths on the booths by the windows and the doors out to the patio were intact.

After ten or fifteen minutes, Jed came back. "It's out. They found the source of the fire," he said. "There's no sign of a break-in, but someone turned on all the burners on the stove and put kitchen towels soaked in some kind of flammable liquid on top of it and more on the floor leading to the pantry. Sloppy, but effective. It spread quickly."

"What?!" Stella said. "You're telling me someone burned my restaurant on purpose?"

"Looks like it," Jed said. "And they didn't care who knew. They're going to want to talk to you, I'm sure." He turned to Natalie. "You, too. Probably everyone who was there tonight."

Suddenly Lily and Janine appeared out of the crowd, still in the black pants and white shirts they wore to serve.

"So it's true. Oh, my God!" Lily started crying.

A fireman pushed toward them. "Mrs. Danielli?" he said.

"Ms. Danielli," Stella corrected. "Yes."

"Could you come with me for a minute? The captain would like to have a word."

Stella looked at Natalie. "My friends are coming, too," she said.

They followed the young man past the barriers to the back of the tanker truck. A tall fireman removed his helmet and gloves and held out a hand. "I'm Captain Pataki," he said. "The fire started by the stove. The kitchen and back of the building are a total loss, but from the bar forward it's mostly smoke damage. I've got men inspecting the roof now."

"Thank you," Stella said.

"Ma'am, this fire was intentional. We have an arson investigator coming from DCI but I'd like to get some basic information. Who was the last one out of the building tonight?"

"That would be me," Natalie said, her voice soft. "I checked and double checked everything and I know I locked the door behind me."

"Did you notice anything different? Anything at all?" He leaned in, the smell of smoke from his gear overwhelming.

She closed her eyes and thought. "The basement light was on," she said after a moment. "I didn't go down there today, so it must have been someone else who forgot to turn out the light."

"And you didn't check the basement before you left?"

She shrugged. "There's nothing down there but sacks of flour, a few cases of wine, and the washer and drier we use. Since we're closed for the holiday I was going to come in one day next week and do the aprons and towels and stuff so I didn't even take them down like I usually do."

"Is the back door unlocked while the restaurant is open?"

"Yes," Natalie said. "We go in and out with garbage, and a couple of people will go out to have a cigarette on their break."

Now he turned to Stella. "You had a party tonight?"

"Yes, the staff Christmas party – just an hour or so to catch up and celebrate before we close for the week."

"So everyone was in the front of the restaurant? No one was in the kitchen?"

"Yes, we were all out front," Natalie said. "Even the dishwashers."

"But the back door was open." Jed spoke up. "You think someone could have come in while everyone was celebrating and hidden in the basement?"

"Who are you?" the Captain said, eyeing him.

"Jed Shaw, I'm an investigator with the state police. Arson isn't my field, but I know the guy they'll send. Stan Whitman. He's good."

"I've worked with Whitman before. What's your connection here?"

"He's my husband," Natalie said. "I'm the executive chef at Sorriso." She paused. "Or I was."

"You still are," Stella said. She set her jaw and glanced back at the smoldering building. "We are not out of business, not by a long shot."

The captain spoke to Jed. "It seems to me like that's the best explanation for there not being a sign of a break-in. Someone who knew the restaurant's habits or who's been watching, came in, hid, and did their work after everyone left." He looked at Natalie. "Probably a good thing you didn't check the basement. Who knows what they might have done?"

Jed's arm came around her, and Natalie reached up and squeezed his hand.

"Ma'am," the captain said to Stella. "Do you have any disgruntled employees or customers that come to mind?"

Stella lowered her head, pressing two fingers between her eyes. It was several moments before she looked up. "I can't think of anyone."

None of them had seen Janine and Lily come up behind them. "What about Dylan Severns?" Lily said.

"Oh my gosh, yes," Natalie agreed with the younger waitress. "He was furious when you fired him."

"Why did you fire him?"

"Glenn, our senior bartender, caught him stealing liquor," Stella said. "He'd suspected for a while, but didn't want to say anything to me until he was sure."

"When was that?"

"Right after Thanksgiving."

"Got an address on him?"

"Yes." Stella gave a sad smile. "On my computer. Which was in my office just off the kitchen."

"Captain?" the young firefighter came up to them. "We've got another call. Can Engine 11 go?"

"Yeah, that's fine. Where are you headed?"

"4783 Inniswood."

Stella gasped. "That's my house!"

Chapter 40

"Just what the hell is going on here?" Mitch asked. "Are you safe? Have they picked this Dylan guy up yet?"

They all sat at the bar in Natalie and Jed's kitchen, large cups of coffee in front of them. The smell of smoke lingered in the air, even though they had all changed clothes.

"No," Jed said. "They haven't been able to locate him."

"At least there isn't much damage at the house," Stella said. "I'm so glad my neighbor looked over when she let her dog out!"

"Is this the guy you told me about? The one you fired for stealing booze?"

"Yes."

"I don't like the idea of you being alone when this character is still out there," Mitch said.

Natalie moved to refill coffee cups. "Please, stay with us."

"You have enough on your hands," Stella said. "I can just get a motel."

"A motel on Christmas?" Mitch said. "That doesn't sound very festive."

"Look," Jed said. "The basement is almost ready. Theo can move down there and Stella can have his room. We just need to get that bed from your folks."

"Aren't you staying here, too?" Stella slid her gaze to Mitch.

"Just tonight and the couch is fine for me."

"Well," Stella began.

Natalie covered the other woman's hand with her own. "Please, just say you'll stay."

"Alright." she nodded. "I'd like to go back to the house and see if I can collect some clothes that don't smell like a bonfire." Right now, she was wearing a pair of Natalie's leggings and a long sweater.

"I'm happy to take you," Mitch said.

"I'll call Dad about the extra bed," Natalie said. "And if you wake up Theo, I'll get some breakfast ready." She yawned. "I think we're all going to need a nap later."

Stella typed into her phone. "I have to make some phone calls, too. The insurance company, the food delivery, the liquor guy…"

"We'll split up the calls," Natalie said. "You'll need to be the one contacting the insurance, of course, but I can help with the others."

They all went their separate ways. Jed took the dogs for their walk. Theo, excited at the prospect of his own space, was happy to help his mom get breakfast ready. He made more coffee and cut thick slices of homemade bread to toast when everyone got back. She had just slipped the egg casserole in the oven when he looked up from his phone.

"Wow, cool. Does Stella know about this?"

"What?"

Theo held the screen so his mom could see.

"Someone started a GoFundMe for Sorriso. They set a goal of $50,000, and it's already at $35,000. Chuck Leffler from Vic's Tavern donated five thousand and there's an anonymous donation of $10,000."

"Wow is right," Natalie squinted at the screen. "Read it for me, Hon, I don't have my contacts in."

Theo read: *"Early this morning, fire heavily damaged a Westfall landmark. Sorriso and Stella Danielli have been a part of this community for over 50 years. I am starting this GoFundMe to help her keep her employees on during what will be a difficult rebuilding time and to say 'thank you' for everything her family has done for Westlake. Brendan Tong*

Jed came in just as he was finishing. "What's this?" Jed said.

Theo explained to his dad.

"Brendan Tong used to work for Stella, didn't he?"

"Yes," Natalie said. "He was the head chef before me. Now he owns Spitfire Grille."

"That's really nice of him."

Natalie agreed. "He's a good guy."

Just then the phone rang. Natalie picked it up and wandered into the other room to talk. After a few minutes, she came back in, a wide smile on her face.

"That was Craig Worthen, head of the board at the vocational school. He offered their kitchen and banquet room for us to use so we don't have to cancel New Year's Eve reservations."

"That's great!" Jed said, reaching past her to steal a slice of bacon from the plate warming on the stove.

She slapped his hand away. "It's very nice of him. My only worry is replacing the food. I'm not sure we can get everything we need in time for the holidays." She chewed her lip.

"Maybe the other restaurants in town would help?" Theo suggested.

"Maybe. Let's not do anything about the reservations yet. After breakfast, I'll make a few calls."

****

"It doesn't smell too bad back here," Stella said as they walked down the hall toward the bedrooms. The kitchen, living, and dining rooms had smoke and water damage. The appliances were okay, but the furniture would probably need to be replaced, even though the fire never touched it. In the bedroom, she pulled open the sliding doors to the closet and sniffed.

"I'm sure it helped that you shut the doors," Mitch said.

"I'm a stickler for a neat bedroom," she said. "I make the bed and put everything in its place before I do anything else." She held a hanger with a white blouse out to him. "Can you smell anything?"

He lifted the sleeve to his nose and shook his head. "Nothing but fabric softener."

"Thank goodness!" she said. "Just give me a few minutes to throw some things into an overnight bag."

Reaching under the bed, she pulled out a soft bag of worn brown leather with handles and a shoulder strap. She opened the dresser drawer and selected several pairs of silky panties. Mitch averted his eyes as she tucked them into the bag.

"Such a gentleman," she said. "I'm sure you've seen ladies' underwear before."

"Not recently." He chuckled and ran a hand over his thinning hair.

"Oh? Really?" She went back to the drawer, choosing a lacy blush-colored bra and giving him a sideways glance before packing it. She added socks, a pair of jeans, black leggings, and several sweaters, topping it off with a nightgown she took from a hook on the back of the door.

"I just need to grab a few things from the bathroom and we can head back to Natalie's."

As Stella moved to pass him, Mitch reached for her hand, catching her fingers and pulling her to him. Before he could second guess himself, he lowered his lips to hers in a brief kiss. "I've been wanting to do that since Thanksgiving," he said.

She smiled up at him. "I've been wanting you to."

He kissed her again, deeper this time, and her hand came up to cup his cheek. "I like you quite a bit, Mitch Morrison," she murmured.

"That's good, because I am growing very fond of you, too."

"I don't think we've done a very good job hiding it. Natalie called me your 'girlfriend' last night."

"She did? And here I thought I'd been so stealthy about it."

They both laughed and Stella stepped away, returning in a few minutes with a flowered cosmetic bag. She lay it on top of everything and zipped the bag shut. Before she could lift it onto her shoulder, Mitch grabbed the handles.

"I've got this."

Chapter 41

Christmas morning started late. Everyone was exhausted from the day before, so it was close to ten before Natalie passed out coffee and pastries and the first present was opened. There were the usual sweaters and pajamas, a new Lee Child book for Jed, and a bottle of Natalie's favorite perfume. Mitch gave Jed a Cubs jacket and tickets to the home opener against the Reds. For Natalie, there was a gift certificate to *Adalina,* one of the trending Chicago restaurants. His gift to Stella was a Cubs t-shirt and one ticket to opening day.

"One ticket?" she said, holding it up. "Why do I only get one ticket?"

"I wasn't about to risk you taking someone else," Mitch said, holding up the second one. He leaned in and kissed her as Natalie beamed at them both.

"It will be such fun to all go to opening day together!"

"Who says I'm taking you?" Jed smirked, winking at Theo. "Maybe I'll take my son." He planted a kiss on her mouth and dropped a small, silver-wrapped box into her lap.

"You'd better not," she laughed. Ripping off the wrapping paper, she held the black velvet box in her hand for a moment before opening it. Inside was a ring with three tiny square-cut citrine topaz gemstones; a perfect match for her favorite necklace and earrings.

"Oh!" she cried, slipping it onto her pinky finger. "I love it!" She lay a hand on Jed's face and leaned in for a kiss.

"I thought you might." He grinned.

"There's one more for you." Natalie took a flat, rectangular box from where it leaned under the tree and handed it to him.

Jed unwrapped it to find the picture Mitch had given them, now in a silver frame. There was his mom, holding Noah with Jed and Chelsea in front of her. He cleared his throat. "This is great," he said, holding it up for Mitch to see. "Thanks."

"It belongs on the wall with the other family pictures," she said.

"Yes," he agreed. "It does."

****

Christmas dinner was at Russ and Connie's. They'd been happy to add Mitch and Stella to the guest list. Snow began falling around noon, and by the time they sat down to dinner, it covered the grassy areas with a light white blanket.

"Want to go for a walk with me?" Mitch asked Stella as everyone was settling into post-meal drowsiness in front of the television.

"Yes," she said, "that's a good idea. Connie refused my help in the kitchen, and if I sit down now after that meal, I'll be asleep in five minutes."

They were both wearing boots, so they donned winter jackets and Stella wrapped a blue cashmere scarf, her gift from Natalie, around her neck. Hand in hand, they headed down the path toward the barn.

Most of the animals were inside, but the donkey, a recent arrival after his farmer owner passed away, stuck his head through the fence railing, begging for a pet.

Stella took off one glove and stroked his velvety nose. "Aren't you sweet," she murmured.

Mitch cleared his throat. "I was thinking," he said. "I'll be heading back to the city tomorrow afternoon and if you wanted, you'd be more than welcome to stay with me for a few days. We could go..."

"Yes." Stella said, smiling up at him. "I would love to come and stay with you."

Their eyes met, and he smiled back as he leaned in to kiss her.

****

"Mama!"

Chelsea woke to a dry mouth and Josie tugging on her arm.

"Mama," Josie hissed, keeping her voice low she didn't wake Cody. "Zora won't wake up."

Chelsea shook her head to clear it and spied the empty vodka bottle on the floor beside the bed. That and the used syringe next to it explained the fuzziness.

"What?" she asked, trying to focus on her oldest.

The child bent lower, her face inches from her mother's. "Something's wrong. Zora won't wake up and she's all sweaty. I think she's really sick." A tear trailed down her cheek.

Chelsea swung her legs over the side of the bed. Her head pounded, then the nausea hit, and she flopped back down. She turned her head. Cody lay on the other side of the bed face-down, his bare ass sticking out from under the sheet. Chelsea pulled the sheet over him, took a deep breath and sat up again, this time managing to get to her feet.

"Okay, I'm coming," she said. She got as far as the narrow door into the hallway before the contents of her stomach emptied, splashing onto the wall and the floor. She sank to her knees, wiping her mouth with the back of her hand while Josie looked on.

"Sorry, baby," she said. "Get Mama a towel."

Instead, Josie ran into the room she shared with her sister. "I told you! Zora's sick!" she yelled. "She needs a doctor!"

Coming back, she pushed past her mother and the mess on the floor, going to Cody's side of the bed. She reached behind a stack of boxes and pulled the cellphone from its hiding place, handing it to her mother.

"Call an ambulance!" Josie was sobbing now.

Chelsea tried to get up, but another wave of nausea hit. She bent over and the puddle on the floor grew. The phone slipped from her hand and Josie grabbed it.

"I'll do it myself," she said. She pushed the emergency call button and walked back into the other bedroom. Chelsea dimly heard one end of the conversation.

"My sister won't wake up. She's five. I don't know. Okay. Okay. Yes, she's here. She can't come to the phone. Okay. I will."

Chelsea made it back to her feet, leaning against the wall. *Shit. Josie just called 9-1-1.*

"Josie! Give that to me. You're going to get us all in trouble."

Stumbling into the hallway, she grabbed for the phone, but her daughter was already moving to the front room of the apartment and Chelsea knew she couldn't bridge the space between them without falling. She felt her way along the wall, back to the bedroom on wobbly legs. As she leaned back against the wall, Cody stirred.

"What the hell is going on?" He sat up, rubbing his eyes.

"Zora won't wake up."

He lay back down, rolling over with his face half in the pillow. "Yeah, you gave her medicine last night, remember?" He yawned. "We were partying, and she woke up so you gave her something to make her sleepy."

"I did?" Chelsea didn't remember much of anything from the night before. She knew it had been Christmas. She'd scraped together enough to buy a used gaming system at the Salvation Army thrift store. That was her girls' only gift. She knew Cody had money, but he hadn't gotten them anything.

"Yeah." He sat up, squinting at her. "You don't remember?"

She hesitated. Maybe she could get the phone and cancel the ambulance. But what if Zora was really sick?

"Um...Josie got scared and called 9-1-1."

"What?" Cody was on his feet, pulling on his jeans. "Where is she? I'm gonna beat the living shit outta her."

Chelsea blocked the doorway. "No, Cody, please!"

"How'd she know where the phone was?" He shoved his feet into his boots and put on a t-shirt. Sirens wailed in the distance.

"Motherfucker," he muttered. "I'm not hanging around to get arrested for kidnapping and attempted murder." He wagged a finger in Chelsea's face. "This is all on you, you stupid bitch," he snarled.

"You're the one who told me to just take them!" she yelled back. "You're the one who shot my brother!"

"How'd she get the damn phone? Can't you even control your own kid?"

"I'm sorry!" Chelsea moved toward him, and Cody reared back and backhanded her across the face. She fell back, banging her head hard on the edge of the door and sliding down the wall, sobbing. Defensively, she curled into a ball as a kick landed on her shoulder. She screamed, and he kicked again, sending pain radiating down her arm. Her head spinning, she saw him grab his gun from the nightstand. For a moment, she was afraid he would shoot her, but he shoved it into the back of his jeans and stepped out the window onto the fire escape.

"Cody!" she called. But he was gone.

****

"Ma'am. Ma'am, can you hear me?"

The voice seemed to come from far away. Chelsea looked up at the paramedic, who flashed a light in her eyes. "It's...it's not me, it's my daughter." She raised the arm that worked and pointed to the other bedroom.

"My partner is with your daughter. Your older daughter said she took medicine. Do you know what she took?"

Chelsea nodded. "Cold medicine. She wouldn't go back to sleep and..."

"Did you give it to her?"

Chelsea nodded.

"Do you have the bottle?"

"In the bathroom."

The paramedic disappeared and came back holding the bottle of generic cold medicine. "This? How much did you give her? What time was it?"

"I don't know. I don't remember!" Chelsea clutched her stomach and retched, but there was nothing left.

"Ma'am, what did you take? Are you injured?"

Chelsea didn't answer. At that moment, another paramedic appeared, carrying Zora, limp in his arms.

356

Chelsea saw Josie hovering in the corner of the living room, watching as he lowered her sister onto the stretcher.

"Will she be alright?"

"BP is 85/40. I'm starting an IV," he said.

"Mom is going to need to be transported, too," the woman kneeling beside Chelsea said. "Broken humerus; possible dislocated shoulder. Who hit you? Ma'am?" When Chelsea stared ahead without answering, she looked at her partner. "Let's transport all three."

"We need to get this one to the hospital asap. I'll call for another ambo and tell protective services to meet us there."

Chelsea slumped back against the wall and closed her eyes.

Chapter 42

The day after Christmas, Natalie stood beside Stella and stared at the gutted kitchen of Sorriso. After the arson investigators examined the area and took pictures that morning, the burned equipment had been hauled out to the alley. All that was left was the charred bits welded to the wall and floor.

The kitchen and office area were a total loss. The bar area had quite a bit of smoke damage, the dining area less. A cleaning service was coming next week, and then they would make the determination of how much they would need to tear out and replace.

The GoFundMe campaign went way past its goal, and the money would keep the staff paid for a month or two. After that, unless insurance came through, it would get tricky. They still weren't sure how long it would be until they could reopen. Jed's connections had gotten Stan Whitman and his team there quickly, but the insurance company would send their own investigators. It could be spring or early summer before Sorriso was back in business.

Though he remained the most likely suspect, there was no sign of Dylan Severns. When Whitman's team interviewed his roommates, the two young men reported coming home the night of the fire to find Dylan's things gone, along with their flat-screen television. They were doubly angry, since he also left without paying his share of the rent.

The investigators were not optimistic about finding him, much less proving he set fire to Sorriso. They discovered he falsified his resume and references, and that his real name was Alex Ferguson. Unlike Dylan Severns, Ferguson had a police record. It didn't include arson, but he had two assault charges, and a protection order against him from a former employer.

"I guess I need a more stringent hiring policy," Stella said. "It's just in my nature to trust people." She dabbed at her eyes with a tissue. "I still can't believe this. It all seems like a bad dream."

"I know,' Natalie said, giving her a side hug. Her cell buzzed, and she fished it out of her purse.

"It's Jed," she said. "Hello?"

"At the restaurant, why?" Her eyes went wide, and she grabbed Stella's hand. "Oh, thank God!"

She turned to her boss. "They found the girls!"

******

Jed tossed the car keys at the hospital parking attendant and grabbed Natalie's hand. Together, they rushed through the sliding double doors into the emergency room. Jed flashed his badge. "Zora Winters," he said. "Where is she?"

The nurse glanced at her screen. "She's in exam room 5D, but you can't..."

"We're her legal guardians," he said. "And we want to see her. Now."

The nurse picked up the phone, turned away, and spoke so quietly that neither Jed nor Natalie could hear.

"Alright," she said, hanging up the phone. "Follow me."

She led them through two more sets of double doors and down a hallway lined with portable equipment. "The doctor will talk to you first," she said.

They turned the corner and a man wearing a white coat over blue scrubs approached them. The tag he wore around his neck read Dr. Adam Pak. He held a clipboard in his hand.

"I'm Dr. Pak," he said, barely looking up at them. He pronounced his name to rhyme with *clock*. "I've been taking care of Zora. She's stable right now and we'll be moving her up to pediatric ICU as soon as the orderly gets here."

"ICU? What happened?" Natalie asked.

Jed followed up. "Is she going to be okay?"

"She overdosed on diphenhydramine," he said. "Basically, it's Benadryl. It caused tachycardia–a rapid heartbeat and low blood pressure. We have her stabilized and on IV saline for dehydration. We'll keep her for a day or two to monitor kidney and liver function."

"An overdose?" Natalie said. "How did this happen?"

"I'll let the police and child protective services fill you in on that," he said. "Now if you'll excuse me..."

"Can we see her?"

"I'll have someone take you up as soon as she's in a room."

"Where's her sister?" Natalie asked. "Where's Josie?"

Yet another set of double doors opened at the other end of the hallway, and a female police officer came through, holding Josie by the hand. Seeing them, the child broke away and ran to Jed, throwing her arms around him.

"Uncle Jed! You're okay!" She started sobbing. Natalie and Jed both knelt and enveloped her in a hug.

"I'm fine," he assured her. "Good as new."

"Can I see Zora? Please?" She clutched at Jed. "She wouldn't wake up! Is she okay?"

Jed glanced up at the doctor, who hesitated, but then nodded. "Five minutes," he said. "I don't know where that orderly is." He moved to the door and pushed it open. "She's still unconscious, but she's responsive. You can talk to her."

Jed put a hand on her shoulder. "You take Josie in. I'll be there in a sec. I want to talk to the officer."

Natalie took the child's hand and quietly entered the small room. Zora looked pale and tiny under the sheet, a glean of perspiration on her forehead. There were tubes and wires everywhere and Josie's grip on her hand tightened.

"Is she going to be okay?"

Natalie knelt in front of her. "Yes. The doctor said they want to watch her, but she'll be fine. She may be in the hospital for a few days."

"Can I stay with her?"

"Not this time, Sweetie," Natalie said. "I know you want to, but Uncle Jed and I think it's better if you stay with us. We're going to get a hotel room right across the street so we can be close."

She expected an argument, but Josie just nodded. "Okay," the girl said. "I'm so tired." She leaned against Natalie. "Can I give her a hug?"

"Sure."

Jed came in as Josie walked over to the bed. She reached her arms through the railing and took her sister's hand, then leaned in and kissed her cheek. "I love you, Zora," she whispered.

"What did you want to talk to the officer about?" Natalie asked Jed as they watched.

"I needed to know what happened to her." He tipped his head back and took a breath. "Chelsea drugged her to make her sleep."

"Oh, no!" Natalie said. She reached for her husband's hand and squeezed.

"Then I asked her where Chelsea was," he said. "They're keeping her here for observation. She has four broken ribs, and a broken arm. Her shoulder was dislocated, but they got it back in."

"What happened to her?"

Jed shook his head. "I'm not sure. Cody maybe?"

"He hit Mama all the time," Josie said, quietly. "He was mad that I called 9-1-1."

"Oh dear," Natalie murmured. "Did he ever hit you?"

"She wouldn't let him."

Jed pursed his lips together. "Well, at least that's one thing she did right," he said, his voice meant only for Nat.

"I'd like to go see her," Jed said. "Can you go over to the hotel and get us a room? I'll be there soon and we'll go get something to eat."

Natalie nodded. "Come on, Josie, let's go."

Josie gave her sister a last backward glance and took her aunt's hand.

****

Chelsea's eyes were closed when Jed entered the room. Her right arm was wrapped with a bandage and in a sling. There was a deep cut on her forehead, held together with two butterfly bandages. Her eyes were sunken and her cheekbones prominent. There were visible track marks on her other arm.

Sighing, Jed took the chair beside the bed, leaning forward with his hands on his knees and waiting. It was several minutes before she stirred, restless, then turned her head and opened her eyes. Seeing Jed, she immediately turned away.

"Leave me alone," she slurred.

"What the hell happened, Chelsea?" Jed said. "You drugged your own daughter? For God's sake, what were you thinking?"

"Is she okay?" She bit her lip, waiting for his answer.

Jed sighed, getting up and walking around to the other side of the bed. "She will be, we hope."

Tears slid down his sister's cheeks, and she closed her eyes.

"Did Cody do this to you?" He waited, arms crossed over his chest, watching her. Finally, there was a quick nod.

"Do you know where he might have gone? The police are looking for him. We can end this. If you help them, things might go easier for you."

She raised her good hand to her mouth and shook her head. "He'd just find me again."

"He can't find you if he's in prison."

"Ha!" she barked a laugh. "He won't be there forever."

Jed sat carefully on the edge of the bed. "Chelsea, he shot me. That's attempted murder, or at least assault with a deadly weapon. He assaulted you. I'm betting he suggested drugging Zora. There were all kinds of drugs in the apartment. If they find him, he's going to do hard time."

Chelsea's eyes stayed closed for so long Jed thought maybe she'd drifted off. When she opened them, she looked at him for the first time. "Why are you being nice to me? Aren't you mad?

"Of course I'm angry with you, but you're my sister and I love you. Mostly, I want you to take some responsibility for all this and one way to do that is to help the police." He took her good hand in his. "The detective said you wouldn't talk to her before. Will you talk to her now?"

Chelsea sighed and rolled her eyes. "I don't know where he is."

"Still, will you just talk to her? Maybe something you know will help."

After a moment, she nodded. "Okay," she said. "Will you stay with me?"

"Of course, I will."

Chapter 43

Mitch leaned forward and put his elbows on the table as Jed set the pizza box on the dresser in the hotel room. The older man covered his mouth with one hand and stared into space. Natalie moved to the loveseat, tucking her feet underneath her. Stella took a seat beside her. Josie was already fast asleep in the suite's other room.

"So," Mitch said, "what did Chelsea tell the cop?"

"She said she doesn't know where Cody went, but she gave her the names of some of his friends and a couple of places he's lived before." Jed took another drink of his beer and paced by the window. "Detective Bradford convinced her to press charges for assault."

"We should get in touch with the attorney that handled things last time," Mitch suggested. "Maybe he could get her some kind of deal for testifying against Cody."

"They'd have to find him first," Natalie said.

"The detective seemed to think they would." Jed looked in on Josie and quietly shut the door. "I stopped back in Zora's room before I left. The doctor doesn't like her kidney function right now. He's hoping it's temporary."

"When will they know?"

"Probably not for a day or two."

"That's it then," Stella said, taking out her phone. "I'm cancelling the New Year's Eve dinner. The school was very nice to offer, but we were going to end up scrounging for ingredients, anyway. I'll call Lily and Janine and have them start contacting people with reservations."

"I hate to do it," Natalie said. "But I think you're right. It's just too much. I want to be here with Zora."

"And you should be," Stella said. "People will understand. Sorriso will be back and we'll do something fabulous for the reopening."

"Maybe Theo will have some ideas," Natalie said.

Stella smiled. "He has a real instinct for promoting the restaurant. I take it he talked to you about it?"

Jed stretched out on the bed, propping a pillow behind him. "He's already put in his transfer papers."

"Wonderful!" Stella said. "I'm happy to have him." She paused. "I think Maddy is going to be happy, too."

Natalie shook her head. "I hope that's not his main reason for wanting to be back in Westlake."

"And if it is?" Jed said. "He's old enough to make that decision for himself."

Stella patted Natalie's hand. "He has a job, a plan for school, and a place to live. He also has plenty of family support. No matter what happens with Maddy, I think Theo is going to be just fine."

****

Zora made a full recovery in time to come home for New Year's. Chelsea was released from the hospital and taken to the Metropolitan Correction Center to await trial. Jed got a call from the Chicago police a few days after that. They'd arrested Cody the night before, a plane ticket to Los Angeles in the glove compartment of his car.

Now, Jed, Natalie, and Mitch took the elevator to the tenth floor law offices of Curren, Edwards, and Blunt, to talk to Chelsea's attorney. After the receptionist showed them into the office, the lawyer motioned to the table and chairs in the corner.

"Help yourselves to coffee and have a seat. Since Chelsea gave me permission to speak with you, I'll go over a few things."

Jed and Mitch declined the coffee and took seats on one side of the table, but Natalie poured herself a cup before sitting down. Alan Edwards had been too busy to take the case himself, but he referred them to a colleague who also worked pro-bono. Leslie Frederick sat down across from them and opened her laptop.

"I'll tell you what I told her this morning. I spoke with Assistant DA Randall, and the prosecutor's office is willing to drop the accessory assault charges in exchange for Chelsea's testimony against Cody Whitlock. *If* she follows through."

"She gave her statement," Jed said.

"Yes, but she will still need to testify if there is a trial." She glanced at something on her computer before continuing. "He may very well plead out, and if he does, they've assured me it will not change the deal with the prosecutor's office. If she follows through," Ms. French continued, "that leaves the kidnapping and child-endangerment charges. Those aren't going away."

Jed drummed his fingers on the table. "How much time is she likely to serve?"

The attorney steepled her hands in front of her. "I honestly think the best we can hope for is three years, even with good behavior. We may be able to get minimum security, but that's not a given."

"Three years in prison?" Mitch shook his head. "Isn't there any way to get her into a treatment program or something like that?"

The lawyer shook her head. "The view of the court is going to be that she's already had that chance, and here she is, back in the system. She's also been in court for neglect and abandonment. The judge is likely to see a pattern here."

Jed nodded. "I get that."

Mitch stared out the window at the grey Chicago sky. "There's nothing we can say to the judge to make this go away?"

"I don't think so." She cleared her throat. "And Chelsea intends to plead guilty. It's probably what I would have advised anyway, but she's determined." She took opened a folder and slid a paper across to Jed. "This is a letter from Chelsea to the court asking them to grant you guardianship of Josephine and Zora Winters during her incarceration, that is, if that's what you want."

"Yes, Jed said, squeezing his wife's hand "it is."

****

By the first of February, the insurance company tied up their investigation, and Stella received a check. Renovations were well underway, thanks to a withdrawal from her retirement account. Theo started classes at Delphi Institute and was helping his Uncle Ian with some of the painting and minor repair work to Sorriso's bar and dining room. At Theo's suggestion, Stella decided to use the opportunity to expand the bar seating, and Ian was building a row of two-seater booths along one wall. With a couple minor adjustments to the seating arrangements, they were able to do it without losing any tables in the main dining area.

Natalie used the time off to work with Kendall on new recipes. She and her sous chef spent long winter afternoons in Natalie's kitchen, putting together ingredients in different combinations, with Jed, Theo, and the girls as enthusiastic taste-testers.

"By the time the restaurant opens, you'll have a whole new menu," Jed said one night as he helped them with the dishes after they'd shared the meal.

"We've got a good start."

"We're keeping some favorites," Kendall noted, "rotating them depending on the season. But I think we have enough new dishes to get some notice, maybe even from one of the city papers."

"Not the Trib," Natalie said, "but maybe one of those restaurant-focused ones. They always like to pick a few from surrounding communities, too."

Jed threw the used dishtowels into the laundry room and turned back to his wife. "Have you set an opening date yet?"

"Stella is hoping for a soft opening on Valentine's Day, just for a few of our regulars." Natalie pushed the button to start the dishwasher. "Then a grand opening the following week."

"Get me the dates and I'll take a few vacation days so you don't have to worry about the girls," Jed said.

Natalie put her hands on his shoulders and kissed him. "Perfect."

"I'm going to take off," Kendall said. "I'll meet you at the restaurant in the morning and we can work on that schedule we talked about."

"Great," Natalie said. "Drive safe. It looks like we're going to get snow tonight."

In the living room, they found Josie bent over a book, as usual, while Zora sat cross-legged on the floor, the huge sketch pad they'd given her for Christmas in front of her. Her tongue peeked out of one corner of her mouth as she concentrated on her drawing.

"I like your snowman," Natalie said, sitting down beside her. "Is that Finn and Charlie?"

Zora nodded. "I don't draw dogs very well yet."

"You did a pretty good job." Jed took a seat on the couch, leaning over to see. "I knew what they were right away."

"Can I send it to Mama?" Zora looked up at them.

Natalie nodded. "Absolutely. We need to send her your new school pictures, anyway. We can go to the post office tomorrow."

Josie got up. "I'm going to write her a letter," she said. "Can we put that in, too?"

Jed and Natalie exchanged a glance. This was a positive development. "Sure," he said. "She'll love that."

Epilogue

Jed sat forward, his hands on his knees. He felt Nat's hand at the small of his back. He looked across at his sister. She bore little resemblance to the broken woman in handcuffs pleading guilty in the courtroom two-and-a-half years ago. He could almost see the contented young woman from the photo album.

Chelsea's honey blonde hair had grown out and hung in waves to her shoulders. Her skin and eyes were clear and there were new curves under the black t-shirt and jeans she wore.

They were sitting in Leslie Frederick's Chicago office again. Chelsea used the time in prison to get her GED and even take some college classes. She had been released earlier that week and asked them to meet her in the city. They all had dinner together the night before, and the girls spent the night with their mother in her hotel room.

During dinner, Mitch and Chelsea filled them in about Infinite Chance, the sober living community Chelsea's counselor heard about near Denver, Colorado. The development was geared towards addicts like her who had failed at sobriety more than once in the past. Mitch did some investigating on his own and discovered they had a higher than normal success rate. Most people stayed two or three years, but others made the community a permanent residence. Although there were options for family living, Chelsea decided to ask the girls what they wanted to do.

Now she twisted her hands in her lap. "I talked to the girls about it last night," she said. "They both want to stay here." She looked away and blinked back tears. "That really didn't surprise me. I told them they could visit me, and we could call and video chat whenever they want. I *think* they're okay." She met Jed's eyes. "But you might know better than me."

"We'll talk to them," he promised. "Are *you* okay?

"I will be. I wish I could stay here and be with them, but I know where I need to be and they're happy here. Josie loves helping with the animals at the clinic, and Zora," she smiled. "That child can't stop talking about her friends and school," she swiped at a tear and reached across the space between them to grab her brother's hand. "Thank you."

"You're family. I told you we'd be here for you. How different would our lives have been if family had stepped up for us, or if Mitch had been able to take us in? I'd do anything to give those girls the home we didn't have."

Leslie French took this moment to slide a file folder across the table to Jed and Natalie. "These are the guardianship papers," she said. "You will be permanent legal guardians of both Josephine and Zora."

"You're sure about this?" Jed asked his sister.

Chelsea nodded. "I'm sure. Are you?" Her eyes slid from his to Natalie's. "You didn't sign up to raise my kids."

"Yes," Natalie said. "We're sure." She grasped her sister-in-law's hand and gave a squeeze.

"Alright. I'll call and tell them I'm taking the apartment." Chelsea turned to Mitch, who sat beside her. "I wouldn't be able to do this without you."

"I couldn't help your mother. I'm so happy that I can help you." He put an arm around her. "Turns out a Pete Rose rookie card is worth quite a bit of money. Who knew?"

"I'll pay you back someday," she murmured, her head against his shoulder.

"No, you won't. I won't take it. You'll stay sober like I have and live a good life. That will be more than enough."

Jed cleared his throat. "When will you leave?"

"The apartment is available now, so as soon as possible. They'll only hold it for ten days. Evidently sober living is in demand." Chelsea picked up her phone. "I'll need to get a plane ticket."

"Actually," Mitch said, "Stella and I have been planning a trip out west. There's so much of the country neither of us has seen, and with the restaurant we haven't had time for a honeymoon. Now that Theo is there, though, we do. Why don't you ride with us, and we'll drop you off?"

Chelsea gaped at him. "I'm not going to third-wheel your honeymoon!"

Mitch chuckled. "Denver isn't that far. We'll have plenty of alone time after we drop you off." His eyes softened as he met hers. "I'd like to see where you'll be living, check it out for myself."

Chelsea leaned in and kissed his cheek. "Okay, then."

Jed looked on, a grin splitting his face. "Nat and I have already talked about coming out next summer to see you. We've never been to Denver. You can see the girls and we can all do some sightseeing together; like a family."

"We really are a family, aren't we?" Chelsea rose, and walked to Jed who stood and wrapped her in a hug. Mitch and Natalie stood, too, and the lawyer excused herself, opening the office door and motioning for Josie and Zora to come in.

"Mama," eight-year-old Zora said, noticing the tears on her mother's face. "Are you sad?"

"No, baby, Mama is happy; as happy as I've ever been."

"Do we get to stay here with Uncle Jed?" Josie asked. Suspicious, her eyes searched her mother's, and Chelsea knew it would take more than one good night together to earn her oldest daughter's trust.

"Yes," she said. "That's what we all decided and that's what's going to happen."

"Thank you!" Josie's embrace surprised Chelsea so much that it took a moment before she responded, hugging her back and planting a kiss on the top of her head. "I love you, baby."

"I love you, too, Mama." Josie ran to Jed and Natalie.

Chelsea watched with tears in her eyes as her brother and his wife embraced her girls. Josie and Zora finally had the home they'd been missing, and maybe, just maybe, so did she.